The Heart
of
Arcrea

Nicole Sager

The Heart of Arcrea
Copyright © 2012 Nicole Sager

Illustrations by Nicole Sager
Back Cover Photo Credits: Amy Hale

Printed in the United States of America

ISBN-10: **1479361887**
ISBN-13: **978-1479361885**

DEDICATION

For Caleb – the "founder" of Arcrea.
Thank you for sharing your ideas with me, and for
allowing me the incredible task of writing about them.

"Let GOD be magnified."
From Psalm 70:4

ARCREA

{MIZGALIA}

{MIZGALIA}

ONE
BONE
BRIK
MOUNTAINS

Oak's Branch
Roughton

Frederick

Ranulf

Tiltman &
Morgway

Quinton

Knavesmire

Rebel's
Lair

Heartland

Saxby
Waterfall
Coswell

Kally

Osgood

Stephen

Dragon
Coast

Clan

Quale

Campbell

Brentwood &
Licklee

Geoffrey

Hugh

Dormay

Arcrean Sea

TABLE OF CONTENTS

LIST OF ILLUSTRATIONS

Nicole Sager

ACKNOWLEDGMENTS

I want to give a big THANK YOU to my family
—Dad, Mom, Christal, Mike, Caity, Caleb, & Caroline—
for being such a wonderful support system throughout the
writing and publishing of *The Heart of Arcrea*! You all have
been so encouraging and loving.
Thanks for being there for me!

Also!
Thank you to the Martin family for all of your help,
encouragement, & advice! You don't know how much I
appreciate you!

And most importantly!
A giant thank you to my Lord & Savior, Jesus Christ,
without whom, none of this would have been possible!
When I am weak, He is strong!

What is this heart of Arcrea?

You must discover it for yourself.

Prologue
* The Arcrean Conquest *

Long ago, during a forgotten time of kings and queens, knights and nobles, wise men and warlords, there lived seven men who were joined together in a quest to discover uncharted lands. Each man looked with anxious pleasure to a future that would bring him a great name and fortune.

In their quest for greatness, these seven became the first to venture south over the broad expanse of Brikbone Mountains, which traced the southern border of the fierce kingdom Mizgalia.

The south side of the Brikbones was reached on a stormy night. The seven explorers stood with their caravan beneath a sheltering outcrop and looked out to the next leg of their journey, shrouded in the darkness of night and blinding rain. Each man wondered what lay below in the shadows of the towering Brikbones. What would they find when the sun rose the following morning—a new land waiting to be explored? or a dead end in the form of a tossing sea? Suddenly, lightning forked a brilliant path across the sky and the seven explorers let out an exclamation of delight as the light revealed a vast landscape that stretched beyond their limited view.

When the sun rose the following morning its warm rays slanted gracefully over this untouched world of tangled forests, broad green meadows, and sparkling lakes and rivers. Birds sailed through the clear morning air, reveling in the newly washed environment. The hearts of the seven explorers swelled with pride as their eyes searched the distant horizon and realized the vastness of this place.

Five years passed as the explorers charted the land, completing a map and dividing portions to each man. When they reached the center of the kingdom, they found a clan of primitive natives who, though startled by the presence of other humans, welcomed the entourage with open arms. The natives knew little of what lay beyond their large encampment, but the clan's elder, Ulric of the Ancients, informed the explorers that his father had called the land Arcrea. The explorers learned much from the natives and cultivated a friendship with the clan, promising that their homeland would not be harmed in the occupying of the rest of the kingdom.

Finally, they continued their journey through the southern half of the new land, taming the lengths of the wild kingdom from the dense forests and vicious plant life to the habitations of dragons and other fierce creatures.

The time came for their families to join them, but when the joyful reunion had finally taken place, all turned their attention to the thought foremost in each man's mind. Who would rule as king in the new

Arcrea? Each man could think only of himself and his own desire to wear the crown. Discussion quickly became heated and soon the long-time friends looked upon each other as rivals.

"Let us go to Ulric of the Ancients and let him choose a man among us," called one man, and the explorers set off for the center of the kingdom, each man sure that he himself would be chosen by Ulric.

The old man listened to the plea of each and saw the pride that clouded the seven hearts. Each man was intent only on the selfish gain to be had through a kingship. Each man craved the power, the wealth, and the greatness that would come from bearing the new title. A quarrel broke out among them and lasted the length of half an hour, and then Ulric raised his hands. The explorers fell silent, waiting to hear which name would fall from the ancient's lips.

A tear slipped from Ulric's eye and found a path down his weathered and heavily wrinkled face. He knew his remaining days on earth were few, and that a new era was dawning for his beloved Arcrea. The choice of this new era's leadership had been left to him, and he would make sure that Arcrea's first king was a man of honor and humility.

"Who will you choose?" One of the seven pierced the stillness with his impatient tone.

Ulric turned to glance at the man and at last spoke in a voice strong with passion, "Do you swear to live according to my choice?"

The explorers nodded and each placed a fist over his heart as they vowed to honor their own request for his decision.

"Well then," Ulric nodded slowly and scanned the group with a steady gaze, "He who discovers the heart of Arcrea and joins the hands of the seven regions will be king."

For a moment no one spoke.

At last, one man asked, "Where is this heart to be found? What is it?"

Ulric eyed him with a wizened arc of his white brow; "You must discover it for yourself."

"How will we know for sure when it has been discovered?"

Ulric reached a withered hand before him, "Only the man who has truly discovered the heart will be able to join the seven regions in a lasting union. All other attempts will fail."

Angered and put out by the ancient's riddles, the explorers vowed that the first man to find the heart would not only become king, but would also be given the land of Ulric's people to do with as he pleased. Being situated in central Arcrea, and now linked to the prophecy of the heart's discoverer, the encampment was thereafter known as the "Heartland".

Years passed and the seven explorers settled their families in the formerly appointed regions, claiming the title of Lord over their own lands. Companies were sent out under their direction in search of Arcrea's heart, but the results were always the same: no man was able to discover the whereabouts of the heart...or even what it was. On several occasions, one or another of the seven lords made an attempt to claim the coveted crown, but always the six other lords joined together in preventing him.

Meanwhile, families flourished and the inhabitants of the kingdom multiplied until several generations had passed and Arcrea was a burgeoning land, well populated and known for its trading routes among the southern port-towns, where the kingdom was bordered by a vast sea. Marriages between the seven regions became common and, eventually, where a person lived was no longer a matter of bloodlines, but of their opinion in politics and the merit of the nobility. Clans were formed in the hills and highlands, keeping alive the spirit of animosity between the seven regions.

The God-fearing natives of the Heartland watched the progress of Arcrea with wary hearts. Some left to join the new people and their ways, but others continued to live as they always had, and prayed that their encampment would be spared destruction during the first king's reign.

The seven founding lords eventually died, leaving their sons and their son's sons to claim each region in their stead. The legend of Arcrea's heart and the prophecy of the first king were passed down through the generations, but many began to wonder if the "heart of Arcrea" had merely been the ramblings of an old man. Perhaps, they thought, the kingdom would be better off as it was: each region ruled by its own lord until the day of his death, and then passed on to the man's eldest son.

Thus life in Arcrea continued for many a year, until the day finally came when one man's curiosity aroused the interest of the long-indifferent kingdom.

Chapter 1
* Druet *

The young blacksmith blinked as sweat dripped into his sharp blue eyes. Giving his head a fierce shake, he drew the tongs from the forge, turned to the anvil, and began to pound the yellow-orange iron with a strength that evidenced his twenty-five years had nearly all been spent in his father's shop.

"Now that's a tune that I can sing to, Druet!" A deep voice sounded from across the room.

The young man glanced up with a grin when his father returned to his own work and began to boisterously sing to the rhythm of the pounding hammer,

> *"A blacksmith's arms are big 'round as a tree!*
> *He bellows and hammers and shapes strange things!"*

Druet laughed, "That didn't even rhyme!"
"And who said that it must?"

"Well, it should at least make some sense. I'm a blacksmith, yet my arms aren't 'big 'round as a tree'."

"Mine are!" Gregory the smith turned to survey his powerfully built son with a playful jutting of his short brown beard, "Don't be so quick to judge yourself, boy; your limbs are near thick as an oak's trunk."

With a grin still in place, Druet turned back to the forge and drove his iron into the flames again, "An oak, eh?"

Gregory's beard split to reveal his teeth set in a teasing smile, "Perhaps a sapling."

Druet shook his head and pulled the bellows, "I still say that it ought to rhyme."

Gregory gave his son a lofty look and began to hum noisily as he reached for his own hammer.

Druet's smile broadened as he shifted his focus to watch with a practiced eye as his iron began to glow red in the intense heat of the forge. As a child, Druet had never doubted that he would follow in his father's line of work. Gregory had always made the work enjoyable, cultivating the evident interest that Druet had shown, and was now pleased to pound iron and steel alongside his son.

Gregory, with his wife, Ruth, and Druet lived in the village of Oak's Branch in Lord Frederick's north-central region of Arcrea. The village was several miles distant from Frederick's castle and was neighbored by the many other villages in the area. Some of the villages had no blacksmith of their own, so Gregory's work had increased as the surrounding peasants had heard of his shop's fine reputation. Even Lord Frederick had, on occasion, preferred the village smith over his own man at the castle.

Frederick's castle was built in the north of his large region in order to be nearer to the wall of Brikbone Mountains and, ultimately, the constantly warring Mizgalians. Along with Lords Quinton and Ranulf, whose regions lay to the east and west of his own, Frederick had led many campaigns against these enemies who dared to cross the border into Arcrea.

As Druet reached for his hammer once again, his thoughts turned to Lord Frederick's campaigns. Each of the seven Arcrean lords was in command of an army consisting of men who were well fed, well kept, and well paid; coddled to ensure their undying loyalty. Druet's teeth ground together when he thought of how the wages to maintain these bribed armies were drawn from the harsh taxes inflicted on the commoners such as his father and himself.

"What sober thought put that frown on your face?" Gregory's sincere tone broke through Druet's thoughts.

The young man inspected the work before him, "Father, how long will our people suffer beneath the tyranny of unjust rulers?"

Gregory was quick to reply, "Until the day of the heart's discovery and the start of our first king's reign. At least, I pray to God that then the suffering will end."

Druet's hammer rested on the anvil, "How can it be that no one has found it? The prophecy of Ulric the Ancient was given over one hundred years ago. How could such a task be so difficult?"

"Had it been a simple endeavor, there would have been numerous claims made to the crown before now. Ulric wisely set a standard that is possible to fulfill, but can only be reached by the man who was

Druet

Nicole Sager

destined by God to do so. It will take a remarkable man to unite the people of Arcrea's seven regions."

Druet gave a small smile of agreement and then continued to think out loud, "Our people are so diverse. We in the north are known to be fierce because of the constant fighting, while the south is acclaimed for its trade at sea, and the people there are much more conformed to a life of peace."

"Aside from the work of the clans," Gregory peered intently at his piece of work and suddenly frowned at an imperfection. Lowering the iron to the anvil, he dropped his hammer in a resounding blow and then lifted it to inspect the results. He gave a satisfied smile and continued, "Why some men are bent on performing mischief I'll never know; but somehow they all find each other and make life harder for the rest of us by rising together and resisting the nobility…trying to 'liberate' us peasants while they fill their own pockets with loot."

Druet mopped the sweat from his forehead, "I heard from Peter that a clan from Rebel's Lair, in Quinton's region, sailed across the bay and harassed Lord Stephen's border…again."

"Fools," Gregory shook his head, "Can they not see that war from within will tear down our defenses against the enemies from without?"

"We need a man to be king; a man who will rule by God's standards and not his own."

"I pray God that this man will reign during my lifetime."

The blacksmith shop was void of conversation for several minutes as the two men fell to their own thoughts.

Druet plunged his iron into the forge again and engaged the familiar bellows in their work. When his piece glowed a bright yellow-orange he drew it out and returned to the anvil. Hefting his hammer in one hand, he let it fall in a steady rhythm that would continue to shape the soft iron. He smiled when Gregory's voice rose in song.

> *"A blacksmith's voice is big as a vessel;*
> *He molds and melts iron, and makes a sharp arrow.*
>
> *"A smith hammers and sweats through all the long day;*
> *Hears echoes of clanging when dreams come his* **way!**"

Chapter 2
* Trouble From Within *

Lord Frederick sat in an oversized chair by the enormous hearth in his castle's great hall. His wife sat silent in a chair opposite, her thin fingers busy with needlework, while his daughter sat on a stool pulled close to his knee and listened as his chief informant, Falconer—just arrived home from an assignment—relayed the information that had been gathered.

"The band seems to be well-organized, my lord. There were at least three hundred gathered when I left the location, and the arrival of more men was anticipated."

Lord Frederick scowled. His own subjects, these wretched clans, were joining together to protest his recent tax law; daring him to crush their attempts and refuse their request for the law's annulment. As if he had nothing better to do! The kingdom of Mizgalia gripped the northern border of Arcrea with dangerous cliffs and Brikbones, antagonizing his army with every opportunity that presented itself. His life had been one of war—war against the Mizgalians, war against the clans and, occasionally, war within his own home.

"My lord?"

Frederick looked up to see Falconer waiting for orders. He glanced at his daughter and saw her eyes flash a familiar spark of wrath.

"Just send your entire army to deal with the peasant pigs once and for all," the girl lifted her nose in disgust, "It will only take a day out of your campaign in the north, and may lend an element of surprise to your situation against the Mizgalians when you return to rout them from the Brikbones."

Falconer bit the inside of his cheek and carefully watched his lord's shrewd expression.

Lord Frederick observed his daughter for a long moment before speaking, "There is something to consider in your plan. I must speak with my knights in regards to the state of the army and their weaponry," he turned to address his agent, "Falconer, you will accompany me to the garrison."

ᔕᓍᲚᲠ

Druet closed his right eye and examined the length of a newly finished sword with his left. Along with a blacksmith's other skills, Gregory had instilled in his son's mind the knowledge of fashioning weaponry; and this, his latest work, was truly a masterpiece.

Druet rested the solid pommel in his firm grip and was pleased to find that he had at last designed a perfect fit. The polished blade caught a ray of sunlight, sending brilliant reflections across the room. Casting a glance around the empty shop, Druet turned and ducked through the back door, stepping into the small yard that was bordered by his home on one side and the smith on another, the two structures being cattycorner to one another.

Setting himself in a swordsman's stance at the center of the yard, Druet took several deep breaths and then delivered several combinations that Gregory had taught him. The sword plunged through the crisp morning air with seemingly effortless speed and Druet found himself smiling when he finished with a lunge. Tilting the glistening blade, he saw the reflection of someone watching him from the cottage doorway.

Druet looked up, "Mother!"

Ruth mirrored his pleased expression and stepped out into the yard, "I was grateful all those years ago when Gregory built his shop beside our home, because I thought that I would see him more often. Now I hear your hammers all day and see precious little of either one of you. It is good to see you enjoying the fresh air today."

Druet was quiet as his mother approached and held out her hands.

"May I see it?"

Ruth took the sword as it was laid gently across her palms; she gripped the pommel and twisted her wrist to study each side, "This is beautiful, son."

"But not as beautiful as the woman who holds it," Gregory's voice boomed as he stepped from the shop.

One side of her mouth tilted upward and both of the blacksmiths knew that Ruth was pleased by the compliment, "You taught him well, Gregory."

The blacksmith stepped forward and took the sword, scrutinizing every inch, "I did, didn't I?" he looked at Druet with a grin, "This is mastery in the form of perfection. Will this be the blade that you keep for your own then?"

Druet dipped his head, "I think so. I am pleased with it."

"Then keep it; there will be others to sell that won't need this one to keep them company."

The three made their way into the shop.

"There's John's pitchfork to be mended, Druet. You set yourself to that today and see whether it will have to be remade."

"Gregory."

The two smiths turned at Ruth's apprehensive tone. She turned with wide eyes from where she stood in the shop's entrance and dropped into a low curtsy as Lord Frederick stepped passed her and into the dimly lit shop. Four knights followed close behind him.

Immediately, the atmosphere became tense as the peasants and nobility exchanged wary looks of indifference.

"Woman," Frederick suddenly spoke to Ruth as he glanced about, "Our horses need water."

"Yes, my lord," Ruth curtsied again and left to obey.

Druet clenched his jaw, sensing the tension in his father as Gregory stiffened and waited for Lord Frederick to speak. The ruler's eyes made another studied pass around the room and then froze on the younger blacksmith. Stepping forward, Frederick took the sword from Druet's hand. Glancing at the weapon, he then raised his eyes to the craftsman.

"Did you make this?"

Druet gave a single nod.

Lord Frederick frowned at the silent response and raised his voice, "Did you make this sword?"

"Yes, my lord."

Lord Frederick gave a slow nod and moved his jaw back and forth.

Slowly, Druet filled his lungs with an apprehensive breath. The fingers on his right hand flexed and then balled into a fist, waiting to grip the pommel of his sword again.

Casually, Lord Frederick shifted and drew his own weapon from its sheath; holding it out to the young man he spoke in a slow deliberate tone,

"My own sword is in need of a good polish and sharpening."

Druet's eyes locked with Lord Frederick's cold stare and the younger man remained still for a moment. His gaze shifted to his own blade, still in the noble man's gloved grasp. Reluctantly he reached to take the dulled sword and then moved to a worktable. Reaching for the grinding stones, he set to work with one eye still focused on Lord Frederick and both ears attentive to the conversation.

Gregory shifted in the uncomfortable silence. Finally Lord Frederick looked up from Druet's sword and spoke.

"I bring you business, Gregory. The weaponry in use among my army is in a terribly sorry state and must be mended immediately. I have come to settle a price with you myself and will send down the arms upon my return home."

"Trouble in the north has proved hard on your blades then?" Gregory questioned; Druet could tell that his father was trying to be lighthearted.

There was a moment's pause.

Druet looked up to see Lord Frederick staring at the floor before him.

The ruler looked up, "This campaign against the cursed Mizgalians has indeed been extended beyond the desired length of time. I had thought to crush them before now, but there was trouble, you know, in bringing Lord Ranulf's army to assist us several months ago. However, my focus turns in another direction now."

The grinding stones suddenly froze, and Druet looked up in time to see his father stiffen at Lord Frederick's last words.

"Another direction, my lord? You're to relinquish your stand against the Mizgalians for another cause?"

Lord Frederick seemed irritated by the peasant's curiosity. His glove strained noisily as he repositioned his hand around Druet's sword.

Druet tossed the stones back to their place and came back around to the group by the door. He held Frederick's sword out with an air of expectancy.

"It was not very bad, my lord."

Frederick glanced at his own weapon and then at Druet's tense face with a thin smile, "Keep it," he studied the sword in his hand, "It will make a fair exchange."

Druet's insides exploded with fury as he watched his sword slide into Lord Frederick's sheath with a metallic sound that grated harshly in the young man's ears.

Gregory saw his son's anger and tried to intervene, "My lord, his sword is not for sale."

Frederick glared at the blacksmith, "Then I suggest that your son accepts my trade before he is left without a sword at all."

"Thief!" Druet lurched forward, but froze when the knights behind Lord Frederick came closer, each laying a hand to the pommel at his belt. Gregory laid a restraining hand on his son's shoulder.

Frederick leaned within inches of Druet's face and glowered, "Do not question my authority, boy, else you find yourself without that traitorous tongue of yours."

The muscles around Druet's mouth were painfully taut as he forced himself to remain silent.

Lord Frederick turned stiffly to Gregory; "I am still willing to grant you the work; the arms will be sent this afternoon."

Gregory's brow creased with wariness, "What is the other direction that you spoke of?"

"Do you also question me?"

Gregory frowned, "I wish to know if these weapons that you want me to mend will be used against the gathering clans…against my people."

Frederick raised a sarcastic brow, "Oh, so you know of them."

"Everybody knows."

"Then you know I am right to put a stop to their foolishness!"

"I only know that a man who possesses everything that money can buy should take a bit more pity on the subjects who have faithfully served him to the point of sacrificing the shirts on their own backs. I think something should be done to stop the clans' foolishness, yes; but it might be done in a manner more gracious and patient than riding ruthlessly over them and leaving destruction in your wake. Will you care for their devastated families when the damage is done?"

His sword forgotten for the moment, Druet's mouth hung open and he stared at his father with new admiration as the blacksmith finished his passionate speech.

Lord Frederick shook with rage, "I will order you to complete the task."

"And I will refuse," Gregory lifted his head higher and looked down on the ruler, "I will not sharpen the sword that may kill my brothers."

A long silence ensued, broken only by the crackling fire in the forge.

Lord Frederick grasped the pommel of Druet's sword and glanced at the knight to his right, "Take him. He should find himself at home in the castle tower."

Two of the knights surged forward to obey their master's command while the other two took hold of Druet's arms, preventing him from rushing to his father's assistance. Druet watched in horror as his father was led outside without the slightest resistance.

"No! My lord, you can't do this!"

Lord Frederick turned with a wrathful glare and pointed a condemning finger at the young man,

"You, too, will pay for your insolence by completing the task refused by Gregory. The arms will be sent as planned and you will mend every last one, or suffer a worse fate than your rebel father."

Outside, Ruth wailed, "No, please! Where are you taking him? Gregory!" Druet closed his eyes and swallowed the agony that rose in his throat at the sound of her helpless screams. The noises of a gathering crowd began to reach his ears as well.

Frederick turned on his heel and marched to the door, Druet's sword clicking impatiently at his side.

Hearing the man's receding footsteps, Druet opened his eyes and for the first time noticed another man who had entered with Lord Frederick. The man stood in the doorway wearing a black cloak that reached the floor. He held himself with an air of confidence, yet his features were tossed with a look that Druet could not read.

The stranger's eyes were taking in the scene unfolding outside but as Lord Frederick stalked by, his gaze shifted to return Druet's stare. Druet rose to his full height beneath the interrogation of the sharp eyes across the room and the stranger's face took on a look of fearful recognition.

Suddenly, Druet felt himself hurled backwards as the two knights sent him reeling with a powerful shove. Frederick's sword dropped from his hand and pain shot through his head and shoulders as he stumbled and crashed into a worktable, scattering tools and bits of iron in every direction.

Druet cried out and clutched the back of his head as the two knights laughed and followed Lord Frederick from the shop. When he could open his eyes again, Druet looked up to see that the stranger, too, had gone, and he was alone.

Chapter 3
* Impossible Quest *

The thunderous sound of Frederick's withdrawing horses pounded in Druet's throbbing head. Through blinding tears of frustration and anger he saw his mother appear in the doorway; franticly she searched the interior of the shop.

"Druet!" Ruth dropped to her knees beside her son and helped him to sit up, "What's happened? Why are they taking your father with them?"

Druet groaned and rubbed his head, "He spoke truth."

Ruth let out a sigh of frustration that startled her son, "Again?"

Druet stared at his mother, "What do you mean 'again'? I never heard him speak out with such passion before today."

Ruth shook her head and wiped at her tears, "It was before you were born. Gregory was a firebrand long before I married him; but he's made an effort to control himself since the time he was forced to spend a night in the stocks," Ruth paused to examine Druet's head and then looked helplessly about, "What will we do?"

Druet rose to his feet, "Lord Frederick expects me to mend his army's weaponry. Father refused because Lord Frederick intends to use the arms against the clans in his region without first attempting to bring peace."

"And your father's brother is among their number…" Ruth watched her son's face, "Thomas' family was starving before Frederick's law increased the taxes. How will they survive if the law is not annulled? Or if Thomas is killed by Frederick's army?"

Druet righted the worktable and pounded a large fist on its surface, "How will anyone survive if this law is not annulled? or if the clansmen are killed in a ruthless battle of hundreds against thousands? They may have acted foolishly in the past, but now they simply join together in hopes that their numbers will sway Frederick's mind, and he intends to annihilate them!"

Druet sat on a stool and buried his face in his hands.

Ruth studied him in silence for a moment and then, as if struck by some sudden realization, she stepped out and made her way to the cottage.

"How long, oh God?" Druet prayed, "how long will our people suffer beneath the tyranny of unjust rulers?"

"Until the day of the heart's discovery and the start of our first king's reign."

Druet froze when his father's words of days before returned to his mind.

"Is this your answer, God?" He asked, "I must wait for a man to go out and find this mysterious heart?"

He was still for a moment, waiting for some divine answer—for lightning to split the sky and point a fiery finger to the chosen man. Instead, a quiet thought was impressed on Druet's mind causing his spine to suddenly straighten in shock. For a moment, he could think only of how absurd this thought was; but then he remembered his father.

"I could free him from Frederick's chains."

Druet rose with a quick motion and went to stand in the doorway, leaning one arm on the frame and rubbing the other hand over his face.

His eyes shifted to gaze heavenward, "But I don't want the crown. I am not worthy to rule such a vast kingdom. I am not wise enough; I am only a peasant. My father said that it would take a remarkable man."

"You are a remarkable man, Druet."

The young man turned to see his mother standing behind him. In her hands were a small leather pouch and a loaf of bread. Druet's eyes widened and then lifted from the articles to search her face.

Her brow rose in question and her voice sounded ragged with an effort to keep from crying, "You are going?"

"How did you know?"

She shrugged and a tear crept from her eye, "The bread is for your dinner. There is money in the pouch—most of several years' savings; I'll live on the rest while you're gone."

Druet's head began to shake in denial, "I can't take...I wouldn't know where to begin! I do not wish to be king, and I must if I find the heart—"

"And join the hands of the seven regions."

Druet stared at his mother for a moment and then turned to look out at the village.

Ruth's eyes became intense as she studied her son's profile, "Do you wish to discover the heart of Arcrea?"

Druet gave a tilt of his head and admitted, "I am curious to know what exactly this legend is."

Ruth nodded solemnly, "Then go and find it. For your father—it is what he would tell you to do. My son, if God has indeed called you to this task, will He not give you the ability to complete it?"

Druet bowed his head with a nod and closed his eyes, "I'll go," he whispered.

"Good," Ruth replied just as softly, unsure whether he was speaking to her or to God. She bowed her head as well and the two prayed for God's protection and wisdom over Druet. When they had finished, Druet looked up and Ruth knew that her son was destined for greatness when she saw in his eyes the willingness to obey God's call.

"What will you do while I am gone?"

The mother smiled, "I will wait for your father to return, and see that no one takes possession of our land."

Druet turned and walked through the shop, gathering several articles of weaponry and accessories for his journey. Lastly, his gaze fell to Lord Frederick's sword, still lying on the floor. With a sigh of resignation he knelt to retrieve it, sliding it into the sheath at his waist.

Turning again to his mother, Druet pulled her into a firm embrace and kissed her forehead.

"I love you, mother."

"And I love you, my son," Ruth took a shaky breath and reached to place a hand on the side of his face, "Remember, Druet, that God alone knows."

"Knows what?"

"Everything. Whether you find the heart of Arcrea or no, God has a purpose for this journey just as He does for all others."

Druet nodded as her words sank into his mind.

"Stand for Him, Druet; even if all others in this kingdom stand against Him."

The young blacksmith turned then and stepped from his father's shop, determined to find the heart of his homeland and so solve the riddle that had baffled the entire kingdom for more than a century.

Chapter 4
* Stranger *

As he began his first day of travel, Druet's mind turned to considering where he should begin his search for the heart. Where had men searched before him? How had they gone about their quest? Had any man gained a clue regarding the heart or its whereabouts? If they had, how could he find them to gain this information?

That evening, as the sun sank low in the sky, Druet turned for the hundredth time to gaze back up the road towards home.

"What am I doing?" he ran a calloused hand through his dark brown hair, "I've never in my life traveled more than twenty miles from Oak's Branch; all I know of Arcrea's boundaries are what I have seen of them on a map."

He turned to face south again, "Why am I going this way?" he motioned down the road with his arms and then dropped them back to his sides; as he did, his left hand struck Frederick's sword and he looked down at the pommel with a slight snort.

" 'It will make a fair trade'," Druet mimicked Lord Frederick's exalted tone and then sighed. He rubbed the bridge of his nose and pressed his hand across his eyes, "Forgive me, God, for my bitterness. I thank You that I have a sword at all. Give me courage to pursue Your will."

The next day, Druet reached the bustling city of Roughton. Making his way to the city square, the young blacksmith wandered among the stalls and shops, studying the faces of the mob that surrounded him. None were thinking beyond the task of filling their bellies with the evening meal. Knowing that he alone was preoccupied with thoughts of Arcrea's ancient riddle made Druet's mission seem even more vast and impossible in his mind's eye.

Feeling eyes on the back of his head, Druet turned to see a young man watching him. The stranger, only slightly older than himself, was standing halfway across the square. He was dressed in the simple but foreign garb of a seaman and had a carefree air about his stance.

Druet returned the man's stare for a moment and then turned to a basket-weaver who was shouting his wares to the oblivious crowd.

"Excuse me, sir. Do you know that man?" Druet motioned across the square with his head.

The basket-weaver squinted, "Which man is 'that man', boy? There are hundreds you know."

"The man standing still in the middle of the square."

"The foreigner?"

Druet nodded, "That's the one."

The basket-weaver squinted again and studied the stranger's face over Druet's shoulder.

"Never saw him before," the man drew back with a sigh, "Care for a basket?"

"No, thank you," Druet shook his head and moved away from the stall. Glancing back, he saw that the stranger's gaze followed him wherever he went.

Suddenly, Druet's attention shifted to the edge of the square and he saw two of Lord Frederick's knights scanning the crowd. Just then, one of the knights caught sight of Druet and pointed; the other knight followed the motion with his eyes to locate their prey.

Drawing his sword, the first knight shouted, "You there! Grab that man!"

All heads turned toward the two knights and Druet took off at a run in the opposite direction. The people of Roughton scrambled to keep clear of the blacksmith's path. Only once did several men step forward to block his way, but Druet shoved passed them and ran from the square.

Through the town's busy streets Druet raced, ducked, leapt, and turned, with the sound of the two knight's pursuit a constant reminder behind him.

At the end of one street, Druet rounded a corner and froze when he saw that the alley was a dead end. Turning back just as Frederick's two knights appeared, Druet drew the sword from his sheath and waited for them to approach. One of the knights laughed at the young man's predicament and Druet thought of their presence in Oak's Branch the day before.

"What do you want?"

The knights came slowly forward and one spoke, "Lord Frederick was not pleased to find that you had forsaken your duty."

"Is that so?"

A quick movement behind the knights caught Druet's attention. He shifted his focus to the knights once more as the other continued the accusations,

"Nor was he pleased by your theft of his personal sword."

Suddenly, the first knight who had spoken shouted with rage as he was tackled from behind. Druet saw the second knight turn to defend his companion; leaping forward, the blacksmith brought his sword up to block the way.

The metallic sounds of clashing swords reverberated through the alley. Druet chanced a glance over his shoulder at the other two combatants and was just able to recognize the stranger from the square before his own opponent rushed forward with a fierce combination.

"Ho, there," Druet's aide suddenly shouted, "Meet at the back!"

Druet's eyes darted to keep up with his mind, which was racing to keep pace with the knight's sword. Inching his way toward the sound of the stranger's voice, he somehow managed to make his way to where the other man stood in combat. Back to back, the two fought until the stranger's rival roared fiercely and backed away, clutching the shoulder of his sword-arm. Druet's companion then turned and maneuvered his way around the second knight, and the two finally managing to back him against the wall.

At the alley's entryway the other knight collapsed and lay still.

"Unconscious," the stranger stated, "From the loss of blood, I presume."

Druet held the tip of his sword to the second knight's chest and spoke in a low tone, "You may inform Lord Frederick that I refuse his work on the same grounds that my father did. And tell him I will gladly trade him this sword for the one that he sheathed in my shop yesterday."

Slowly and cautiously, Druet and his aide left the alley and quickly disappeared up the street. When they had gone a safe distance, Druet turned to his companion.

"Thank you for your help."

"You're most welcome, mate."

"I'm afraid I know more of crafting a sword than of wielding one in combat."

"You did well."

Druet could sense that the stranger kept trying to study his face as they walked side by side. Finally, Druet stopped walking and the other man came to a halt beside him. The young blacksmith's brow was creased with caution as he turned to face the other man.

"I saw you in the square today."

"And I you," the stranger's gray eyes were penetrating.

Druet held out his hand and it was taken in a firm grasp of greeting, "I am Druet of Oak's Branch."

"Here in Frederick's region?"

"Yes; a day north of here."

"I'm Nathaniel of Dormay, in Geoffrey's region."

"In the far south? Then you are a foreigner to these parts."

31

"That I am; and this is a place just as fierce as the rumors I've heard. I've lived a life on the seas myself, and only just came ashore in search of a man."

"Here in Frederick's? Who are you looking for?"

A curious look crossed Nathaniel's face and he glanced up the street; running a hand through his sun-washed brown hair he turned back to Druet, "I believe I'm looking for you."

"Me?" Druet stepped back in shock, "I never heard of you before today!"

Nathaniel went on slowly, as if treading cautiously with his words, "On my last voyage I did a lot of thinking over the old prophecy; you know, the one of Arcrea's heart."

Druet's eyes widened.

"I prayed that God would send the man who was to search for it. God worked in my heart and slowly convinced me that I was to search for and join the man on a quest to discover this legend of Arcrea. Once on shore I struck out and let God lead me where He would," Nathaniel flashed a smile, "and here I am today, a month later!"

Druet blinked, "A month?"

Nathaniel nodded.

"But I left Oak's Branch only yesterday."

Nathaniel cocked his head to one side, "Then you *are* in search of the heart."

Druet could only stare in shock.

Nathaniel searched his new friend's face and nodded, "You're the man, I'm sure of that now."

"A month ago," Druet murmured.

Nathaniel grinned and slapped Druet's shoulder, "God knew, Druet."

Nathaniel

Nicole Sager

Druet's thoughts turned to his mother at home and he nodded, "God alone knew."

"Will you accept my company then, mate?"

The young blacksmith stared at the seaman for a moment as a grin slowly spread across his face, "I'd be pleased to have you join me, Nathaniel."

The two shook hands over their new alliance and then started up the street at a brisk pace, heading south out of Roughton.

Chapter 5
* The Ignispat *

Druet and Nathaniel were soon fast friends, each considering the other to be the brother he had never had. Druet discovered that his friend's hometown of Dormay was a coastal town, built on the shores of the vast Arcrean Sea, which Druet had never seen. Nathaniel lived there with his father, mother, and two younger sisters. As they traveled, Nathaniel regaled the hours away with many tales of his sailing days. Druet, in turn, shared stories of his life near the border wars against Mizgalia, and the reasons behind his current journey from home.

As he talked aloud about his father's unjust imprisonment, the young blacksmith became more confident in his mission to discover the heart. Finally, he allowed himself to anticipate the day when, God willing, he would solve the ancient mystery and satisfy not only his own curiosity over the legend, but that of the entire kingdom as well. The crown that would be given to the heart's discoverer still held little interest for him.

The two friends continued south, thinking that the first place one ought to search for a heart would be the Heartland itself. They took the time, however, to search every place they passed along the road, and so three weeks soon passed and they had still not reached the natives' central region.

As their search progressed, news quickly began to spread and the kingdom of Arcrea was roused by the quest of this unknown blacksmith. Some shook their heads and declared him a fool for trying to unlock the secrets that one hundred thirty years of searching had failed to produce. Others reveled in the story, glad for a fresh but harmless topic to consume their thoughts and conversation.

"News travels fast," Nathaniel spoke wryly one day, "Lord Frederick has no doubt heard of your quest by now."

"Our quest," Druet corrected as he studied a map of Arcrea.

Nathaniel looked at his friend with an amused twist to his smile, "*Your* quest. I'm just along for the adventure, mate."

Druet shook his head with a tolerating grunt, "You may be the man to find the heart, Nathaniel."

"Of course," the seaman muttered; his gray eyes shifted back to the road and he shook his head in a manner that proved he was unconvinced.

Druet moved to a large rock beside the southbound road and spread the map over its surface.

"I think we're somewhere in here," his finger traced a circle halfway between Oak's Branch and the

Heartland, "Or perhaps a touch more south. How is it we haven't progressed farther?"

"Because we searched to the east and west of the road," Nathaniel indicated a broader circle, "We took quite a few detours."

"What if the heart was hidden somewhere in the forests back here, but we missed it?"

Nathaniel shrugged.

Druet ran a hand through his hair, "Arcrea is a place vaster than I ever knew."

Nathaniel took the map and studied it before turning to face the south again, "It looks as if we may be approaching another patch of dense forest...beyond those hills there."

Druet looked to where Nathaniel was pointing, "Let's start, then. Perhaps we'll find a cave or such in the forest—someplace logical to search."

They reached the forest late in the afternoon and continued on the worn path that twisted into its depths. As the sun began to lower and the light became scarce Nathaniel fashioned two torches and Druet used a flint to light them.

"We'll need to find a place to stop for the night."

An animal cried in the distance, sending a chill through the trees.

"Perhaps we should turn back and wait until morning," Nathaniel's gaze was glued in the direction of the cry, "I don't know much of the forests, mate. What kind of creatures dwell here?"

Druet paused, "I don't know. I've heard of the fierce plant life and dragons that the ancient explorers tamed, but—"

"Plant life? You mean our worst enemy may be the grass beneath our feet?"

"Not grass; Carnatur Plants."

"Carnatur, eh? What are they, man-eating daisies?"

Druet grinned, "You're close."

"I've heard of the dragons, too," Nathaniel hopped onto a fallen log and jumped down to the other side, "They dwell on the western border of Lord Hugh's region, though, so we shouldn't find any here. They were subdued in the ancients' time, but have multiplied since then. Lord Hugh knew nothing of their vast reproduction until it was too late. Now all he can do is ensure that they keep to their coastal caves and away from the people."

"Perhaps their caverns hide the heart."

Nathaniel turned to his friend with a wary grin, "I'm not sure I'm ready for that just yet."

Druet froze.

"What's the matter, mate?"

"Something moved behind you. I saw something drop—"

Druet's words were cut short when a long, snakelike creature landed suddenly on his torch-bearing arm. With a cry, Druet whipped his arm, forcing the creature to drop to the ground. His torch also flew from his grasp, extinguishing with a hiss when it landed in a small pool of water at the base of a tree.

Druet's eyes never left the slithering creature. When it hit the ground a hundred tiny legs, like those of a centipede, emerged from its underside and carried it over the ground with effortless speed. The tail of its four-foot long body terminated in a sharp tip, while the other end rounded into its snakelike head, which was flanked on either side by thin flesh that fanned into a fierce-looking collar.

"What is that thing?" Nathaniel held his torch high and took a single step closer.

The creature reared on its miniature legs, hissing loudly, and a small burst of flame escaped its mouth.

"Ho, there; it ignites!"

"It's an ignispat."

"A what?"

"Ignispat! I've heard of them once before," Druet's hand found the pommel of his sword and he drew it from the sheath, "My father told me of an encounter with one long ago. It was unusual that it was alone, he said; they normally travel in large numbers."

"Then that means—" Nathaniel drew his own sword and turned around to search for the fallen creature that Druet had spotted moments ago.

Suddenly, the first ignispat's hissing came to a halt and both young men turned to stare at it. Slowly, the sound began again, growing in volume and intensity as hundreds of ignispats surrounded them in answer to the call of the first. Druet and Nathaniel looked up as spurts of flame began to spot the canopy of branches overhead and the ignispats scurried to be nearer to the ground and their human prey.

The first ignispat, coiled on the ground, suddenly lunged for Nathaniel; Druet quickly brought his sword in an overhead slice. The creature dropped to the ground, severed in two, and the two men exchanged a wide-eyed look when the hissing overhead quickly increased to an unbearable intensity.

"God help us," Nathaniel rasped.

An ignispat appeared suddenly between Nathaniel's feet and he moved to deal with the hissing reptile while Druet swung at another that dropped from overhead.

The two friends tried to move from their position, but quickly realized that the swift creatures had the ability to follow their progress in the treetops. One after another the ignispats dropped or lunged from tree or ground, spitting fire as they attempted to overwhelm Druet and Nathaniel.

One leapt from the trunk of a tree and spit its flame as it neared Druet's face. Surprised by the close proximity of creature and fire, Druet sidestepped from its path. Tripping over a root and landing flat on his stomach, Druet opened his eyes to find himself face-to-face with yet another ignispat; the creature hissed and spit just as Druet rolled out of the way. Once on his back, Druet saw two spurts of flame escape a couple of ignispats that had just abandoned the trees above him. Swinging his sword-arm, Druet succeeded in severing one before it reached him; the other landed on his chest and flared its one remaining side of flesh-fan. A hundred legs emerged and dug into Druet's tunic as the ignispat drew its head back and prepared to spit another flame.

Hearing a dozen more of the creatures landing with soft thuds around him, Druet grabbed his present attacker just behind the head and sat up in one swift motion. Turning the ignispat away just as it spewed fire, Druet directed the reptile toward one of those that had just dropped and scorched the second creature with the flame of the first.

The other ignispats suddenly shifted their attention from Druet, and the young blacksmith realized that their glittering eyes were following the creature in his hand—the one that had unwittingly struck one of its own. The reptile loosened its grip on Druet's tunic and thrashed franticly in his hand. Druet dropped the ignispat and jumped to his feet just as the surrounding reptiles slithered to trap their supposed traitor.

Aiming to take advantage of the chaos, Druet adjusted his grip on his sword and prepared to make quick work of the battling dozen before him.

"Ho, there, mate!"

Nathaniel's shout caused Druet to look up.

The two young men watched in shock as the horde of spitting ignispats converged on the dozen who still fought viciously on the ground before Druet. The young blacksmith slowly backed away as the mass of slithering creatures grew and all began to battle against one another. The noise was incredible, but in another moment all was silent.

Druet and Nathaniel, still breathing heavily, stared at the motionless mound of ignispats that had all fought to the death. The smell of overcooked meat hung thick in the air and the sudden quiet in the forest was strangely unnerving.

Druet sheathed his sword, "A man once came to Oak's Branch and preached the word of God—he actually owned a copy of the scriptures. He read that a house divided against itself cannot stand."

Nathaniel sheathed his sword with a sharp snap, "Well, these disgusting creatures kindly illustrated that point today," he studied the ignispats and sniffed several times.

Druet grinned, "Hungry?"

Nathaniel's glance rolled sickeningly, "I miss my mother's fine cooking."

Druet slapped his friend's shoulder and the two turned away from the sight of their skirmish, "Were you injured?"

"No...perhaps a bit singed, but still whole and hearty all the same! You?"

"Other than gaining a healthy apprehension for forest creatures, I believe I survived this encounter unscathed."

Nathaniel's brow lifted at his friend's eloquently spoken words; he opened his mouth to comment but suddenly clamped his jaw on the words, choosing instead to say, "I'm sure your father will enjoy hearing of this ghastly encounter."

Druet's smile saddened and he nodded. The object of his quest—Arcrea's elusive heart—somehow seemed farther from his reach than before; his reach seemed somehow more limited. With the battle against the ignispats behind him, he wondered for the first time if his mission would be futile—not because he couldn't find the heart, but because he may not live to discover it.

Praying for God's wisdom in his life, Druet brought his attention back to the present and to Nathaniel's comment.

"I'm sure he will, friend...I *know* he will."

Chapter 6
* Unlikely Companions *

The following day, the two travelers continued their search within the forest, examining a cave and several clearings that seemed unusual amid the regular dense surroundings. Unfortunately, nothing of the heart was found.

"At least we didn't run into another horde of ignispats," Druet leaned against a tree and pulled the folded map from a pouch at his belt.

Nathaniel finished dunking his head in a pool of cold water and then came to peer over his friend's shoulder. "Where are we?"

"Here is where the forest ends; we're nearly there. It looks as though we may be approaching a city, too."

The city of Tiltman sat atop a hill that rose from the forest's edge. When they entered the city the two young men were greeted by citizens who, upon learning of their identity, exclaimed delight over Druet's quest. They were told of several other men who, inspired by his mission, had also set out in search of the heart.

It was there that they also learned that the gathering clans of Frederick had dispersed the week before, after receiving a warning of the ruler's plans for utter devastation.

Druet received this last news with a small smile, thinking that his mother had, no doubt, played a part in sending word to his uncle Thomas.

As they approached the gates on the south side of Tiltman, Druet became aware of an unusual commotion.

"What's happening?"

Nathaniel craned his neck to look ahead, "Seems to be a feud at the gate."

Druet scanned the street ahead and saw that a growing crowd of spectators was forming a wide ring before the open gateway. In the middle of the ring two young men, both several years younger than Druet, circled one another with swords drawn.

Making his way to the inside of the crowd, Druet studied the two warriors. One, slightly taller than his opponent, had extremely blond hair that seemed nearly white in color. He held a sword in each hand— their sheaths crossed at his back—and wore a black doublet studded with silver. Druet recognized the colors as those belonging to Frederick's army and knew instinctively that the tunic had been looted. The young man's bright green eyes were glaring furiously at the second warrior who, in appearance, seemed to be his opposite.

The slightly shorter, solidly built young man had his nearly-black hair pulled back in a short club that reached just below his shoulders. His dark brown tunic was tied at the waist by a yellow sash that Druet saw was a strip carelessly torn from the standard of Lord Hugh's region. The young man's alert brown eyes followed his two-sworded adversary as his large fist clenched the pommel of his own weapon.

"Your clan at Rebel's Lair asked for trouble when you crossed to plunder Stephen's border!"

The green eyes flashed, "What do you care about that? You're not from Stephen's region!"

"I'll defend any region that I like! Especially when it means aiding them against you!"

The shorter man swung at the other and the three swords clashed several times. The crowd began to shout—some calling for an end to the fight, while others cheered one man or the other on. Druet glanced up the street and wondered why no soldiers came to stop the riotous behavior.

The blonde crossed his two swords and shoved the shorter man back several paces, "You're one to talk! Your clansmen at Knavesmire attacked Hugh's border so often he built a fortress on the shore across from your encampment!"

"There's no fortress there."

"What, did you sabotage that too?"

With an enraged growl, the shorter man renewed the vicious attack and the metallic ringing echoed in the gate's archway. The crowd's shouting heightened furiously and finally Druet could stand the insanity no longer.

The blacksmith took several steps toward the center of the ring.

"Ho, there, mate!" Nathaniel's cry was nearly lost in the chaos that surrounded them.

Bracy

Nicole Sager

Druet took one final step and halted several yards from the swordsmen; his hand rested prudently on the pommel of his own weapon. The crowd began to grow quiet as their attention slowly shifted to Druet, and a curious murmur raced through the ring, along with several calls for him to step back.

The two opponents continued their fight for another moment until the taller man's green eyes shifted and saw a powerfully-built stranger standing several yards away…glaring at him. With a twist, the blonde maneuvered out of the shorter man's reach and stood staring at Druet.

Druet eyed them both, "Excuse me, good sirs; I'd like to pass through to the gate."

"Are you the blacksmith?"

Druet froze and his face became the picture of surprise.

The shorter clansman spoke up, "The blacksmith from Oak's Branch?"

The first man raised one of his swords, "*I* was asking him, you chicken liver!"

"Well, I was asking him too, you maggot!"

The two snorted at each other and turned simultaneously to wait for Druet's answer.

Druet stared back at them, still surprised by their knowledge of his identity, "I'm Druet of Oak's Branch—a blacksmith, yes, but…how did you know?"

The blonde shrugged and motioned with his two swords, "All of Arcrea knows of you. I just supposed you were the man."

"I knew for certain the moment I saw you," the dark-haired man spoke confidently.

The green eyes rolled in disgust and then shifted back to Druet, "I've been in search of you and wish to join your quest."

"You?" the other cried, "I've been wandering through Frederick's for days now, seeking to join him!"

The taller man laughed, "You think you're cut out for work such as his?"

Nathaniel approached Druet from behind and gave his comrade a questioning glance. Druet gave his friend an uncertain look and then turned to the two clansmen.

"What are your names?"

"I'm Talon of Rebel's Lair, in Quinton's region," the blonde stated proudly.

"I'm Bracy of Knavesmire, in Ranulf's region," the dark-haired man made a bow.

Druet crossed his arms over his chest and spoke firmly, "And what gives you two foreigners the right to disturb the peace here in Frederick's region, not to mention the fact that you're blocking the gate?"

Talon glared, "He started it!"

"Liar," Bracy growled.

Druet glared, "What is it you're fighting over?"

Both clansmen started talking at once and Druet struggled to catch bits of what they said.

"His clan... Attack... My clan... Scoundrels... Border..."

"Alright," Druet held his hands up, "I gathered that much from your accusations earlier. Now tell me, why do have to deal with it through swordplay? Don't you realize that innocent blood may be spilled that way?"

"Innocent! His clan crossed—"

"He was among the number—"

Talon and Bracy fell silent under Druet's steady gaze. Slowly, Bracy sheathed his sword and Talon made a habitual twist of his wrists that sheathed both of his. The two cast a final glare at one another and then glanced sheepishly around at the awe-struck crowd that still stood in a ring around them—their focus now riveted on the young man who had put an end to the fierce fight.

Oblivious to the amazed stares, Druet turned to Nathaniel and motioned onward with his head.

A smile played at the corners of Nathaniel's mouth as he glanced once more around the ring and then followed Druet's firm step toward the gate.

Just as they reached the archway, Druet and Nathaniel turned at the sound of Talon's voice.

"I would join you still, Druet."

Bracy stepped forward, "I too."

Druet's authoritative glance passed between the two, "I will not stop you. Only know that if you do come, I will not tolerate in my band what I saw here today; long-fought clan disputes or no."

Druet turned without another word and passed through Tiltman's south gate with a grinning Nathaniel close behind. Talon and Bracy exchanged a near-savage glance and then followed, leaving the citizens of Tiltman with a new bit of gossip to share over their evening meal.

Nathaniel came up beside Druet and his grin broadened into a look of fascination, "You were meant to be king, Druet."

Druet glanced at the two clansmen behind him, keeping as far apart from each other as they could without surrendering the road. He turned to face forward again and his chest rose in a fraction of a laugh.

Suddenly, Druet's gaze focused on the stretch of road ahead and his mouth gaped in disbelief at what he saw.

Chapter 7
* Morgway *

A s they neared the base of Tiltman's hill, the four travelers gradually slowed, finally halting at Druet's lead. The young blacksmith's eyes swept over a makeshift village built to either side of what had once been the main road from the city, but was now a dirt street creased in the center by a shallow trench of sewage. A second road now skirted the village, gradually fashioned as travelers had sought to avoid the unpleasant community.

Druet's eyes began to sting, a result of both the putrid air and the tears that suddenly sprang to his eyes.

A haggard woman sat on the threshold of the first hut and gently, languidly, rocked back and forth, apparently trying to comfort the starving child in her lap. Down the street a dog yipped as two children chased it from the crate of a scant chicken. A woman appeared in her door, tossing the strange contents of a pail into the dirt, and then wiping tears from her eyes as she reentered the hut. Druet could hear the faint sound of another woman shooing her husband from the house to find work; a moment later the man stumbled out into the street and mumbled that there was no work to be had, before sinking to sit against the doorframe with his graying head buried in his hands.

Druet blinked to clear his vision, overwhelmed by the sights before him and the constant sounds of agony that filled the air. Whimpering children, crying babies, and the moans of men and animals alike collided with Druet's sense of justice as he realized that this place was a result of Lord Frederick's steadily increasing and unnecessary taxes.

Druet turned to gaze up at the city of Tiltman, remembering the sufficient, if not plenteous, provisions that he had seen there.

A sudden commotion pulled Druet's attention to the newer of the two roads, where a man was approaching on his way toward Tiltman. A small crowd of poorly-clad children rushed from the village to beg a coin of him.

The man shook his head and continued his steady pace, forcing the little ones to dodge out of his way, "These are hard times for all of us, children," he murmured.

A wail escaped the group of youngsters as they watched the man's back move up the hill and through the city's gates. Their sights then fell on Druet's band and they surged forward again; palms held up, they pleaded for a coin with eyes that held even more anguish than their high-pitched voices.

Druet laid his work-roughened hand on a small boy's head and lifted his face to the sky, taking a moment to blink back his tears.

Nathaniel watched his friend for a moment, knowing of Druet's anger toward injustice and wondering how the young blacksmith's abilities would amaze him this time. He glanced to see Talon and Bracy at a loss for what to say or do.

Druet finally looked down at the small face beneath his hand, "What is this place?"

The boy wrinkled his nose and scratched at it as he answered, "It's called Morgway, sir."

"How many people live in Morgway?"

The little fellow shrugged and a girl beside him spoke up, "I can't count that high."

The boy tugged at Druet's tunic, "Sometimes we have to share huts when the roof falls."

Druet glanced at Nathaniel, "This place distresses me."

"I know the feeling," Bracy scratched his head, "What do you say to moving on now?"

Druet turned to stare at the clansman, "Bracy, I need you to gather a count of the homes in Morgway, and bring the number back to me with haste."

Bracy's jaw dropped.

"Now."

Slowly, Bracy pulled away from the group and headed down the dirt street, counting the huts on his fingers. The crowd of children watched him go and then turned to face Druet, waiting to hear what strange command would next be issued.

"Talon," Druet turned again, "I need wood gathered and a large fire built…over there, in that cleared space. Nathaniel," Druet faced his friend and found the seaman grinning expectantly; he made a motion to indicate the cluster of children, "Will you tell them a story?"

Nathaniel gave a rumbling laugh and then bent so that he was eyelevel with his audience, "Who would care to hear of the day I nearly fell into the icy Arcrean in the midst of the fiercest gale recorded this side of the Brikbones?"

Druet watched as several mouths gaped in fascination and the children began to drop in place to sit on the dirt road.

Bracy approached with a guarded look and murmured, "Twenty-three huts."

"Come with me," turning back toward Tiltman, Druet climbed the hill at a fast pace and strode through the city gates with a determined glint in his eye.

€€€

Lord Frederick finished a turn and gently brought his sword around to meet the one held by his daughter. She flashed him a confident smile and the two continued through the intricate pattern of steps that comprised the Arcrean Sword Reel, a dance introduced by the land's ancient natives and passed down to the subsequent generations. When the last step had been completed, the two sheathed their swords and Lord Frederick made a low bow.

"Beautifully done."

The girl curtsied and then both looked up as the heavy oak door was opened and Falconer stepped in.

"What news, Falconer?"

"The rumors have been true, my lord; the blacksmith's son is traveling south and all of Arcrea waits each day for further news of him."

Lord Frederick's hand gripped the pommel of Druet's sword at his side, "And what is known of his mission?"

"He searches for the heart of Arcrea, my lord."

Lord Frederick turned away and muttered a curse, "And Gregory's wife; does she stay at Oak's Branch?"

Falconer nodded, "I have two men posted nearby to track any activities she may attempt beyond the smith."

"Good."

Falconer waited a moment in silence and then glanced at Frederick's daughter; she too was watching her father, waiting for him to speak.

"Are there any further orders, my lord?"

Lord Frederick drew his sword and studied the impeccable blade with a shrewd eye, "I still have a score to settle with this boy. The blacksmith must not discover the heart. I am sure that my fellow Arcrean lords would agree with me and even join me in putting a stop to this boy's quest if the need should arise; but for now his aimless wandering can only be harmless."

Falconer dipped his head in acknowledgement and Lord Frederick finally turned to face the informant.

"Follow him, Falconer."

છ૭૯૨

An hour passed.

Nathaniel gave three more stories and then told his audience that he needed a rest. Moving to the spot where Talon had built a fire pit, the seaman leaned against an outcropping of rock and looked toward Tiltman.

Kneeling by his growing project, Talon followed Nathaniel's gaze, "What's he up to?"

"I don't know him well enough to have that figured out; but I do know him well enough to say that it will be something good."

Talon rose, "I thought I was joining a man on a quest to find the heart."

"You did. But you'll soon find, as I did, that Druet is as clueless about Arcrea's heart as the ancient explorers were."

Talon lifted a confused brow.

"Druet is in search of the heart, mate; but his sense of justice won't pass up an opportunity to put something to rights…even if that means a detour."

A shout was heard as the children raced from the village yet again.

"He's coming! He's coming back!"

Followed by Talon, Nathaniel moved to meet Druet and Bracy, advancing toward Morgway with a small entourage of help behind them.

Two men carried a large black cauldron between them and, at Druet's request, moved to hang it over the fire that Talon had built. Three women, carrying bushels of fresh vegetables and thick broth, followed the cauldron to the fire and began to prepare a stew, throwing confused glances first at Druet and then at the village.

Curious villagers began to emerge from the huts, looking with confusion and alarm at the group of strangers.

Druet spoke with a man who had brought a crew to cover the sewage trench, asking him to let the men of the village assist in the work.

"I believe this will cover the cost of your labor," he slipped several coins into the stunned workman's hand, "Thank you for your time."

Talon watched the crew move away toward the village, and then shifted his gaze back to Druet,

"You paid for all this out of your own pocket?"

Druet shifted a silent gaze to Talon and the clansman saw a look of satisfaction in the blacksmith's blue eyes.

"You actually find pleasure in giving, then?"

"I do."

Druet turned as a man approached from the city, pulling a cart, "Talon, I need you and Bracy to deliver these—one mantle to each house. I wish it could be more, but this will at least afford some essence of warmth to these people."

Moving to the back of the cart, Talon met Bracy coming from the other side. The two exchanged looks of complete bewilderment and then reached to take up a pile of thick mantles.

"Not so close. Don't touch me, Bracy."

"Just grab a stack and be sure to take the opposite side of the street as me."

As the sun sank in the west, Druet looked up at the orange sky and was reminded of his hot irons at home. Bringing his gaze to earth again, he watched with a pleased smile as the long line of starving villagers finished passing by the steaming cauldron of stew. His stomach growled and Druet thought of the pleasure he would take in having to hunt for his own supper later. The money from his mother's pouch had been exhausted enough for one day; he would need to save what remained for the journey ahead.

A woman approached the spot where he stood at the edge of the firelight; Druet recognized her as the woman who had sat on the stoop of the first hut. Her contented child toddled along behind her and looked up at the blacksmith with a shy stare.

The woman looked at Druet and suddenly burst into tears. She dropped to her knees and clutched at his hand, laying her forehead to the back of his rough fingers. Druet knelt on one knee and waited until the woman looked up again. Her lips moved to speak her gratefulness but only a fresh flow of tears came. Druet gave an understanding nod and the woman moved to pull her child into an embrace that Druet knew was meant for her own consolation.

Standing again, Druet was met by several men who, overwhelmed by his day's work among them, could only grasp his hand and nod their thanks. The small boy who had stood beside him earlier came to place his hand in Druet's, following the blacksmith as he took an evaluating walk through the village.

The next morning, Druet and his three companions took the road through Morgway heading south. Behind them, a throng of villagers watched their departure. Some wept openly while others blinked fiercely at the tears that would come. Some called out blessings on the retreating figures while others could only stand motionless and stare after them.

৪০০৪

Deep within the Heartland, the natives' elders gathered with all haste for the council meeting that had been called only two days before, giving the men little time to travel from their various encampments to Olden Weld, the central village of their homeland.

Leland, the natives' chief and a direct descendant of Ulric the Ancient, lifted his hand to bring silence. After opening the meeting in prayer, he slowly looked from one face to another before finally speaking.

"You have all heard of the blacksmith, Druet, and his mission to discover the heart."

All heads nodded warily.

"We are all aware that it was proclaimed in olden days that the first king of Arcrea would possess the Heartland, thereby casting our people from their homes."

The elders nodded and began to murmur among themselves.

One man half-rose from his seat, "Something must be done!"

The chief nodded, "I wish to send one from among us to search for Druet of Oak's Branch."

The elder to his left studied Leland's face knowingly and finally asked, "You have someone in mind?"

Leland answered with a small smile that revealed his plan to the other elders.

"Leland, you can't be serious!"

"You wish to send—"

"What are you thinking, man?"

Leland held his hands up for silence, "All is well. The one I have chosen wishes to go—as I'm sure you can well imagine."

"When?"

"Tomorrow at daybreak."

Chapter 8
* Observations *

Nathaniel lifted his face to the wind and breathed deeply of the scent that had become ingrained in his senses, "Its going to rain, mates."

Druet's eyes lifted to search the cloudless sky for a long moment and then lowered again to the map in his lap, "I'll trust you, Nathaniel."

Nathaniel gave a small laugh and then turned to observe the other two travelers. They had traveled two days from Tiltman and Morgway and had just stopped in a fairly shaded place, with patches of trees dotting a wide valley.

Talon gave a vicious growl as he tried again to light the fire that he had built. Two freshly-skinned rabbits sat on a flat rock beside him, waiting for the spit.

Bracy laughed as he stretched with his back to a tree, "Having trouble there, Gallon?"

The green eyes flashed as he murmured, "It's *Talon*, you pig."

"Did you just call me a pig?"

"No, worse than that: a Mizgalian pig!" Talon huffed at another fruitless effort with his flint, "Where's a flaming ignispat when you need one?"

Druet glanced at Nathaniel with half a smile as he moved to stand next to Talon,

"Here. It's not a fire-spitting reptile, but I guarantee it's a bit friendlier."

The blond head came up and Talon took the offered flint from Druet's hand.

"Thank you."

Bracy watched Druet with a studied expression, "Have you met with an ignispat, then?"

"*An* ignispat?" Nathaniel sank to a seat by the fireside, "I wish it had been just one!"

With the rabbits finally roasting over Talon's fire, the two clansmen listened as Druet and Nathaniel told of their war against the ignispats.

"And you're still after the heart?" Bracy looked from one to the other when the story was done, "I wouldn't have thought a blacksmith and a water-legged ship's man would have had it in them to go on after such an encounter."

Talon scoffed, "You just say that because you *think* you would."

"I've seen worse than ignispats!"

"The reflection of your own face, perhaps?"

"Ho, there!"

Talon and Bracy turned from glaring at one another in answer to Nathaniel's shout. The young seaman and Druet both sat frowning at the clansmen until Druet spoke in a firm but quiet tone.

"The next man to start a quarrel doesn't eat tonight."

It was quiet for the span of several breaths as each settled back down and searched for a different topic to discuss. The sun had dropped low in the sky and the crickets were beginning their evening chorus.

"So," Talon cast a sidelong glance at Bracy and then cleared his throat as he looked across the fire at Druet, "Where have you searched for this heart?"

"Most everywhere in Frederick's region, south of Oak's Branch that is. We found several caves, forests, overgrown paths...I don't know what else to do."

"Has anyone ever come close?" Bracy asked, "Many have searched for the heart before and others are searching now, inspired by your quest; but has anyone ever found a clue? Or is it a hopeless trail with no end in sight?"

"I believe it is hopeless..." all turned in surprise at Druet's words, "to a point. My father taught me that many men will seek to be Arcrea's king, but only one man has been chosen by God to fulfill Ulric's prophecy and satisfy that coveted role."

Druet leaned his head back against the trunk of the tree behind him and stared up at the stars that were beginning to peek through the dark canvas of sky, "I sometimes wonder if I *am* on a hopeless trail—there is a great likelihood that I am not the chosen one. But if I don't search—if I don't try—I'll always wonder then if I might have succeeded...if perhaps I was the man God had chosen, but in rejecting His call I was casting off this great honor to another."

Druet brought his gaze down to return Bracy's, "That is why I must continue to search for Arcrea's heart, though no man has ever come close to discovering it, or even a clue to its whereabouts, in the past."

Bracy nodded slowly and then lowered his gaze, "I cannot say that I believe God cares enough about this place that He would appoint a man as our king...but I will say that you seem a noble man, and able for the fight it will take to earn the crown."

Druet dipped his head in a single nod, "I pray that by our journey's end, your estimation of God will be greater than your kind opinion of me."

When the rabbits were at last removed from the flame's heat and served, the young blacksmith spoke again.

"You know, in all of this searching for Arcrea's heart, I've never given much thought to the heart itself, or what it may prove to be other than some place or an object that represents an actual heart," he looked around at his comrades with a thoughtful expression, "Really, apart from being the prize of this quest, what is a heart?"

Nathaniel swallowed his mouthful, "It is the very depth of a man."

"It is his inner self," Talon added, "that which is hidden from the world's view, yet expressed in his desires and actions."

Druet looked to Bracy and the young man responded, "It is the core or reason behind a matter."

Druet nodded, "Interesting. I'd like to record these thoughts on the back of our map."

Nathaniel habitually lifted his face as the breeze pulled at his hair, "I think we should head in another direction, mate. Among the last few cities we've traveled through, I've heard talk that the natives in the Heartland do not take kindly to men who scour their encampment in search of Arcrea's heart, as if it were a written rule that every man may pillage the land to his soul's contentment as long as the heart is his excuse."

Just as he finished speaking, a web of lightning blossomed across the sky to the west, followed by a distant roll of thunder. Nathaniel made a funny smile when a drop of rain landed on his nose.

"Told you."

ഈകഃ

Falconer stood at the head of a dirt street and gazed in well-hidden shock at the village before him. He knew what Morgway had once been, thanks to Frederick's taxes, and that the sorry place was still a far cry from pleasant; but to see that the achievement of one day's work—of one man's work—had put a smile on the faces of these oppressed people! This blacksmith had earned more respect in one day than the lord of the land had earned in nineteen years.

A woman's voice rose in absentminded song from within the first hut to his left; a child sat on the front stoop and gently rocked a doll made of sticks. A dog followed two children across the street, ambling over the mound of dirt carefully packed over the trench and into a home where a man's laughter suddenly sounded.

Falconer turned at the sound of someone approaching from behind. The newcomer was a tall, spindly man with yellow hair hanging roughly to his shoulders and a billowing tunic a size too large. His leggings were red and yellow, a color to each leg, and his short boots were fringed at the ankle. A well-used lute hung from a strap over his shoulder, draping across his back, and he was whistling a simple tune.

Falconer stroked the nose of his ebony-colored mare and nodded as the whistler drew closer; the other man responded with a dramatic wave of his long arm.

"A fine day to you, sir! And such pleasant weather is it not?"

"It is."

The man glanced beyond Falconer, "Have you been observing the good work done in Morgway? Such a story, such a story."

"I heard that Druet the blacksmith ordered the covering of the trench and fed the villagers a good supper."

"So he did, good sir! And bought a new mantle for each home; so lending warmth to the people from his heart and hand. I am in search of this charitable blacksmith, for I wish to join his band. You see, I am Blunt, a traveling minstrel from Lord Hugh's region, and the people of Arcrea wish to hear nothing but tales and songs of Druet."

"And you will join him in order to learn more of his doings firsthand?"

"Correct! I have already written a melody about his work here in Morgway; would you care to hear it?"

"Thank you, no; I'm afraid I cannot stay in this place long," Falconer turned and took a step toward the village; a thought struck him and he turned back to ask in a casual air, "Where will you search next for the blacksmith?"

"I heard that he went south from here, but that was a week ago. Since then, news has trickled into Tiltman that he turned southeast toward the region of Stephen."

Falconer nodded as he turned and mounted his horse; he would travel south for several miles before doubling back to follow this minstrel on his trek to find Druet.

"Good journey to you, then, Blunt!"

"And to you, good sir!"

Chapter 9
* Dangerous Venture *

D ruet's band searched the south portion of Frederick and crossed the border into Lord Stephen's region two weeks after leaving Tiltman. Everywhere they went, news of their coming had preceded them and the citizens of each town, village, hamlet, and farm wished to express their favor of the young man whose charitable work at Morgway had earned him the respect of every Arcrean peasant.

When passing through the cities, Druet made it a point to inquire about the local landscapes, forests, and other places that might prove a wise location to continue his search. Each spot was visited and searched by the four travelers, but always the cave, clearing, outcropping, forest, valley, abandoned cottage, embankment, or dried riverbed was left without success.

The heart was nowhere to be found.

In a dense tangle of forest a mile beyond the city of Saxby, Druet used his sword to cut away a thick hanging vine that blocked what appeared to be the only recognizable path to follow. Behind him, Talon growled at a bush that insisted on snagging at his pants and tunic.

"This cave had better offer something worth the effort it's taking to get there."

Bracy snorted from somewhere off to the left, "Do you always complain when physical activity is asked of you?"

"Keep your mouth shut, Bracy. I wasn't complaining about the travel, just these accursed plants!"

"At least they're not Carnaturs," Druet interjected.

"Or ignispats," Nathaniel shouted from behind, casting a wary glance to the thick canopy overhead.

"I'm hungry," Bracy suddenly announced.

Talon gave a disgusted look and leaned forward to glare at the other clansman, "Who's complaining now?"

"I'm simply stating a natural fact!"

"But you grumble every time I bring back food!"

"I only mentioned the fare when we had eaten rabbit seven meals in a row! Can't you catch anything different?"

"You just watch me catch a lizard for your next meal," Talon murmured; raising his voice, he added, "Bracy, you play the hunter for a few days and see if you snare a better critter."

Nathaniel gave a dramatic sigh, "Oh to be perched in the rigging of the *Seabird*, with no griping land-lovers about and only wind and sail to care what you had to say!"

Druet's shoulders shook with a laugh and Talon rolled his eyes.

"Very funny, Nathaniel."

Suddenly Druet froze and tilted his head to one side, listening to a strange sound that was coming from somewhere up ahead. The other three men joined him and listened as well.

"Do you hear that?" Druet whispered.

They nodded and the four started forward again, cautiously watching where they stepped and ensuring that they made as little noise as possible.

It was not long before they came to a place where the ground dropped away some fifteen feet into a clearing that was approximately fifty feet across. The area was littered with giant boulders and shrubbery that grew from the nearly vertical walls in several places. A pool of water collected in the middle of the clearing.

The four men silently lowered themselves to lie on their stomachs, scanning the clearing with alert eyes.

"There," Bracy pointed to a spot across the clearing where a pack of creatures, each the size of a large dog, were feasting on the carcass of another larger animal.

The savage beasts had long cat-like tails that constantly whipped the air, and large feet that were webbed between the toes. Their heads were a pointed affair, with a sharp-looking snout, and their large ears looked able to catch the sound of a leaf dropping in the forest. Occasionally, one or another of the creatures would snarl and make a clicking sound with the back of its tongue, warning the others away from its own portion of meat.

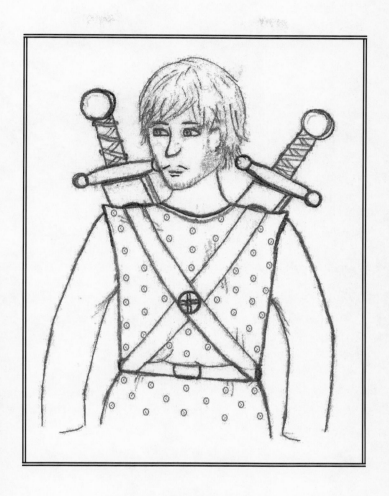

Talon

Nicole Sager

"What are they?" Nathaniel asked.

"It's the Catawyld Beast," Talon replied, "They migrated from the eastern Brikbones fifty years ago when a band of Mizgalians drove them south, seeking to fill Arcrea with these fierce creatures. They live in packs such as this one and are adept at climbing; whether tree, rock, or castle wall. Their greatest assets are their dirk-teeth; a double set of finely-sharpened fangs."

"Look down there."

Druet pointed below them and slightly off to the right where the entrance to a cave opened out onto an overhang five feet from the ground in the clearing…ten feet below the band's position in the trees above.

"Yep," Nathaniel scratched his right ear, "There it is…with dangerous beasts to guard it and all."

"The catawylds no doubt make their home there."

"But what if the heart is hidden there?"

"Druet, we're dead men when they catch sight of us! Even could we scale the clearing walls in seconds they are twice as fast."

"Then I'll go alone. They're distracted with the carcass just now; if you all help lower me to the overhang, perhaps they won't take notice of me."

"Druet, we would all still be in danger."

Druet was silent for a moment. Something inside of him desperately wanted to search the cave below, yet he was certain that God would not call him to purposefully put others' lives in danger.

"God, what do I do?" Druet rested his forehead on the backs of his hands, waiting for an answer to come.

To one side, Nathaniel watched his friend, feeling that he was witnessing the making or breaking of a man.

Suddenly, in the trees on the other side of the clearing, a deer stumbled to a halt at the top of the vertical drop. The catawylds looked up in unison and gave a fierce shriek that sent the deer back the way it had come. With another shriek of anticipation, the catawylds left their nearly cleaned carcass and gave chase to the deer, scrambling effortlessly up the walls and into the forest.

"Go!" Druet rasped.

Without a second thought, the four young men lifted to their feet and found footholds to begin their downward trek. Half-slipping, half-running they quickly made their way to the overhang in front of the cave's entrance.

Druet landed and immediately turned to enter the cave, but froze before he could go any further. His three comrades quickly came to a halt around him.

Standing just inside the cave was a snarling catawyld.

The animal's tongue clicked in warning and it crouched as if to pounce, but did nothing more. Behind it, Druet saw the motionless form of a dog, no doubt the catawyld's next meal.

"Its right fore-leg is wounded," Talon whispered of the catawyld, "It should be an easy—"

Druet's hair stood on end when another snarl suddenly sounded from behind them. Slowly turning, but keeping the wounded catawyld in sight, the four shifted to see a second large beast perched at the edge of the overhang. The rest of the pack had not yet returned, and so Druet supposed that this creature had been left to guard the carcass and the clearing.

Druet's mind raced to form some sort of plan, "Talon and Bracy, as the better swordsmen, will take the one outside the cave. Nathaniel and I will take the wounded one inside."

"When?"

The second catawyld crouched with a click of its tongue and Druet's heart thundered in his chest.

"God help us," Nathaniel whispered as each man laid a hand to the pommel of his sword.

"Now!"

The four split in opposite directions as the catawyld pounced and the five swords were drawn.

Druet and Nathaniel hurried to flank either side of the wounded beast. The angry catawyld used its hind legs to leap at Nathaniel and received a cut across its shoulder in return. With a shriek it shrank back and bared its teeth at the seaman. Seeing that the beast was preoccupied with Nathaniel, Druet rushed up from behind. The catawyld turned at the last second and snarled at Druet, but before it could move, the blacksmith's sword had found its target and the beast was immediately still.

Outside the entrance, Bracy howled when the larger catawyld clawed at his tunic, ripping a hole in the course fabric. Talon wielded his twin swords and whistled for the beast's attention; when the catawyld turned for an instant, Bracy leaned into a plunge and delivered a thrust to its side. Talon then leapt forward and finished the creature off from the other direction.

Sheathing his swords with a quick twist of his wrists, Talon panted, "Look for the heart, quick; before the pack returns."

The other three sheathed their swords as well and Druet turned to scan the cave with a disappointed sigh.

"It looks no different than the other caves we've seen."

"I need a new tunic," Bracy grumbled.

Druet's gaze traveled upward and around the cave, finally landing on the motionless dog by the wall. Its side lifted and then fell in a forced breath, and Druet saw that its eyes were open.

"Its still alive," Druet knelt for a closer look.

Panting, Nathaniel came to peer over his shoulder.

"A dog?" Talon's arms stretched in disbelief, "We went through all that for a dog?"

The animal in question lifted its head then and tried to lick its back leg, obviously broken.

"Why didn't they kill it before bringing it here?"

"They're coming!" Bracy called.

The snarling and tongue-clicking of the nearing pack grated on each ear as the four men turned to look across the clearing. At the top of the wall, a catawyld suddenly appeared and spotted them instantly; shrieking to alert the rest of the pack, it dove from its perch and flew down the wall.

"This way," Nathaniel shouted at the back of the cave, "it tunnels farther."

"What if it's a dead end?"

"Its our only chance now!"

Talon and Bracy ran to follow Nathaniel while Druet, with a swift glance at the approaching catawyld, quickly scooped the wounded dog in his arms.

"Leave it, Druet," Bracy shouted.

The dog began to thrash as a fresh burst of pain shot through its leg. As gently as he could, Druet situated his arms as he stood and began to move after his comrades; finally, he gained a good grip and clutched the dog firmly to his chest.

Talon waited for Druet to pass him and then took up the rear with both swords ready. Using sticks and shrubbery that had been dragged inside by the catawylds, Nathaniel and Bracy managed to construct and light a makeshift torch as they ran.

The tunnel twisted and turned, climbed and dropped for several hundred yards before suddenly opening into a vast cavern of cone-shaped rocks and luminous green water. As the young men pulled up short in surprise over their surroundings, the pursuing catawyld leapt from the tunnel behind them and shrieked fiercely at Druet while eyeing the dog in his arms. The dog jerked and Druet tightened his hold on its middle.

"Talon?"

The light-haired clansman nodded silently, his eyes never leaving the beast before them. In the next instant, the catawyld leapt forward and Talon simultaneously threw one of his blades spear-fashion. The catawyld dropped mid-leap, clicked it tongue once, and died.

"Will others follow?" Nathaniel asked.

Talon shook his head as he bent to retrieve his sword, "They didn't see us. It sounded as if they caught their deer, so their senses will be filled with the fresh meat for a while. By the time they catch our scent we will already have traveled farther from their haven than they will care to follow."

Talon sheathed his sword and his green eyes shifted to Druet. He shook his head, "You had to bring the dog."

Druet was silent.

"Why?" Nathaniel asked sincerely.

Druet's gaze passed from one face to another.

"I don't know."

Chapter 10
* The Healer *

The cavern's green waters were fed by an underground stream that eventually broadened into a river. As Druet's band followed this, the question on everyone's mind was finally voiced by Bracy.

"Is this place the heart?" His voice echoed along the strange chamber, as if daring him to answer his own question.

"It may be," Druet spoke slowly, "But...something about it doesn't seem right. There's no reason why this place should be the heart more than any other Arcrean cave or river."

"Its green," Talon noted with a glance at the water.

Bracy wrinkled his face, "So are your eyes, but that doesn't signify anything special."

Without warning, Talon's arm shot out and delivered a stiff shove to Bracy's shoulder, nearly sending the surprised clansman into the river.

"Talon! What was that for?"

"Don't talk about my eyes."

Bracy made an annoyed grunt, "You're so provoking!"

"*I'm* provo— You're the one who just provoked me!"

Druet rolled his eyes while half a smile reached his lips in spite of his aversion to their relentless arguing.

Shifting his attention to the animal in his arms, Druet gently shifted his hold and studied the nervous dog. It was a scruffy light-brown creature with a collar of white fur around his neck, a black muzzle, and ears that appeared far too furry for his breed.

When the group stopped to rest, Druet wrapped the dog's broken leg and then positioned the animal over his shoulders when they were preparing to move on. Bracy smiled and shook his head at the sight,

"You look like a shepherd."

"Have you given your black sheep a name, then?" Talon called laughingly.

Druet grinned, "Anvil."

Nathaniel laughed and gave his head an amused shake, "Only a blacksmith."

Before much longer, the four men began to hear a thunderous noise coming from up ahead. As they drew nearer, they saw an opening in the cavern wall where the river poured through and cascaded to a pond several hundred feet below. The sunlit landscape of Arcrea stretched before them as far as the eye could see. Clouds drifted in their windswept path overhead, casting deep shadows on patches of earth below.

"Feels as if you could see the whole kingdom from here."

The others nodded at Talon's words as they scanned the breathtaking view.

Bracy sighed, "So this wasn't the heart…it's the head."

"Bracy, don't try to be poetic; it doesn't suit you."

"That wasn't poetry! It didn't even rhyme."

Druet squeezed his eyes shut when their words reminded him of his own lighthearted bantering over his father's poorly-worded songs. What he wouldn't give to be home again, pounding steel and enduring Gregory's booming voice in the sweltering smith shop. What he wouldn't give to laugh with his father again.

"Let's go."

Druet stepped forward and began his descent, using a narrow ledge that protruded from beside the waterfall and zigzagged its way across the cliffs to the valley below. Behind him, his three companions followed carefully. Above him, Anvil settled his chin on Druet's head with a pig-like grunt.

Druet's eyes widened, "Hey, up there," he waved a hand in the dog's face, "no drooling, mutt!"

They made it to the valley floor with little trouble; the only scare being when Bracy tripped forward and nearly tumbled off the path with Talon in tow. Fortunately, Talon had the wherewithal to dig his heels into the rock and duck, and Nathaniel, standing firmly in front of them, locked a preventative grasp on Bracy's wrists as the clansman flew forward over Talon.

As their shouts echoed across the cliff walls, everyone remained frozen, allowing their minds to process the fact that they were still alive and well. Nathaniel then slowly helped Bracy to a standing position and they continued their descent, Talon giving a quick slap to the back of Bracy's head.

At the pond below, each filled his own water flask and then stared silently at the glittering water, preparing for the next leg of their kingdom-wide search. Anvil hobbled on three legs to the water's edge and lapped up a drink while looking at Druet from the corner of his eye.

"He seems to be doing better already; perhaps the catawylds had only just brought him to their clearing before we arrived," Druet glanced at Nathaniel and saw that the seaman's eyes were still locked in a stare on the water, "Are you alright?"

Nathaniel offered a silent nod and then suddenly reached down to take off his boots. Tossing a swift glance of anticipation at Druet, he shrugged his vest off and dashed toward the water, jumping out over the pond without the slightest pause of preparation and plunging into the water with a wildly shouted whoop.

Standing on the embankment, Talon and Bracy watched the splash and then both turned to stare at Druet with startled expressions. Druet grinned and then bent to remove his own boots. For the rest of the day, the four travelers swam in the pond and rested on its banks.

The water was fed into a stream that meandered south, and was bordered on both sides by a light forest that reached to the base of the waterfall's cliff.

Late in the afternoon, Talon reminded Bracy that it was the dark-haired clansman's turn to find food. Bracy gave the blonde a withering look and then set off into the forest. When he returned some time later, Talon looked up with a shout,

"What did you get?"

Bracy grimaced, "Three rabbits…"

"Ha!"

"…and a squirrel."

"A squirrel!? What'll we do with that…?"

"Ho, there," Nathaniel spoke from his lazy position in the grass, "You two are too hard on each other. You need a bow to hunt anything bigger…I'm surprised you've managed rabbits."

Some distance away, Druet swung his sword in several combinations. It felt good to use his arms in swinging a heavy object…even if it was Lord Frederick's sword. Thinking of the hammers in his father's smith, Druet hefted his sword in one hand and brought it around in an overhead slice. He let it fall within inches of the grass and then lifted it for another cut. Over and over, Druet imitated the action of pounding his hammer over a scrap of yellow-hot iron. In his mind he heard the sharp twang and thud that his hammer produced, and he saw the malleable iron take shape beneath his blows.

"Druet!"

The young blacksmith looked up with a start and gasped for breath; he hadn't realized he was panting.

Nathaniel quirked an eyebrow, "I said the rabbits are cooked and ready to eat."

Druet nodded and took another deep breath. How long had he been lost in thought? Giving his head a shake to clear the cobwebs of memory, Druet wondered why today had been harder than all the previous days. He missed Oak's Branch, his father, his mother, and the constant hard work in the shop.

"Are you alright, mate?"

Another nod and Druet sheathed his sword, "I need a rest."

Nathaniel nodded but eyed his friend uncertainly as they walked toward the cook fire. Clearing his throat, he suddenly grinned, "We gave the squirrel to your dog."

Druet chuckled, "I'll have to thank Bracy for his gracious contribution."

An hour later, the band sat talking around the fire. Druet was using a small grinding stone to polish one of Talon's swords. Beside him, Anvil suddenly lifted his head from the blacksmith's knee and barked at the nearby trees.

Druet lightly tossed the sword and Talon caught it by the pommel as the four young men stood in unison and turned to face whatever the dog had sensed.

"Who's there?" Druet called out.

They waited in silence for a moment, the sudden tenseness as obvious as the crackling fire.

"Maybe its nothing," Talon whispered; he glanced at Anvil, "That's the first time he's barked all day—maybe his senses were muddled by the catawylds' attack."

"SH!" Druet brought a finger to his mouth and leaned forward.

The sound of someone talking gradually drew closer until two forms, a man and a woman, emerged from the forest. Each carried a small sack slung over their shoulders and the man used a tall walking stick that helped to propel his steps forward. Druet was about to ask again for their identity when the man lifted his scraggly gray head and a gap-toothed smile split his features.

"Well, hello there!"

Bracy's mouth dropped open at the man's enthusiasm.

The man turned to the woman, "My dear Sarah, I believe we found them!"

A smile spread across Druet's face, "Who are you, sir?"

The man did not respond, only continued to advance toward the group with quick steps. Talon cast a confused look at Druet.

The elderly Sarah looked up with an apologetic smile and then, leaning close to her husband's ear, spoke with a loud voice, "Rodney, the blacksmith asked who you are!"

The old man stopped suddenly and brought his head up to stare at Druet, "Oh! I am Rodney of Saxby, dear boy, the city which you passed through only this morning!"

Sarah smiled endearingly at Rodney and then added, "He is a healer."

Rodney nodded emphatically, "A healer hard of hearing! Ha ha!"

Druet invited the couple to share the fire and everyone soon seated themselves around the warming flames. Talon sheathed his sword and was the last to sink to the ground.

"You are—" Nathaniel began and then, with a glance at Sarah, leaned toward Rodney and raised his voice to nearly a shout, "You are a healer?"

"That I am, good sir! But only by word of mouth."

When Nathaniel looked confused, Rodney explained, "I began my work years ago, using medicinal herbs and such to make natural remedies of the plants that God has provided for our use here."

Druet saw Bracy shift uncomfortably at the mention of God's provision.

"There were many healers in Arcrea then," Rodney shook his head sadly, "When the seven lords heard that our remedies were working—some even more effective than the harsher ways of a physician—they banned the practice of healers and passed a law that decreed any man working openly as a healer would be condemned to death."

"Why?" Druet asked loudly, "Why forbid a practice that was helping to keep the people healthier?"

"Why indeed? It causes one to pause and think, does it not?"

Talon leaned forward, "How did the seven lords excuse their actions, then?"

"They charged us with working magic among the people..."

"With plants?" Bracy interjected.

"...they proclaimed that we were using dark powers to move the commoners in rebellion against the nobility."

Talon scoffed and sat back, "We're in rebellion against the nobility anyway."

Bracy sat up straight, "Against the nobility! The only thing your clan has ever done is badger the coast of Stephen!"

Druet cleared his throat before Talon could respond and the two clansmen fell to silently glaring at one another.

The blacksmith turned back to the healer, "You have been condemned to death if you are open about your work, and yet you told us straight away that that is your profession?"

Rodney shrugged his thin shoulders, "I'm old. What can they do to my aged bones other than break them and so send my soul on to eternal glory? Besides, I know of you Druet; you are not a man who will betray one to injustice, I know."

Sarah turned to Druet, "We have come to offer our services to your band and join you on your quest."

Talon and Bracy turned looks of shock to Druet and waited for his answer. Druet smiled at their concerned looks and thought of the recent day when he had made the same face in response to the clansmen's similar offer.

"I will not stop you and your wife from joining us, Rodney. I'm sure you already know that the journey will be hard, so if you are willing to undergo this hardship, then I welcome you to our band."

"What a pleasant boy he is, Sarah!"

Druet pressed his lips together and dipped his head. From the corner of his eye, he could tell that Talon and Bracy had yet to close their dropped jaws.

Druet lifted his hand and tussled Anvil's furry ears. The dog responded by placing his chin back to rest on Druet's knee and staring up at the blacksmith with large black eyes.

"You know," Rodney suddenly spoke again, "that dog wandered through Saxby every day for a month. It disappeared only a week ago, and I wondered where he had gone to. I'm so glad to see that he is in good hands, aren't you, Sarah?"

Druet saw the woman nod and then listened as Nathaniel conducted the rest of the group's introductions.

Anvil yawned, a high-pitched wheezing sound, and Druet watched the dog's eyes slide shut. Leaning back against a large rock that had been serving as his makeshift chair-back, Druet stared at the shifting flames and listened absently to the pleasant chatter of Rodney and the good-humored replies of Nathaniel.

Thank you, God, for such friends. I pray that Your presence would become real to Bracy; for, if nothing else comes of this search for Arcrea's heart, a man brought to repentance before You would make my journey successful.

Druet's eyelids began to droop.

The fire before him became the heated forge in Oak's Branch and once again he heard the clang of hammer on iron.

Chapter 11
* Of Laymen & Lords *

Father!" Druet's voice sounded empty, "Father, where are you?"

Racing through the unfamiliar dark stone stairways and corridors, Druet finally reached a door and flung it open. Within the prison cell, Gregory sat helplessly chained to the wall.

"Father, I've come to help you! I've found the heart!"

Gregory looked up with a defeated gaze and spoke in the same hollow tone as his son's, "No, Druet; it will take a remarkable man."

"You don't understand!"

Druet rushed forward to strike the chains that bound his father. His hammer struck the links in powerful strokes until a hand was calmly laid on his arm.

"Druet," his mother spoke from beside him, "God alone knows."

"But I found the heart! I found it! Look for yourself mother!"

She began to shake her head slowly, and Druet realized that the cell and his parents were slipping away from him. He tried to race back along the corridor, but the cell door only pulled farther from his reach. The floor swept from under his feet.

A course laugh sounded behind him, and Druet turned to see Lord Frederick glaring down at him. The laughter turned into a strangely warped sound and Druet turned to run, but found his path blocked by the stranger who had stood in his doorway, watching Gregory's arrest.

Lord Frederick pulled Druet back around to face his ugly snarl, "You can cease your foolish quest now! It will take a remarkable man."

"But it's done—I found the heart!"

With a fierce growl, Lord Frederick pulled Druet's sword from his sheath and raised it over his head.

"*NO!*"

Druet jerked forward and opened his eyes. Sweat was pouring down his face and his hand was clutching the pommel of his sword so tightly his knuckles were white. Glancing around the circle, he saw that the others were fast asleep...except for Nathaniel.

"You're troubled today, mate."

Druet sighed and ran a hand over his face and through his hair, "I miss my father."

The ripples in the pond, created by the cascading waterfall, slapped gently at the water's edge.

"I look forward to meeting him," Nathaniel finally spoke; Druet looked up to return the seaman's steady gaze, "Your father will be very proud when he hears of all that you've accomplished."

"I've only done what any ordinary man might do."

"No, Druet, not ordinary—*extra*ordinary. Any man who 'might' do what you have done has failed when he doesn't go and do it. You obeyed the call of God, and are still working to complete His plan for your life," he grinned, "Not to mention you've become the toast of every Arcrean table."

"Except the nobility," Druet thought of the intimidating picture that Lord Frederick had presented in his dream.

"Hmm," Nathaniel gave a sideways nod of agreement, "You may not be exactly a toast at their tables, but I'm sure they talk about you just as often as the peasantry does."

"That's not much comfort, you know."

Anvil's ears suddenly slanted upward and his head quickly lifted to stare across the pond. Druet's gaze followed the dog's but he saw nothing to cause alarm.

"I don't hear anything, do you?" Nathaniel whispered.

Druet shook his head.

Anvil rose stiffly and hobbled to the edge of the pond. Raising his head, he sniffed the air for an unusually lengthy time and then made a noise that sounded like a dismissive sneeze. Lowering his head to lap up a drink, he returned to sit by Druet, seemingly content but with his eyes glued to the opposite shore.

Druet's eyes shifted to Nathaniel, "I'll stay up to watch for a time."

Nathaniel nodded, "Wake me in a while and I'll take a turn," he leaned back and began to situate himself comfortably, "On second thought," he grinned mischievously, "Wake Talon or Bracy...and they'll take a turn."

Nothing unusual occurred during the night, and the next morning Druet woke the band to start before the sun had risen. Following the stream for a short distance, they soon followed a path that cut through the forest and emptied its travelers onto the main road from Saxby.

They made quite a picture as they walked. Druet led the band with Anvil on his shoulders, and studied the road ahead with alert eyes. Nathaniel came close behind him, peering into the trees on either side and occasionally glancing to ensure that the others were following. Talon and Bracy remained on opposite sides of the fairly wide road, alternately pelting pinecones at each other when an opportunity was provided and watching the elderly couple behind them with curious glances.

Rodney and Sarah walked along one side of the road, frequently pulling up various plants, tying the stems together, and dropping these bunches into Rodney's sack. The gray-haired man used his staff to encourage his legs into forward motion and he muttered the name of each specimen to Sarah, who carefully scratched the list into a piece of smoothed bark.

At about noon, they came to a crossroads and stopped to eat some bread that Sarah had brought from Saxby. Anvil barked and looked down the road they had just come by and Druet soon became aware of someone singing.

It was not long before a tall spindly man, perhaps a decade older than Druet, with shoulder-length yellow hair and brightly colored leggings came into view. He was absently strumming the strings of a lute and singing a song that Druet quickly realized, to his embarrassment, was about his work at Morgway.

Anvil barked again and the bard interrupted his song to exclaim with obvious delight, "Ah! And so I find you at last, Druet!"

Bracy's eyes grew abnormally large while Talon slapped a hand to his forehead and muttered, "Oh, no."

৪০෬

Flickering torches brilliantly lighted the great hall, with help from a multitude of chandeliers that dripped wax into the hair of the gathered nobility below. The servants moved about carefully, wary of the raucous laughter and angry shouting that varied with each topic of conversation.

Lords Ranulf and Quinton had gathered with their knights in Frederick's castle to discuss the border wars against Mizgalia; but as the discussion progressed it became apparent to all that each lord was having difficulty in refraining from starting a war with his fellow Arcrean rulers.

Lord Frederick pounded a fist on the table and sent his wine-filled goblet careening to the floor, "We might have put an end to this campaign months ago if you had brought your men to help reinforce my northern border, Ranulf!"

"And leave my own border with minimum protection? Quinton might have sent his men instead!"

"I sent as many as my knights could spare at the time," Quinton growled.

"I had none to spare," Ranulf retorted, half-rising from his chair, "Not only do I have the Mizgalians to watch for, I have the clans to deal with as well! Lord Hugh is constantly sending me complaints regarding the clan at Knavesmire. I have trouble finding an adequate number of soldiers to settle my own border, let alone Frederick's."

"I have more clans in half my region than you have within your entire border. The gathering at Rebel's Lair alone has more members than the occupants in five of my cities, and they pillage Stephen's border more times in a year than I care to know. Let Hugh protect his own border—he doesn't have Mizgalian-laden Brikbones to cover."

Ranulf dropped back into his seat and yelled for a servant to refill his goblet. A fresh cup was placed before Lord Frederick as well and the conversation soon continued when Lord Quinton spoke.

"What news of the wandering blacksmith? I hear nothing but praise is spoken of him among the common masses."

"He is in Stephen's region," Frederick replied with a disgusted tone.

"Then I say let Stephen have him. Why bother ourselves over a fanatic that is sure to fail?"

"He comes from Frederick's region," Ranulf spoke with an antagonistic tone.

"And he chose to leave Frederick's region, what of it? I say this war with the Mizgàlians has lasted long enough, and ought to bare more weight in our minds than some stupid peasant on a hopeless mission."

Frederick's hand moved unwittingly to clutch the pommel of Druet's sword. This "stupid peasant" and his mission bore more weight in his mind than the other lords knew.

"Druet the blacksmith is being followed as we speak. I sent a man after him and will continue to watch his movements. His father is imprisoned in my tower just now for an act of rebellion."

"Wonderful," Quinton swallowed the contents of his goblet and motioned for a servant to refill it, "Just be sure to keep him there and you'll have an excellent motivation to persuade this Druet to give up his foolishness should the...ah...need arise."

Frederick tipped his goblet in acknowledgement, "My thoughts exactly, Quinton."

Chapter 12
* Change of Plans *

D ruet's band of seven, which now included Blunt the minstrel, sat at a generous supper that had been provided for them by an innkeeper in the city of Coswell. The blacksmith's mangy dog lay with his upper-body between Druet's feet, and Falconer was certain the animal's eyes hadn't stopped watching him from the moment he had slipped into a seat across the room.

Lord Frederick's chief informant studied the group of travelers and wondered that the ruler was so concerned about this man. Many others had searched—were even now searching—for Arcrea's heart, but the seven lords had simply left them to fade unsuccessful from the kingdom's memory; but not the blacksmith from Oak's Branch. Falconer realized that Lord Frederick had, no doubt, discovered what he himself had known from the very first: that this blacksmith—

Falconer looked up as the innkeeper's young apprentice appeared and held out a rolled scrap of parchment.

"For you, sir; delivered at the back door."

Falconer nodded and sent the boy away with a small coin. After reading the message's contents, he rose and quickly left the inn, traversing several dark streets before finally turning to enter a narrow alley. The author of the private message was waiting for him there, silently handing him another parchment, sealed by Lord Frederick, as he approached.

Falconer moved to catch a bit of light from an upper window and his eyes scanned the second message. A look of surprise crossed his usually controlled features, and then he frowned and turned back to the other figure, cloaked in the shadows.

"This is not what we had planned."

"Plans change."

"I don't like it," Falconer hissed.

"That matters little. What Lord Frederick says is law; you have no choice in the matter."

"I will not be held responsible."

"There will be nothing to hold you responsible for."

Falconer clenched his fist around Lord Frederick's message and the parchment severed in his grasp.

The messenger watched the two pieces fall to the ground and then spoke again, "Burn it, and then leave this place before we are discovered."

Falconer watched the figure disappear around the corner before bending to retrieve what remained of the message. For a long moment he studied the pieces in his hand and then, casting a swift glance after the messenger, slipped the parchment into his doublet.

ഹ൱ജ

Druet dropped a piece of meat to Anvil and then drew his map from its pouch. Leaning forward, he addressed his three new companions.

"Rodney, Sarah, Blunt, tell me what you think a heart is."

Rodney blinked at him and Sarah leaned close to his ear, "What is a heart?"

"Oh, why that's simple, my dear boy. A heart is a delicate yet powerful member of the body, without which one cannot survive."

Druet finished copying the healer's words onto the back of the map and then glanced at Sarah.

"It is the organ which drives life through the body."

"Blunt?"

"The heart is that which carries the weight of one's emotions; whether hatred or love, triumph or defeat," the minstrel finished with a dramatic drop of his clenched fist onto the table's rough surface; several platters clattered and his clay mug shifted precariously.

Bracy glanced at Talon and rolled his eyes.

"Thank you, Blunt," Druet finished writing and then replaced the map.

Nathaniel leaned his head back against the wall behind him, "Where do you plan on heading next, mate? Coswell offers a road for every direction."

"I've been praying about that," Druet picked at a roll on the platter before him, "I think its time we head west."

Chapter 13
* Threads of Tension *

The shrill sound of a feminine scream woke Druet's band several mornings later. Druet, Nathaniel, Talon, and Bracy buckled their swords in place while Druet quickly ordered Blunt to stay and keep watch over the elder healer and his wife. Blunt placed a hand over the pommel of his short-sword and gallantly vowed that he would not take his duty lightly.

As the four younger men stealthily made their way through the forest in the direction of the continuing screams, Druet heard a second feminine voice followed by the coarse sound of men cursing. Listening to the various timbres of voices, he guessed that there were four men.

Druet motioned for two of his comrades to circle around and Nathaniel and Bracy silently obeyed.

The distinct sound of an arrow whizzing through the air was followed by a savage bellow and the thud of a fallen man.

"That does it," another man snarled, "Clancy, just circle around and grab her; she's a child!"

"Back off!" the girl shouted threateningly, "Or you all follow your comrade to the dirt."

"You think you can take the three of us, lass?"

"I took him, didn't I?"

"Brone wasn't much of a fighter, lass. Now hand over your money and we'll be on our way."

"If I have any money, I'm not about to drop it into your filthy hands."

With his back to a tree, Druet peered around the trunk at the stretch of road where the three remaining ruffians stood with their backs to him. Beyond them a young woman, several years younger than Talon and Bracy, stood with an arrow pulled taut in her bow and a glare on her face that would have sent Druet running had he been the one facing her.

The girl's black hair was pulled into a long braid that refused to hold all of her hair, and she wore the black dress of a huntress, with an embroidered belt that matched the trimming at the neckline and sleeves, which were also laced with blue string. Her large, violet-colored eyes were fixed intensely on the three men before her.

Behind her another girl, the same age or a bit younger, sat huddled against a tree—the screamer, Druet guessed. Her dark hair hung in loose curls that nearly hid her frightened face, and she wore the simple russet tunic and dark-red over-tunic of a commoner.

The man called Clancy began to circle around as he had been ordered and Druet realized that waiting for Nathaniel to circle around would not be wise.

103

Druet stepped from the trees and Talon followed his example. The brutes turned at the sound of his voice.

"Leave them be; weren't you ever taught that its dishonorable to frighten women?"

"And who are you?"

"Does it matter?"

"It does to me, sir."

Druet stalled, praying that Nathaniel and Bracy would appear soon, "In that case, I'm Druet of Oak's Branch."

"Ha! I should have known it," the brutes' leader scowled, "The man after Arcrea's crown. Are you already supposing the role of king, to be ordering us about like your subjects?"

Druet clenched his teeth, "I'm simply acting as I hope any other man would to protect his fellow Acreans, let alone women, from the disgraceful likes of you."

Taking advantage of the shifted focus, the huntress suddenly swung her bow low and knocked the leader off his feet; pulling the string back again, she turned to keep Clancy at bay.

The sudden commotion sent the whole group into a frenzy of activity. The leader regained his feet and lurched toward Druet as the blacksmith drew his sword. Talon drew both of his own weapons and trained his focus on the third ruffian.

The swords had only clashed several times before Nathaniel and Bracy appeared. The huntress noted their approach with a wary eye and turned her bow on them.

"No!" Druet shouted at her as his sword slashed through the air to meet his opponent's; the girl's eyes shifted to meet his in response, "Those two are with me!"

She gave the slightest nod and flashed a look of frustration at the wide-eyed girl behind her.

The fight didn't last long. Talon and Bracy alone possessed more skill with the sword than the three brutes could muster together. Druet and Nathaniel held their own well, and the young woman with the bow covered the fight from behind while keeping in position before the other girl.

Clancy fell heavily to the ground with a deep wound and the four young men prepared for another bout. The leader eyed them warily and motioned for his comrade to lift their wounded friend while he watched the other swordsmen.

He glared bitterly at Druet; "We'll cause you no more trouble if you'll let us go in peace, then. And here's a toast..." he spit savagely at the blacksmith's feet, "to his majesty."

Out of the corner of his eye, Druet saw the huntress turn to watch for his reaction. Keeping his steady gaze on the brutes as they backed away into the forest, Druet finally turned and sheathed his sword when they had disappeared from sight. He approached the two young women by the tree.

"Were either of you hurt?"

They shook their heads, and the girl who had screamed rose to her feet, her closely set eyes still wide with fright, "Thank you for your assistance! I was sure that I was done for."

The huntress slung her bow over her shoulder and turned to glare at the other girl, "What else did you expect? What were you thinking, walking alone through a forest guarded by the clans of Stephen?"

"Aren't you alone?"

"I can protect myself. You had no idea what you were doing! You could only stand there and scream in their faces."

"Well, my screams brought *you* running from somewhere in the forest, and then brought more help in Druet and his friends," the other girl countered with a hurt look on her face; she turned to Druet and dropped a curtsy, "I am deeply indebted to all of you. My name is Elaina; I come from south Ranulf."

"But why are you alone?" the huntress demanded.

Elaina bowed her head, "My parents both died of a fever that ravaged our village. I left several weeks ago and decided that I would seek to join Druet's band of travelers."

Bracy cleared his throat noisily and Talon shot a glance at Druet that clearly stated his opinion of Elaina's words: her presence would be of no help to them.

"We're sorry for your loss," Nathaniel offered and Druet nodded his agreement, unsure of what else should be said about the matter.

His gaze then shifted to the huntress and he saw that she was still glaring at Elaina.

"And who are you?" He asked.

She turned to scowl at him, "Renny."

Druet waited for her to continue; when she remained silent, Talon blurted, "That's it?"

Her eyes sparked like a purple storm, "That's all you need to know!"

Druet cleared his throat and shot a glance at Talon, "Well, thank you, Renny, for your hand in the fight. Nathaniel," he turned and stepped away, "signal for Blunt and the others, will you?"

Nathaniel nodded and then gave a shrill whistle. Several minutes passed before they heard Anvil's approaching bark and the summoned trio came into view, Rodney and Sarah plucking herbs from their surroundings, and Blunt strolling behind them and singing a song about "Druet's valiant band".

"What is he?"

Druet turned to see Renny standing behind him, watching Blunt with a skeptical expression.

"He's a traveling minstrel, lately joined to our band."

"Does he ever stop singing?"

Druet grinned, "Hardly; but he's been very kind in watching over Rodney and Sarah; they too were recently added to our number."

Renny paused to distinguish the lyrics of Blunt's song, "Do you like to hear him sing about you?"

Druet's face flushed and he lowered his voice, "It comes to be embarrassing at times. However, I know that the songs are his livelihood, and as long as he doesn't sing words that are morally wrong and evil, I'll not keep him from his work any more than I would keep you from using your bow."

Renny's nose wrinkled as she considered his words.

A sharp bark announced that Anvil had spotted Druet. The dog hobbled quickly over and sat before his master for a rough pat of welcome. His tongue hung in a contented pant as he turned to study Renny. Hauling to his feet again, he moved in a complete circle around her and sniffed the hem of her dress. He lifted his head to sniff her skirt for a long moment before giving a short snuff through his nose and returning to sit at Druet's feet.

Renny watched Anvil's antics and glanced at Druet, then, puffing a strand of black hair from her face, she turned to walk away, eyeing Rodney and his wife as she went.

"We're ready to go, mate," Nathaniel came up beside Druet and gave a sideways nod to indicate the others; he glanced beyond the blacksmith to where Renny stopped to lean against a tree at the road's edge, "Is she coming?"

Druet shrugged and turned to Renny. Her gaze was moving suspiciously from one person to another.

"Renny!"

She snapped her head up in answer.

"We're heading west...you're welcome to join us."

Her head lifted slightly in a cautious tilt and for an instant her eyes flickered warily to Elaina, "I might as well."

"Good. Let's go."

Druet turned and immediately started off down the road at a brisk pace that was just slow enough to allow Rodney and Sarah to keep up.

As the travelers fell into step, Talon advanced to walk beside Druet. The two exchanged glances, Druet's one of question, and Talon spoke in a low tone.

"You think they'll slow us down?"

"Renny and Elaina?"

Talon nodded.

Druet shrugged, "I've prayed much during the past weeks of this journey and I believe that God will send to us those who He will use to complete this mission. I will not argue His plans for whoever that may be."

"But you think they may slow us down?"

"If they slow us down it will only be to the pace that God would set for us. I don't see, though, how 'slowing down' would make much of a difference in this quest. We walk, we search, we walk some more, and we search some more. What does the speed matter?"

Talon was silent for a moment, "You really believe that God cares for the little things in life, don't you?"

"We are His creation, Talon; He delights in paying heed to the slightest details."

Talon stared at the road ahead, "You were wise to confront those brutes when you did, rather than wait for Nathaniel."

Druet raised an eyebrow; "I decided that the odds weren't looking favorable for Renny...no matter how emphatically she says she can take care of herself."

Talon grunted.

"You know," Druet grinned, "you and Bracy make a formidable force to reckon with. I would hate to fight against the two of you as a team."

Talon shook his head, "I tolerate him for your sake, but he's too pig-headed to make any sort of aide in combat."

"I am not!" Bracy shouted from several paces back.

Talon's green eyes shot an angry look over his shoulder, "Stop eavesdropping, you inconsiderate piglet!"

Bracy quickened his pace and came to walk at Druet's other side, "I'm just as skilled with the sword as you are and you know it. Admit it!"

"I wield two!"

"That doesn't mean I couldn't!"

Druet held up his hands for peace but the action went unnoticed.

"I'd like to see you try, Bracy."

"Would you? Well, maybe I could work on it if you would do the hunting for a while!"

"Do the hunting? I *did* the hunting!"

"That's just like a man from Rebel's Lair; pass the work off and never shoulder it again."

"Don't you speak against my clan! I can think of several things to say that would remind you of the repulsive behavior at Knavesmire!"

The two suddenly froze when they realized that Druet was no longer between them. Turning, they saw he had stopped several paces back, and that the rest of the band had come to a halt at various points behind him.

Druet stood with his arms crossed and his jaw clenched in an unrelenting manner. His steady gaze remained locked on the two clansmen until they both had to look away. He moved forward and each muttered an apology as he approached.

"Talon, Bracy; I give you my word, I will tie your ankles together with a cord and force you to walk together for a day if you can't learn to be pleasant to one another."

The horrified looks on their faces told Druet that he had suggested the worst possible punishment that he could inflict on them.

Moving past them, the young blacksmith continued his walk up the road. Nathaniel watched as Talon and Bracy exchanged hostile glances and then separated as they moved to follow Druet. Blunt and Rodney were deep in discussion behind them, and Sarah was chatting happily with Elaina, pointing out her pleasure in having a female companion.

Slowly starting forward again, Nathaniel looked over his shoulder to where Renny still hung back, away from the others. Her observant gaze moved from Bracy to Talon in confused amazement at the scene she had just witnessed.

"You coming, Renny?" Nathaniel called pleasantly, hoping to quicken her pace.

Her brow lifted and she gave several quick nods, "Yes," she fingered the string of her bow and her gaze shifted ahead to Druet, "I'm coming."

Chapter 14
* Renny *

Renny eyed her target and slowly pulled back on the string, careful not to attract attention with the movement. Following her practiced instincts, she released the arrow and watched as it cut a path through the trees and directly towards the desired mark. The young buck dropped to the ground and Renny stepped out from her hiding place.

The young woman went to stand beside the deer. She leaned on her bow and looked over the animal's quality; it wasn't very big, but she had to take her strength into consideration. She had wandered at least a mile from the other travelers, moving deeper into the forest as well as ahead of them. She was hoping they had come within half a mile by now; it would grow dark soon, and the deer would need to be prepared.

Slinging her bow over her shoulder, Renny bent to tie the buck's legs together.

෨෧

Druet scanned the road in either direction and then lowered his gaze to the seven faces waiting for his decision.

"I knew she'd be trouble," Talon muttered.

Druet glanced at Nathaniel and ran a hand through his hair, "We'll move on a short distance and find a place to stop for the night."

"What about Renny?" Sarah questioned with a searching glance into the trees.

"I don't know where she went," Druet held his hands out, "She may have decided to part from our group and move on in another direction."

"But what if she's in trouble?" Elaina asked.

Anvil barked and shot off toward the trees as quickly as his stiff leg would carry him. Druet started off in that direction, hearing Nathaniel coming behind him.

A moment later, Renny appeared dragging a deer and Anvil began to circle around the prize. Renny stopped when she saw Talon and Bracy's hostile expressions.

"I thought you might have made it farther along the road. Since you stopped, it took me longer to find you."

"We wouldn't have stopped if we'd known of your plan to wander off!"

"Bracy!" Druet warned, but his voice was drowned out by Renny's hiss.

"I'm not required to report my actions to you!"

"You could at least tell Druet," Talon put in.

Renny grit her teeth and narrowed her eyes, "I don't have to if I don't want to."

"If you can't cooperate, maybe you should wander farther next time…and don't come back!"

"Maybe I will!"

"Enough!"

Everyone started at Druet's bellow. His blue eyes splashed like a cup of cold water on the combatants and his words fell sharper than a whip.

"Talon and Bracy, I told you before that I wouldn't tolerate aggressive behavior. I've borne you're lesser disputes in hopes that you would grow out of them and learn to appreciate each other, but I will not let you spread your antagonistic venom to the rest of the group. Renny, if you do not wish to travel with us, then I will not force you to stay. If, however, you would continue with us, you're welcome to; I would appreciate knowing, though, if you plan to wander from the group for the simple fact that your absence causes us to worry when we don't know for sure where you've gone off to."

Renny's mouth dropped open.

The atmosphere in the group was stifling.

Druet took a deep breath and closed his eyes; he wasn't fond of confrontation and couldn't understand how these others seemed to thrive on tension and discord.

Lord God, give me wisdom and strength.

Druet opened his eyes and glanced at Renny's burden; bringing his voice to a friendlier tone he asked, "Did you bring that to share or should I set out for something more to feed the rest of us?"

"It's to share," she shot a glance at Bracy and Talon, "if anyone wants it."

"Thank you. I'm sure everyone will enjoy it."

Druet readjusted the ties around the deer's legs and then lifted the animal to his shoulders.

"Let's find a clearing to stop for the night."

"There's a spacious place a fourth of a mile up the road and thirty paces into the trees," Renny muttered.

"Then we'll head that way," Druet started off, trailed closely by Anvil.

Slowly and silently, the rest of the group followed.

By the time Renny's deer had been consumed, the tension had abated and laughter had slowly trickled its way into the conversation, primarily induced by stories and songs told by Blunt.

Finally, Druet pulled the map from its pouch and looked up to ask the newcomers his usual question.

"Elaina, Renny, what is a heart?"

Elaina pursed her lips in thought, an expression that seemed to naturally take residence on her face whenever she sat still long enough.

"A heart is essential."

Druet wrote the word on the map's reverse side and then looked at Renny. Her intense gaze studied his for a long moment until Druet wondered if she had heard his question.

Finally she spoke, "A heart is a thing too easily broken and then never restored to its former state of perfection."

Elaina sadly placed a hand on Renny's arm, "Oh Renny, has your heart been broken?"

Renny jerked her arm away, "I said *a* heart, not *my* heart," she then rose from her seat and walked across the clearing to sit alone.

The others watched her go and then Bracy spoke in a low tone, "There's something not right with her—something she's not telling us."

Nathaniel stretched his arms over his head and yawned, "Bracy, have you told us every detail of your own past?"

The clansman drew his head up in defense, "I've told you more than just my name."

Nathaniel brushed a hand dismissively through the air and turned to the man at his right, "Blunt, good fellow, do you know any sea-faring tunes?"

Blunt's face lit up with a wide smile, "Ah, I should have thought of it before! I shall play the song and you shall sing! Do you know 'Clouds o'er an Arcrean Sea', my friend?"

"Ho, there," Nathaniel elbowed Talon, sitting to his left, and grinned, "Its one of my favorites."

The minstrel and seaman began a rousing tune that told of a storm recorded in Arcrea's ancient history. They produced more than one smile as Blunt attempted to harmonize his softer voice with Nathaniel's boisterous one.

As the song continued, Druet saw Elaina turn and glance at Renny. The young huntress sat with her back to a tree and her lips moved in silent speech as she stared at the ground before her. Elaina turned back to the circle and glanced questioningly at Druet; his gaze shifted to see that Talon, too, was watching Renny. The blonde clansman darted a look at Druet and slowly shook his head.

Druet sighed.

Bracy was right: there was something more to Renny than the young woman wanted to admit. He wanted to believe that that something would prove to

Renny

Nicole Sager

be harmless, but as the leader of this small band should he risk waiting to find out?

When Renny stood quietly and moved beyond the clearing and into the trees, Druet rose and stepped back, pulling one of Talon's swords from the crossed sheaths. The green eyes widened in confusion and Druet motioned for the other man to stay seated.

"I'll bring it back."

Whistling for Anvil, Druet strolled in the direction that Renny had gone. Behind him, the untroubled laughter of his band rose to fill the clearing and he smiled in spite of himself.

When he had walked several yards into the trees, Druet paused and called for Renny. His eyes searched the area by the light of the fire behind him and the traces of moonlight that managed to penetrate the canopy of trees. When no answer came, he walked another short distance, into a smaller clearing, and called again. This time he was answered by an irritated sigh.

"Over here."

Druet turned to see Renny sitting on a fallen log at the clearing's edge. Anvil went to sniff her skirt and then dropped to lie in front of the log.

"I thought we agreed that you were going to tell me when you planned to wander off."

"I didn't agree to anything," Renny's voice cut sharply through the air, and then seemed to soften reluctantly, "I'm not used to telling people where I'm going."

Druet nodded silently, praying that this conversation would be a means of confirming what he needed to know.

He cleared his throat, "You don't like being around people?"

"Why do you ask?"

"You left our circle to sit by yourself."

Renny leaned forward, "Because Elaina is far too meddlesome for her own good! She pestered me with questions all day, and I'm tired of her façade of innocence."

"Façade?" Druet frowned in confusion.

Renny sat back again and stared at the ground, "I don't like her."

Druet ran a hand through his hair; now he was even more bewildered. His gaze shifted to Talon's sword and he suddenly looked up.

"Are you familiar with the Arcrean Sword Reel?"

Renny's head shot up and she looked from Druet to the sword in his hand and then back again, "Yes, I am."

Druet motioned with his head and held the pommel of Talon's sword out toward Renny. The girl slowly rose and came forward, taking the sword and testing its weight in her hands. Druet drew his own sword and Renny's quick gaze studied the blade.

"That's not a commoner's sword."

"No," Druet agreed, "It belongs to Lord Frederick. I'm holding it for him until he decides to return the one that he took from me."

Renny lifted an eyebrow and took a step back to prepare for the dance. Anvil watched as the two set themselves in the beginning stance and, at Druet's nod, they began to move through the complicated steps.

"My mother taught me this," Druet commented.

"Your mother did? My father taught me."

"But you don't want to tell me who he is?"

Renny shook her head with a frown; though focused on the dance, she was still wary of her partner.

"Then tell me this…"

Druet's sword gently pushed Renny's to one side and they each turned in a full circle; Renny waited in skeptical silence for his question.

"…Does your hair ever stay tucked in its braid?"

Renny's face was a picture of bewilderment at the random question, "No," she was silent a moment and then decided to explain, "When I was little—ten or eleven—my father suffered an injury to his head. In order to cleanse the wound, they had to shave off his hair. I felt sorry for him and didn't want him to go through the shame of a bare head on his own…so I cut my own hair."

Druet raised his brow in surprise and swung his sword gently down and to the right, "You cut your hair?"

Renny nodded.

He grinned, "How short?"

"Short," Renny brought her sword up and then crossed it to tap Druet's, "My mother was devastated. She stared at me in shock for a long while and I finally started to cry. I wouldn't let anyone try to fix the terrible work I had done, and so my hair grew back unevenly."

"What did your father say?"

"When he finally regained consciousness, he took one look at me and then ran his hand through the little hair that I had left. He told me…"

Her words slowly faded and she quickly swiped at her eyes as she made a turn in the dance.

Druet eyed Renny as they continued to move through the reel. She confused him. One minute she seemed more dangerous than an ignispat, and the next she was as harmless as Anvil.

"You love your father dearly," Druet noted; his gaze carefully watched Renny's sword and he decided it was time for a change of topic, "You know these steps far better than I do."

"You are a blacksmith?"

"Yes."

"I'm surprised you know the dance at all."

"Being a blacksmith doesn't make me illiterate or unrefined."

"Is that what you're trying to prove by searching for Arcrea's heart?"

Druet raised an eyebrow as he brought his sword across and turned under his own arm, "No...I'm not trying to prove anything with my search. My first motivation is to free my father from his unjust imprisonment."

"Why is he in prison?"

"He refused to improve Lord Frederick's weaponry in preparation for an attack on his own people."

"The clans that gathered to protest the tax law?"

"Yes. His brother—my uncle—was among their number."

"Do you sympathize with the clans?"

Each stepped to their right and then forward, completing a box step and moving to the opposite side.

"I don't sympathize with the clans' lawless actions against the peasantry, nor do I approve of their aimless uprisings when there is no cause to defend; but in this case Frederick planned to destroy the clans simply because they had joined together in a common protest against him."

"Weren't they gathering for an insurrection?"

"Perhaps; but Lord Frederick never took the time to find out; he just planned a skirmish that would destroy a multitude of his own subjects."

"And your father would have none of it."

Druet shook his head, "And neither would I."

The two were silent for a moment and then Druet spoke again.

"You're sure you won't tell me where you come from?"

Renny shook her head and gave a faint smile at his attempt to ply for information.

"Not even if I swear to keep it a secret?"

Another shake of her head and Renny brought her sword up to complete another step.

"Though I will tell you this," she spoke slowly, "only because I know that none of you trust me…I'm not here to harm anyone."

The two swords locked at the cross-guard and Druet paused to search Renny's face. Her violet gaze returned his without hesitation until he finally nodded.

"I believe you."

She looked surprised as she pulled back to complete the final steps, and Druet silently prayed that his instinct was correct. The last combination was performed, and Druet bowed as a voice suddenly spoke from the edge of the clearing.

"Beautifully done!"

The two turned in surprise to see Elaina smile as she clasped her hands in delight.

Renny's lip curled ever so slightly and she scowled as she handed Talon's sword to Druet.

"I'll head back to the clearing now."

Renny started off and Elaina matched her pace, "I'm so glad that you're here, too, Renny; it wouldn't be the same without another girl my age to talk to. I know we'll be good friends."

Druet watched them go and then lifted Talon's sword to study it for a long moment. Whistling for Anvil, he too started back toward the larger clearing.

No matter what he said or did to prevent it, the tension in his band of followers was rising as more people of diverse backgrounds joined him. Eventually—one way or another—someone was going to burst.

Chapter 15
* An Unresolved Past *

Lady Alice of Brentwood Castle sat down to a private evening meal with her uncle, Lord Osgood. The young woman's light blue eyes studied the bounty before them to ensure that her servants had not forgotten anything. She had been careful to survey her appearance before coming down; from her loose honey-colored curls to her simple gown of emerald green with golden embroidery and buttons that stretched from her wrists to just above her elbows, everything was perfect.

It had to be.

Osgood seldom came to visit his niece on the southern coast of his region; but when he did, he expected perfection.

Alice had been her uncle's ward since the day of her parents' mysterious disappearance at sea nineteen years ago. She had been seven years old. Rumors had swarmed like bees through the kingdom and most of

Arcrea had pointed a finger at Osgood, blaming him for the loss of his elder brother—the rightful heir to the region's lordship. However, no positive proof had been unearthed to convict him of any misdeed, and so Osgood had become lord of the region and Alice had had no choice but to try and forget the past, which had proved to be impossible. Everywhere, constantly, she was faced with the memory of her great loss.

Alice bowed her head and whispered a prayer of gratefulness for the food, and then sat with her back straight and head erect as she waited for her uncle to signal that he was ready to eat.

The middle-aged lord now shifted his trencher until it sat directly in front of him. His goblet was filled and then placed at just the right angle from his trencher.

Alice's stomach growled its impatience over the wait and she cast a swift glance at her uncle to see if he had heard. His gaze swept across the table and at last came to rest on her face.

"Alice, my dear niece, you've spread a lovely table for me."

She smiled, "I'm glad you approve."

With a nod to the servants, Alice set the meal in motion and was soon relieved by the sight of food piled on her trencher.

Lord Osgood started on a leg-of-mutton and smiled, "Alice, your aunt always asks after you when I return home from these trips, and each time I am forced to reply that you are prettier every time I see you."

"Thank you, Uncle; you are kind," Alice took a bite of chicken and wondered why her aunt Rose never came to visit Brentwood. It had been eight years since the two women had last seen each other.

Osgood finished the mutton and licked his fingers completely clean before picking up another, "You know I would visit you more often if I didn't have to lug my own drink down here with me."

Alice smiled graciously, "You know I don't drink wine, Uncle; and the fact is you *don't* visit me more often…why then should I store it for you? And if I did have it here for you, how could I honestly encourage you to stop the habit of taking it?"

"Oh, Alice," Osgood chuckled, "You've always been pious like your poor mother before you."

Alice's smile faded at the reminder of her mother and Osgood realized his error. Tearing off a chunk of bread, he muttered,

"She was a good woman."

Alice picked at her own piece of bread. It bothered her that Osgood never looked her in the eyes when he spoke of her parents. Was he truly guilty of causing their disappearance in order to claim his brother's title?

Forcing herself to think of other things, Alice placed a pleasant look on her face and asked, "What news of Arcrea? I hardly ever receive word of the kingdom's happenings here, and I never leave Brentwood to find out for myself."

"Oh, its all the same—border wars to the north, clan rebellions everywhere, and disputes among us lords," Osgood finally brought his gaze up to look at Alice again, "There is also the story of the blacksmith from Frederick's Oak's Branch."

"A blacksmith? What of him?"

"He's after the heart."

Alice frowned, "The heart? You mean the one in the prophecy? Spoken by Ulric the ancient?"

"That's it for sure. He left Oak's Branch after some rebellion against Frederick, and has been on this quest for...oh, I'd say for two months now. The entire kingdom can talk of little else."

"I don't understand, Uncle. There have been many heart-seekers before, and I'm sure there will be many more to come; what makes this blacksmith so different from the rest?"

"Most would say it's his character," Osgood spit the word as if the idea was overestimated, "He's a charitable young man who's touched the heartstrings of the common masses. The commoners sing his praises and make a hero of him; he even has a band of followers who travel with him."

"Where is he now?"

"That's the worst of it," Osgood sat forward in his chair until his generous paunch rested on the table's surface, "He's been in my region for two weeks now, and I hear nothing else but news of his every step. He's northeast of here; several days south of the western Heartland. Personally, I could not care less if the man searched every nook in Arcrea, so long as I didn't have to hear of it; but as far as the other lords are concerned—especially Frederick—this Druet of Oak's Branch is a nuisance and a threat to Arcrean society. They will not bear much more of his silly quest."

Osgood tapped the rim of his goblet and Alice watched in silence as it was refilled from the supply that Osgood had brought with him.

Alice's mind began to wander as her uncle lost himself for a moment in the food and drink. She didn't know much about the world outside her castle, but from what Osgood had said of this blacksmith, she had the idea that the young man in question was not the villain her uncle would make him out to be.

The seven lords of Arcrea were an evil set; she hated to admit this of her own lot, but it was true. And if the seven lords were opposed to the blacksmith, then the blacksmith must be their opposite...and that would make him a good man.

"Alice, did you hear me?"

Lady Alice started and turned to look at her uncle, "I beg your pardon; I was lost in thought."

"Pray, do not lose yourself, my dear," Osgood pointed a meaty drumstick at her, "The kingdom would never forgive me the loss of such a charming young woman."

Alice watched a clump of fat drip from the chicken and wondered whether Osgood had been referencing again to the loss of her parents; she quickly refocused when he continued to speak.

"I was asking if you might be of a mind to journey north with me tomorrow and bless our castle with your lovely presence. Rose would be delighted to see you."

Alice wasn't sure if she ought to laugh with relief or cry out in frustration at Osgood's declaration that he was leaving the next day. She never wanted him to stay overlong, but she also felt slighted when her only visiting relation seemed so eager to leave Brentwood. Then again, she never went to visit them either.

"Alice?"

"I'm sorry, uncle..."

"Perhaps you'd like to think it over; it was a rather sudden suggestion."

"No," Alice shook her head and a honey-colored curl fell across her forehead; brushing it aside with the back of her hand, she went on, "No, I don't need to think it over; I…I couldn't be ready by tomorrow. Perhaps…maybe in a month or two—"

"A month or two?" Osgood laughed and reached for his goblet, "My dear niece, how much will you be packing?"

Alice smiled at the thought of a thousand trunks forming a caravan from Brentwood to her uncle's castle.

"Its not that I need to pack so much as…" Alice looked down and flicked a breadcrumb across her trencher. How could she say that seeing him and Aunt Rose settled and happy in their noble status had always opened afresh the wound in her heart that had been made by the loss of her parents?

"I'm not ready," she repeated the words half-heartedly, feeling like a child clinging mournfully to the past and refusing to let go. She longed to have a good cry over the matter and move on with her life, but the grief insisted on remaining bottled up inside of her.

Osgood didn't seem to notice his niece's sudden misery. With a shrug, he licked his fingers and reached for more meat.

Her own appetite lost, Alice watched her uncle's oblivious consumption and decided that, if she had not felt like crying over the memory of her parents, she would have laughed with relief at Osgood's impending departure from Brentwood. Perhaps tomorrow, when she had regained control of herself, she would.

Chapter 16
* A Fresh Start *

During their first three weeks in Osgood's region, the relationships in Druet's band began to fall into a pattern. Blunt, Rodney, and Sarah were practically ignored by everyone except Nathaniel and Druet. Talon and Bracy, though still intent on driving each other mad, joined forces when it came to antagonizing Renny. Elaina spent her time asking Druet questions whenever he pulled his map out to study; she also continued to try to get Renny to talk. Renny continued to keep her distance from the others, studying their words and actions as if her observations may unlock the key to some mystery. When she did concede to merge with the group, it was to walk the road with Druet.

They scoured a larger portion of Osgood's, searching unsuccessfully for the heart and discovering many places that resembled the village of Morgway. Druet wished he had the means to provide even some of the simpler needs in these places, but the money from his mother could only go so far and the pennies that Blunt kindly offered from his simple minstrel earnings was never a substantial amount.

It was nearing the end of summer and the first traces of an autumn breeze were begging to tug the leaves free from their branches to toss them about.

Druet finished exploring the strangely tunneled root cellar of a dairy farmer and stepped out into the sun. The man had brought Druet to the place and offered to let the famous blacksmith search to his heart's content for anything unusual.

"It was dug that way when I came here," he'd said, "Perhaps it's the work of the ancients."

Nathaniel was leaning against the cellar's makeshift doorframe; he lifted his head as Druet appeared from inside.

"Nothing," Druet shook his head.

Nathaniel watched his friend's gaze wander to the rest of the group, scattered across the farmer's yard. Rodney and Sarah, along with the farmer and his wife, were listening with delight to Blunt's new song. Renny leaned against a fence, studying the rolling landscape and trying to ignore Elaina, who was chattering beside her. Talon and Bracy sat on the back of the farmer's cart, not exactly pleased to be keeping each other company, but linked by their common aversion toward the others—and especially their dislike for Renny.

Druet sighed, "Something must change, Nathaniel. I feel like I'm wandering on an aimless trail and forcing these poor people to wander with me."

Nathaniel grinned, "You need to take control, mate."

"What do you mean?"

The seaman shrugged, "You're so humble about your position, Druet, but you need to understand that these people," he stretched an arm toward the others, "have come to *follow* you—we haven't come as co-heart-seekers, but as a group of men and women who believe that you are the chosen one and who want to witness your journey and assist you to the point of discovery."

Druet's brow furrowed, "That's very flattering, my friend, but I don't understand…"

"I suppose—to put my limited seaman's knowledge to good use—what I'm trying to say is: Everybody needs, and even wants, a captain; someone who will tell them what's expected of them. We've, most of us, come to you willingly, but so far we've each traveled as individuals. Don't be afraid to make us travel as a unit. You were meant to be a leader, Druet; take control of your band."

Druet stared at Nathaniel for a long moment. His mind grasped at the words just spoken and he felt as if he'd just been given a great opportunity—a chance to begin again. He whispered a prayer for strength before leaving the shade of the cellar door and walking toward the others with a purposeful stride.

"God, help me."

Blunt finished his song with a flourish and bowed as his audience rewarded him with applause, and then all eyes turned to Druet. Talon and Bracy left the cart and came to stand nearby. Elaina stopped her chatter and both she and Renny waited for the blacksmith to speak.

The farmer stepped forward, "Did you find anything in the cellar?"

"Unfortunately, no, good sir," Druet dipped his head to the man, "I wonder if I might ask a great favor of you?"

"Anything, sir blacksmith."

Druet smiled at the title, "I would like to stop here for the day, if you would let us camp and hunt on your land?"

The farmer's face brightened as if Druet had handed him a sack of gold, "My wife and I would be honored, sir! And you will please sleep in my hay barn, just down the hill; it should prove dry and warm."

"Thank you, sir; we will."

The farmer and his wife scurried away, saying that they would return with fresh water for their guests to drink. Druet watched them go and then motioned for his followers to join him.

"Make a circle."

When the shape was complete, Druet took a deep breath and spoke slowly, "There is something that we have not yet done as a group, that I believe is a very important thing to do," his eyes scanned their faces, "I'd like to pray."

Everyone stared back at him in silence; some pleased, some wary, some surprised. Druet made a fist with his right hand and held it out to Sarah; she gripped his wrist with her left hand and held out her own right fist to Rodney. This pattern was followed all the way around the circle until the nine travelers had linked together in a ring. Druet bowed his head and the others did the same.

The farmer and his wife returned from the well to find the travelers bowed in prayer. They stood back and watched the circle in awe, listening as Druet lifted a simple prayer to God in complete faith that the Creator heard him—a simple blacksmith—and truly cared for the petitions brought before His heavenly throne by the work-roughened hands of a commoner.

When Druet finished, half the circle jerked their wrist from the hand to their left and stepped back a pace. Druet turned and eyed the two clansmen off to his left. Finally choosing one he called, "Talon."

The blonde straightened at the authoritative tone, "Yes?"

"You'll do the hunting for the evening meal."

Talon nodded and glanced to mark the sun's progress in the sky, "I'll go now, then."

A slight smile itched the corners of Druet's mouth, "And Talon…"

"Sir?" the respectful title slipped out unconsciously.

"You'll take Renny to help you."

"What?"

Both Talon and Renny stared at Druet in shock, and the girl stormed a step closer, "What did you say?"

"You're going with Talon to hunt."

"He hates me! I'd rather go alone!"

Talon glared at her and grit his teeth, "The feeling is mutual."

Druet crossed his arms. Behind him, he could sense that Nathaniel was having trouble keeping a laugh down, "You will both go. Talon will lead this hunt and Renny—you will be his assistant. I want your word that there will be no foul play from either one of you."

Renny scowled, "If you don't trust us to keep peace, then why send us together?"

"Because our band needs a few lessons in working together."

"We've had such lessons," Talon growled.

Druet sighed and pivoted on his heels, "Bracy, would you like to take Renny hunting?"

Bracy's mouth dropped open and he stuttered, "I…I…"

"You can't replace me!"

Druet turned a wide-eyed look to Talon, "I didn't think you wanted to go."

Talon clamped his mouth shut and exhaled slowly through his nose.

"Talon, I can't lead a group of people who hate each other. My options are to cultivate unity, or remove those who simply won't accept peace."

Renny's gaze of amazement finally left Druet and swung around to Talon. Her violet eyes were still fierce, but her words were sincere when she spoke.

"I'm willing to do this for the group if you are."

Talon studied her and then glanced at Druet, "Alright."

The clansman started off down the road and Renny followed several paces behind.

Nathaniel cleared his throat and stepped up to Druet's side, "You do follow advice in a hurry."

Druet clapped his brother-like friend on the shoulder, "Only good advice, mate. Thank you. Blunt! I need you and Elaina to start a cook-fire. Bracy…" Druet's gaze shifted beyond the clansman and he started off toward what he'd just spotted, "Bracy, I believe Rodney mentioned that he needs help mixing his herbs. Anvil; come, boy!"

Nathaniel shook his head with a smile and called after the band's captain, "Where are you going?"

"I'm off to herd the three cows that just escaped the back pasture! Care to join me?"

Chapter 17
* Injustice *

*"I sing of young Druet
Who, humble and meek,
Does travel the land,
A heart for to seek…"*

Druet's face flushed crimson as Blunt's song carried across the marketplace of Quale, the city of Osgood's residence. The musical tales of his quest enraptured the bard's audience and induced applause at each song's close. Across the open square, the heralded blacksmith leaned against a wall in an alleyway, waiting for his companions to complete their various errands throughout the city. Nathaniel was the first to return, closely followed by Elaina.

Nathaniel smiled and nodded his head toward Blunt, "This is one of my favorites. We sound more admirable every time he sings it!"

Renny appeared at the alley's entrance. Her eyes darted from one face to another and finally paused when they rested on Elaina. The other young woman smiled under the scrutiny, but Renny's expression remained unaffected. The violet eyes shifted to glance at Druet and then Renny moved to lean against the wall in silence.

Rodney and Sarah appeared at the edge of the square and stopped to listen to Blunt. Druet smiled. The elderly couple never tired of listening to the minstrel.

Druet's smile faded when Blunt's song cut to a stop and the crowd suddenly shifted as three soldiers in Osgood's service pushed to the center of the square.

"Rodney of Saxby in Stephen!" the soldier at the forefront bellowed, demanding a reply from the summoned name.

Rodney stepped forward with a surprised look on his aged features, "I am Rodney of Saxby, my good man."

The soldier's glare never softened, "By order of Lord Osgood, at request of Lord Stephen—under whose regional rule you belong—you are under arrest for opposing the law of Arcrea."

"No, please," Sarah cried.

"What has he done wrong?"

The soldiers turned at the sound of the questioning voice off to their left. Druet had left the alley and a murmur began to spread through the crowd at the realization that the blacksmith was among them.

Druet marched steadily forward until he was only three paces from the soldiers, between them and

Rodney. He stood with his hand resting on the pommel of Frederick's sword.

"What has Rodney done wrong?" he repeated.

"Who's asking?" the soldier growled.

"Druet of Oak's Branch."

The soldier pointed a gloved finger at Druet, "You keep to your own business, you cocky upstart."

"This is my business; Rodney is numbered among my party and so I take responsibility for him. He is under my protection. Now I ask you again; what has he done wrong?"

The soldier glanced to where Nathaniel and Renny had come up behind Druet. Talon and Bracy appeared then and also came to stand with the group.

"The man Rodney has disobeyed the lords of Arcrea in continuing the practice of healing—"

"What is wrong with healing?"

"The man is a magician dissenter who uses dark powers to twist the minds of the Arcrean people!"

A gasp surged through the crowd and the townspeople studied Rodney warily as they backed further away from him. The healer stood quietly, listening as Sarah repeated everything he could not hear. Druet lifted his voice loud enough to be heard over the crowd's murmurs of shock and disgust,

"I have traveled with Rodney for weeks now, and he has never once used magic or evil powers. He speaks instead of the good to be done through the use of Arcrea's God-given vegetation."

"It is forbidden!" The soldier shouted.

Druet lifted an eyebrow, "Why?"

The soldier's face began to redden with rage, "I do not make the laws, you insurgent dog; I only enforce them."

Rodney & Sarah

Nicole Sager

Druet knit his brow and drew closer to the soldier, "I will not allow you to arrest a harmless old man from my company who has done no wrong."

"You cannot speak against an order of Lord Osgood."

Druet remained firm, "If the lords of Arcrea have a matter of question that concerns a member of my band, then let them come and speak to me in person. Go now and tell Lord Osgood that I will remain here for one hour; if he wishes to discuss this matter further then let him come within that time; but if he does not come, then Rodney will remain with me."

The soldier stood still, considering the situation. If he tried to gain access to the old man by force, he would not only have Druet and the four behind him to deal with, but also the crowd in the square who sympathized with the blacksmith and his cause. Turning on his heel, the soldier stormed off toward the castle, followed by his two silent subordinates.

಄ﻬ

An hour passed and Lord Osgood stood at a palace window, watching as Druet's band left the city of Quale. Behind him, his captain stood seething; unable to comprehend why he had not been sent back to collect the old healer.

"Do not fret, Captain," Osgood grunted as he stepped away from the view, "This was a matter of Stephen's, just as the blacksmith is a matter of Frederick's. I will not risk my men and the anger of Quale over foreign issues."

"But my lord, the people will now consider you to be a soft ruler—cowardly even! They may—"

"Let them think what they will!" Osgood yelled; his voice echoed along the corridor, "It matters little," he motioned for the captain to leave and when he was alone muttered, "These people have no more power over me than my pathetic brother did."

❧❧

"That was a bold risk," Renny appeared at Druet's side as the city of Quale disappeared from view behind them. A rolling landscape stretched before them, waiting to be explored.

"I know," Druet replied.

"They had a legitimate reason for Rodney's arrest…he does disobey the lords when he continues as a healer."

Druet's eyes scanned the road ahead, "You're right; if Osgood had returned with soldiers there would have been little I could have done. My hope, though, is that his lordship was forced today to realize that the law against the healers is wrong, and that he could not punish Rodney justly without reintroducing the issue of healing to the minds of the people. There would have been inquisitive questions for him to answer."

Renny considered his words, "I suppose, if you find the heart and become king, that you will annul the law against healers?"

"I hadn't thought of it, really; but I suppose I would," Druet was silent for a moment and then spoke as if to himself, "I wonder how Lord Stephen learned of Rodney, and that he could be found with us."

Renny watched Druet's face as he considered these thoughts and then she glanced back at the others, "Elaina seems unusually quiet."

"You didn't seem too happy to see her in the alley earlier today."

"I saw her meet with a stranger in Quale."

"Is that all?"

"There was something odd about it. I don't trust her."

"Have you asked her about it?"

"No."

"Would you like me to?"

"No," Renny's violet gaze shifted to his, "I don't want her to know that I saw her."

Druet frowned in confusion but shrugged, "Alright, I won't say anything this time...but if you two continue to be at odds with one another I will address the issue."

That night, Elaina glanced across the campfire at Renny and then announced to the group that she had met a man in Quale traveling north to Ranulf's region; he had promised to deliver a message to a dear friend whom she had known there.

Druet caught Renny's eye for a split second and knew that she didn't believe a word the other young woman had spoken.

"She will be happy to know that I am well," Elaina added with a soft smile as she remembered her friend.

"I'm sure she will," Sarah smiled at her and then looked across at Renny, "It is good to have you join our circle this evening, Renny."

The girl gave a small nod, "Thank you, Sarah."

The older woman turned to smile at the two young men who sat opposite one another, "Talon, Bracy, thank you for the meat this evening."

They nodded and Talon rolled his eyes to Druet, "That is the last time I hunt with him as the leader."

"Was it really that bad?"

"Awful."

Bracy shook his head, "Stop your complaining—we got a deer!"

Talon reached to scratch his neck and, shifting his face away from Bracy, he whispered to Nathaniel, "*I*...got a deer."

Nathaniel shook his head and then looked at Druet, "Do you think we'll have more trouble over Rodney's occupation?"

Druet shrugged and Rodney spoke up, "I will not endanger you all with my work...I will leave you tomorrow and return to Stephen."

"Rodney, no," Druet leaned forward and shook his head, "I meant what I said today; I consider you under my protection and I will defend you against an unjust arrest."

Rodney nodded sadly, "But it is just, Druet, my boy; I am a healer against the wishes of the seven lords."

Druet stood to his feet in an agitated manner, "When were the seven lords given the right to impose injustices on the people of Arcrea? It should be the people's choice where they go to receive medicinal service—I never heard of anyone telling Lord Frederick where to take his children when they were ill."

The others sat in slight shock at Druet's sudden outburst.

Elaina cleared her throat to interrupt the silence, "But the lords would not act against their own laws."

"Of course not," Druet threw his hands up, "because they only establish laws that make life better and easier for themselves," he pointed at Rodney, "The healers' work brought no profit to the lords and so it was proclaimed unlawful; but if Rodney's medicinal ways had lined Stephen's purse with silver, then Rodney's work would not be forbidden today."

"Well said, well said," Blunt pointed a finger into the air, "Your words inspire me to write a sonnet that will inform the common people of this injustice!"

"And I look forward to hearing it, mate," Nathaniel smiled, "The ways of a learned healer can be no more dangerous than the common practices of leaches and bleeding…I'd much rather swallow one of Rodney's tonics than have a common physician insist on spilling my heart's life."

Druet stared at the seaman, "Why did you say it that way—'Heart's life'?"

Nathaniel shrugged, "The heart needs the blood as much as the blood needs the heart…they give each other purpose and keep each other active."

Druet was still for a moment, and then he quickly sat and made a note on the reverse side of the map.

Chapter 18
* A Meeting in the Night *

Renny was motionless as she kept her position in the shadows. The forest was quiet, except for the occasional hoot of an owl and the lulling noise of a few crickets. The moon was high and only half-full, casting a bluish glow over the trees.

A soft whistle, easily mistaken for the call of a bird, sounded off to her right, and Renny answered with a call of her own. A shadowy form appeared and Renny emerged from her hiding place to approach the newcomer.

"You were hard to track," the cloaked figure whispered, "It is good for you that all of Arcrea knows the whereabouts of Druet the blacksmith."

Renny lifted an eyebrow, "Perhaps not good for Druet, though."

"Perhaps not, but little I care. Are you ready to leave?"

Renny looked down at the ground for a moment and then returned her gaze to the man before her, "I'm not going back with you."

He drew back in shock, "What? Are you mad, Aurenia? What will I tell your father?"

"Tell him the way is clear, and I will return, but that I would continue for a time with Druet's band."

" 'The way is clear?' "

"He will understand; now you must go before they discover that I've left the camp and come searching for me."

"Are you a prisoner?" the cloaked man asked with concerned anger.

"No," Renny lifted an eyebrow and shook her head, "Now go."

The man sighed as heavily as their quiet setting would allow and then turned to go.

"Your father will not be pleased, but I will do as you say only because I know you will not listen to me. But know that I will not be held responsible…"

"There will be nothing for you to be held responsible for. Father will understand better than you know," Renny whispered, "And remember; the way is clear."

He nodded, "The way is clear."

Renny watched as the messenger disappeared through the trees. A slight breeze played with the hair that had slipped from her braid to frame her face, and she heard the monotonous tongue-clicking of a catawyld beast from somewhere off to the east. The creature sounded miles away, nevertheless Renny quickly turned and melted into the shadows of the forest, heading back toward camp.

Chapter 19
* Carnaturs *

Elaina screamed the next morning when two catawyld beasts appeared at the edge of their campsite. Renny's arrow killed the first and Talon managed to eliminate the second, but not before Elaina had fallen in a faint.

Talon rose from ensuring that the beasts were dead and turned to Druet, "It's unusual to see only two."

"You think there are more nearby?"

"It's possible," Talon sheathed his swords with a twist of his wrists, "We should move away from here before the others—if there are more—smell the fresh kill."

Sarah succeeded in helping Elaina to regain consciousness and the motley crew was soon on their way.

As they walked, Blunt complimented Renny on her quickness with the bow. The girl responded with a small nod and an even smaller thank you and then fell silent again. Druet gave her a curious look when Blunt had moved away to talk with Nathaniel.

"You don't seem to enjoy it when the others include you."

Renny kept her eyes on the road, "They're very kind."

"But you don't want to get to know them," Druet's eyes scanned the road, habitually searching for anything unusual.

There was no response from the young woman beside him.

"Why don't you?" Druet pressed.

Renny gave him a studied look, as if trying to decide how much she could tell him, "I can't get to know them."

Druet looked down at her and countered, "You *can*...but you *won't*."

Renny heaved a frustrated sigh, "I can't afford to become attached to them."

"Everyone can afford to make new friends, Renny."

"Except me—I can't!"

Her tone had been louder than she'd intended it to be. Renny closed her eyes and took a deep breath.

She lowered her voice, "You don't understand. I have already become attached to...some extent," she turned to look at him, "and that worries me."

"For what reason?" Druet shook his head with a confused frown.

Renny stared at him for a long time before shaking her head stubbornly and turning back to face the road.

"Ah..." Druet shook his head, "more silence."

Behind them, Bracy inched closer to where Talon was walking.

The blonde frowned, "What are you doing on this side of the road?"

"Don't be ridiculous," Bracy rolled his eyes, "Say, why do you think we haven't gone to search for the heart in the Heartland? It seems an obvious location, don't you think: *Heart*—land?"

Talon shook his head, causing his hair to shift in ragged layers over his ears, "That doesn't mean the heart is hidden there."

Bracy shrugged and looked down to study the spot where his tunic had been ripped during the first catawyld encounter. He shook his head woefully at the sight of his own sorry attempt to patch up the material.

Talon cleared his throat noisily.

Bracy looked up, "What is it?"

"Are you done speaking?"

"Yes…"

"Then…" Talon motioned with his hand for Bracy to back away, "keep your distance, man."

"Ugh," Bracy muttered and sidestepped two paces, "Talon, you're pathetic."

Four days later they reached the southern coast of Osgood. Nathaniel, who had begun to grow excited the closer they came, was nearly giddy with delight when the group finally stood on a cliff that overlooked the vast Arcrean Sea. The seaman took great gulps of the salty air and then turned with a grin to Druet.

"What do you think of it, mate?"

Druet stared out over the endless expanse of tossing waves and smiled, "It's beautiful; unbelievably vast. I see now why you love it, and I wonder how you could leave it so easily to join me on my quest."

"Only by the grace of God, my friend," Nathaniel grinned and looked past Druet, "What do you think, Renny? Have you ever seen the sea before?"

The girl shook her head as she gazed at the glassy surface below.

"You haven't?" Druet asked with sudden alertness.

He grinned when she turned wide eyes to him. Everyone knew that southern Arcreans depended heavily on the merchants' sea-trade for their economy—nearly every man, woman, and child who lived in southern Arcrea had, at one time or another, been to the coastline.

"So you're from somewhere in the north?"

Renny opened her mouth to reply, but then seemed to decide against the action; instead she scowled and shifted her eyes back to the sea.

The travelers headed west along a worn coastal road that bordered the cliffs. Soon, trees and shrubbery began to appear on either side of the path, providing some shade from the afternoon sun. When they reached a sort of clearing, where the road suddenly turned from the coast and headed north, they paused to consider which way they ought to go—with the road, or along the unmarked coast.

A lone tree stood in the crook of the path, while tall grass-like plants some six feet high dotted the coastal side. Blunt went to stand beneath the bending grasses of one of these, pulling his lute around from the back to play a song.

Druet's eyes studied the well-used map in his hands and then glanced up when Blunt began his song of their recent encounter with the catawylds. His gaze immediately shifted above and beyond the minstrel and his eyes widened. Quickly dropping the map, he suddenly rushed forward with a shout.

"Blunt, move out of the way!"

Everyone turned with a start and Anvil raced after Druet with a sharp bark.

Blunt froze and looked up in puzzled answer to the blacksmith's cry. Druet reached the spot and shoved the minstrel out of the way just as a large green head lunged from a height of eight feet and snapped its jaw over whichever human prey it could reach. With a howl of pain, Druet was forced to drop to the dirt.

"Druet!" Renny shrieked.

Anvil began to bark ferociously and for a moment the others stood frozen in shock; in the road before them Druet's right shoulder was being held by the mouth of a strange bulb-shaped plant! Its thick eight-foot long stem served as a neck that traced back into the tall grass plants that disguised it. As the other men drew their swords and rushed forward, three more heads rose from the plant to stop them and Anvil in their tracks. Each head hissed like a snake and was reinforced with short razor-like teeth. Several smaller heads—the vicious plants' offspring—peeked from the grass at the plant's base.

"Carnatur Plants!" Rodney's eyes grew round, "I did not know that they still infested the southern coasts."

"What do we do?" Nathaniel shouted anxiously.

The healer scratched his chin, trying to remember what he knew of the ancient plants.

Druet was struggling to pull his sword out, but with his shoulder pinned to the ground and the three other large carnaturs swaying closer to his face, it was proving a difficult task. The strange plants continued to keep Druet's friends from reaching him, stretching their necks and hissing angrily whenever someone came too close. Anvil began to whine pitifully amidst his growls.

Renny held an arrow to her bow but couldn't shoot at the one holding Druet for fear of hitting the young man himself; the other plants moved constantly, making it difficult to track her target.

Druet tried to pry the carnatur's jaw from his shoulder.

"Druet, what do we do?" Talon bellowed.

Druet winced and growled in pain, "The heart!"

Bracy gave the carnaturs a look of uncertain disgust, "That thing is the heart?"

"No," Druet kicked as another plant brought its head closer, "take out the heart!"

"The carnatur's heart," Rodney offered, "If you take it out at the head it will replace itself with another. You must go to the root to destroy it."

"How?"

Renny's eyes flew to the cliff, "Talon! Come with me!"

The two rushed toward the cliff while Nathaniel and Bracy tried to distract the vicious plants, and Anvil ran in circles barking frantically. Circling out of the carnaturs' reach, Renny and Talon found footing to lower themselves to a place that opened in the cliff's side, directly beneath the plant's location at the edge of the drop. Within this opening, a network of roots three to five inches in diameter stretched from ceiling to floor.

Renny moved to let Talon pass inside, "You cut the roots; I'll guard the opening."

As soon as Talon's swords started their work on the roots, a carnatur's head appeared over the edge of the cliff. Renny pulled back on her bowstring and tried to follow the shifting plant as it lunged and then pulled back several times, its wide mouth open to reveal its dangerous teeth.

On the road above them, Druet roared in pain and Nathaniel shouted for Bracy to grab Druet's sword.

Renny's eyes remained glued to her green foe as she called over her shoulder, "Talon, hurry!"

"Trying!"

Talon grunted with satisfaction as he severed one of the thick roots. The frustrated carnatur pulled back to strike and Talon suddenly shouted, "Renny, duck!"

"What?"

"DUCK!"

Renny ducked in the opening just as the wild plant lunged forward with open jaws. Talon ducked a second later and the carnatur snapped its sharp teeth over several of its own roots. With a hiss, the giant plant pulled back to regain its bearings.

As soon as the carnatur retreated from the root cavern, Talon dropped one of his swords and put all of his strength to the second. With a fierce cry, he thrust the blade upward into the dirt where the roots of the plant were concentrated. The carnatur's numerous heads shrieked and the one that had come to protect its roots became still before slowly pulling away and disappearing up over the cliff wall.

Talon worked quickly to sever the rest of the roots, with Renny using her dagger to help. The clansman then used his sword to carve up and around the heart of the plant, removing the massive bulb and tossing it out to the foaming sea far below them.

"Let's go," Talon sheathed his swords and the two started back up the cliff.

They found that the plant's heads had all retreated back into the grass to wilt and die. The first carnatur had at last relinquished its hold on Druet when Nathaniel and Bracy had managed to sever the stem several feet beyond the plant's head. The young blacksmith still lay in the road; the shoulder of his tunic stained a deep red and a look of sheer pain twisting his features. Rodney was kneeling beside him to examine the wound and Anvil was lying beside Druet's head, watching the healer's gentle hands and nosing Druet's hair.

Blunt stood like an inquisitive bird behind the healer. His forgotten lute had been left on the road nearby—crushed from the fall he'd taken at Druet's saving shove, "Will he live, Rodney? Tell me, man! If he dies, I shall never be able to forgive myself."

Druet grimaced as Rodney fingered the skin around his wounds, "Blunt, it—Ah!—it wasn't your fault."

"Not to worry, Blunt," Rodney comforted, "he will not die."

"Will he lose his arm?" Renny asked as she knelt at Druet's other side.

Blunt groaned and threw his head back at the possibility she had presented. Anvil watched the minstrel and then howled in turn.

Rodney glanced at Renny, "I pray not. I would that I had a cleaner place to tend the wound properly. If infection sets in…"

Nathaniel leaned over the group and pointed at a spot on the map, "The castle Brentwood lies several hours east of here along the coast."

"Castle?" Talon peered at the map over the seaman's shoulder, "I doubt the nobility would welcome Druet into their homes."

"I've heard of Brentwood," Elaina approached, "Lord Osgood's niece lives there. She is his ward and rarely ever leaves the castle."

"Let's go, then," Renny urged.

Rodney looked up in confusion, "Go where, my dear?"

Sarah leaned down to loudly fill him in on the murmured plans, "Castle Brentwood, Rodney…on the coast."

Elaina looked down at Renny, "But if Lord Osgood hears of our presence there and decides to take advantage of Druet's helpless situation… Druet would be in greater danger then."

"It sounds like a fine place to tend his wounds," Rodney smiled brightly.

"Nathaniel, what do we do?" Bracy asked.

Everyone turned to face Druet's closest friend as their natural choice for a substitute leader.

Druet suddenly jerked under Rodney's gentle prodding of his shoulder; sweat covered his face and he drew a sharp breath through clenched teeth.

"Nathaniel, take me to Brentwood."

Chapter 20
* Choice of Allegiance *

Falconer's eyes studied the boisterous occupants of the great hall in Osgood's castle at Quale. From where he stood in the shadow of a pillar at the room's outer edge, he had a clear view of Lord Frederick's intense face. Lord Frederick eyed the other arguing lords and from time to time would cast an annoyed look at his alert spy; things were not going according to plan.

Finally, Lord Osgood set his goblet down in a "just so" manner and then lifted his hands for silence. When this failed to produce the desired effect, he hefted his bulk from his high-backed chair and stood to his feet with a bellow that rung in the rafters for several moments after.

"SILENCE!"

The room became still, but only for a moment.

Lord Geoffrey stepped forward, "I was only saying that—"

"We've been listening to your 'only saying' for the past half-hour!" Lord Stephen shouted.

Frederick rose to his feet and slammed his goblet down on the table's surface, "We did not come to Quale to discuss the matters of southern trade," he cast a sour glance at Ranulf, Hugh, and Quinton, "Or the issue of clans."

Quinton glared, "You began the talk of clans!"

"That's of little matter now! I wish to bring before you all the issue of Druet the blacksmith."

"What of him?"

Lord Ranulf dropped into his chair, "His quest for Arcrea's heart will die away as all the others' did."

Frederick turned, "It has gone on for several months now, which is far longer than the others lasted."

"He comes from your region, Frederick; you deal with him!"

"It is true that he hails from my region, Osgood, but his quest will affect every one of us. You should know this as he is currently traveling your lands."

"Still?" Osgood reached to pluck a greasy drumstick from the trencher before him, "I stopped listening to the rumors of young Druet weeks ago."

Frederick rolled his eyes in disgust and reached to slap the food from Osgood's grasp. Osgood started up in anger but was met by Frederick's furious gaze above him.

"You fool! We all know about your despicable behavior five days ago, when you refused to carry out a request of Stephen regarding the healer. Why? Because the blacksmith dog said 'no'! That is where the trouble begins—if we decide to ignore this young rebel then he will overthrow us as soon as our backs are turned."

The other lords observed Osgood with dark looks.

Osgood sputtered at the condemnation, "But he is one man against our vast armies!"

"Wrong!" Frederick shoved Osgood back into his chair and turned to address the room's other occupants, "The people of Arcrea love him. They consider him a hero—worthy to claim our crown. Should he give the word, all of our people would rise up against us in his name to remove us from our rightful place in the seven seats of Arcrea."

He turned a fiery gaze to Lord Osgood; "You say that he is but one against *our* armies; yet how many of us have committed to lift our banner against his cause when the time comes?"

"I say the time may never come," Quinton lashed out.

"I say it will come and has even already begun," Frederick answered.

Eager to defy Quinton, Ranulf rose to his feet, "I agree with Lord Frederick. The blacksmith's endeavors have already lent courage to the peasantry; they question our authority and right to rule our own regions."

"His trouble has lasted long enough!"

"He has disturbed the peace and traditions in Arcrea," Geoffrey added, "I say this truth should make void his right to search for the kingdom's heart and gives us reason enough to put a stop to his quest," the southern lord drew his sword and lifted the blade into the air, "I will pledge my sword and my army against this Druet, and swear to end his foolish errand when the time is right."

Stephen, Ranulf, and Hugh drew their swords and repeated Geoffrey's oath of allegiance. Quinton and Osgood showed only a slight sign of annoyance before adding their swords to the promise, and then all turned to Frederick, waiting for him to join them in answering his own call for obligation.

Satisfied to have secured his desire, Frederick reached to clasp the pommel at his side and froze for an instant when he remembered the blade's designer. With a feeling of intense pleasure, he lifted Druet's sword from the sheath and thrust it into the air in an oath against the young blacksmith.

"For Arcrea!"

The six other lords gave a shout and echoed the cry with enthusiasm.

Falconer turned and left the great hall, his mouth set in a grim line as he traversed the halls of Castle Quale and made his way outside. He had done his duty, had delivered the latest news of Druet's whereabouts and conditions to Lord Frederick, nevertheless the agent felt that he had failed somehow.

It is because you know the truth.

The words rang continuously in Falconer's mind as he mounted his black mare and turned the horse's head toward the gates of Quale.

It is because you know the truth, and yet you still refuse to act upon it. You know the truth, Falconer.

Falconer reined his horse to a stop in an alley off of the city square. He had heard of the incident in this place just days before, when Druet had resisted the soldiers sent by Osgood for the healer in Druet's company…and Osgood had done nothing.

The truth.

Falconer closed his eyes and willed the voice of his conscience to be silent.

"I do not know the truth…" he hesitated, "for certain."

A memory suddenly flashed across his mind's eye and Falconer saw again the sultry blacksmith shop in Oak's Branch. He heard the cries of Gregory's wife as the blacksmith was led away and saw again the determined look in Gregory's eyes. Then his mind shifted, as had his focus on that day months before, and again he saw young Druet lifting himself to his full and powerful height.

It was at that moment, as Druet had returned the agent's sharp gaze, when Falconer had known that the young blacksmith was the man chosen to fulfill Ulric's prophecy.

Druet would be Arcrea's first king.

Falconer's eyes studied the square. He was sure that Lord Frederick thought the same of the young blacksmith; why else would the ruler fear the simple peasant? Lord Frederick would not rest easy until Druet had been deterred from his innocent mission or destroyed.

Then why do you continue to serve Frederick? You know the truth.

"But what if…?"

Falconer sighed. It was this question that always brought him back to serving Frederick. What if Druet was *not* the chosen one? What would happen to him then? Most assuredly Lord Frederick would put him to death for treason against the nobility and loyalty to a rebel.

Falconer dug his heels into his mare's flanks and had soon left the alley and the city of Quale behind him.

You know the truth.

"But what if…?"

The truth.

"But what if…?"

What if Druet is the chosen one?

Falconer's gloved hands clenched tightly around the reigns as his horse thundered down the road heading south. He hadn't considered this side of the question. What would happen to him if he continued to serve Frederick, and Druet truly were crowned king?

Falconer brought his horse to a stop at the top of a rise and his eyes shifted to see a filthy village in the valley below. His mind traced back to Morgway and he wondered how many other places had been touched by Druet's kindness.

"I must make a choice," the spy muttered to himself, "Whom will I serve?"

You know the truth.

As the words echoed through his mind again, Falconer's hand slowly came up to feel for something hidden in his doublet; a moment later he drew out the message that he had received and torn in Coswell. Placing the two pieces together, Falconer's gaze perused the written words once again and his eyes narrowed in familiar disapproval.

Returning the parchment to his doublet, Falconer urged his mare forward again and continued on the southbound road.

You know the truth.
You have a choice.
"But what if...?"
What if...?

A gentle breeze cooled the evening air and shifted the tall grasses that stretched away from the road. The wind's hollow sound drew Falconer's mind back to the seven lords' fervent cries of loyalty and duty. Habitually, the dark-clad spy placed a hand over his heart—and the torn message—in a solemn salute.

"For Arcrea."

Chapter 21
* A Refuge & A Secret *

Lady Alice sat by the large hearth in Brentwood's great hall, in one of several high-backed chairs that had been set within reach of the flame's warmth. Over the hearth was a large detailed tapestry of two ships in battle; Lord Osgood himself had ordered it to be made and hung years ago, to Alice's dismay. Adjusting the cushion at her back, Alice tapped her forefinger on the chair's solid arm and took a moment to watch her servants moving slowly about their evening tasks.

Her eyes shifted back to the book in her lap but refused to concentrate on the familiar words. Uncle Osgood had kindly sent her a worn work of literature for her last birthday and, it being the only new piece to read, she had already read it five times.

She had lately begun to wish that she had accepted her uncle's offer to accompany him to Castle Quale. Perhaps there she would have learned more of the traveling blacksmith from Frederick's region. The little that she had learned from the people in Brentwood's villages had reinforced her opinion that he was an honorable man, but there was still much of his story that she would like to know.

Lightning forked the sky and Alice looked to the window. This storm had come on quickly.

"My lady, would you like me to prepare your chambers so that you might sleep?"

Alice looked up when the voice sounded by her chair, "I don't know, Bess," absently, she plucked at the light blue fabric of her dress until she realized that her personal attendant was still waiting for a clear answer, "I'm not tired."

Suddenly a soldier approached with an urgent step and Alice could see by his soaked attire that he had been outside.

"What is it, Captain?"

"My lady, there are strangers at the gate seeking refuge."

"Strangers? They did not tell you who they are?"

"One answered and said that they are Druet the blacksmith and his band, and that they seek clean shelter for a wounded man."

Alice felt her mouth drop open, "Druet the blacksmith?"

"Aye, my lady."

Alice rose to her feet and tossed her book onto the mantel, "Let them in."

"Lady Alice, what if it is a trap?"

"You may question them in the courtyard, but let them in."

"But—"

"My lord uncle told me that Druet has been in Osgood's region for some time now; I will trust that it is him. Let them in."

The captain left to obey and Alice turned to Bess, "Prepare the fire in the spare room and make it ready for the wounded. Have the other servants build some cots by the fire here, and tell Cook to prepare some food for the travelers."

The elderly Bess dropped a quick curtsy and then scurried away to obey her mistress.

The great hall quickly became alive as several more torches were lit and set in sconces. Maids rushed to move the high-backed chairs and arrange blankets near the fire for the weary travelers. Lady Alice watched them work and gave directions when needed; then, when the hall's outer door finally opened with a rush of wind and rain, she turned to welcome her guests.

The captain of Brentwood's small garrison ushered in nine travelers and a dog, each shivering and soaked to the bone. One of the men had been placed on a makeshift cot that was being carried by two others; a section of his bloodied tunic had been cut away to reveal a harshly torn shoulder.

As soon as the door had been pushed shut behind them, the young man at the head of the cot looked up with an anxious expression and caught sight of the castle's noble lady. Alice's eyes widened when she saw that he wore the attire of a seaman; would she forever be faced with reminders of her parents' sea-faring tragedy?

The seaman's concern for his friend was clearly revealed in his tone as he asked, "Where can we put him please, my lady? We need a clean place to lie him down."

"This way, quickly," Alice motioned to a side door and led the way.

The seaman and the other cot-carrier, a young man with starkly blond hair and green eyes, followed Alice up a single flight of stone steps and into a room on the right of a short corridor. Behind them came a gray-haired man with a sack and a walking stick that appeared to be pulling him along; the scraggly dog and an elderly woman walked beside him.

Alice ushered them into the spare room and then watched as the others entered; a tall spindly man with yellow hair reaching his slumped shoulders and a slightly shorter man with black hair tied back in a club stepped into the room with solemn faces. After them came two young women; the first wore the common clothing of a peasant and kept her saddened gaze on the floor. The second was dressed in attire that was unfamiliar to Alice; her dripping black hair hung loosely where it had escaped her braid and her violet eyes shifted alertly over the dark corridor before colliding with Alice's gentle gaze.

Alice felt compelled to speak, "Welcome to Brentwood."

The girl nodded and muttered something that Alice suspected was a sort of thanks and then the two followed the others into the room. The captain stood guard at the door.

Alice quickly gathered that the wounded man on the cot was Druet the blacksmith himself. She watched with wonder from her place by the wall as his followers carefully lifted his unconscious form onto the bed and did their best to make him comfortable; she had never seen such care shared among people. Even the dog whined sadly as he found a place to lie by the room's hearth.

The sound of muttering drew Alice's attention to the elderly couple to the left of the bed's head. Inching closer she could just make out parts of the man's speech as he pulled bunches of dried plants from his sack.

"The centaury...but the chamomile...fever...fox's clote or marigold...yarrow for infection...pasque...pain. My dear did you gather the oak?"

Alice's eyes widened with quick comprehension, "He is a healer?"

Her hoarse whisper drew the attention of the entire band, except for the healer himself, and Alice flushed at the room's sudden and silent pause.

The seaman's steady gray-eyed gaze never wavered, "He is a healer, yes, and harmless. If you wish us to leave then say so, but Rodney is our choice for medicinal help."

Alice glanced from the healer to Druet and then turned back to the seaman. All her life she had been taught that healers were evil magicians who had rebelled against the nobility in order to practice evil magic among the commoners; and yet, this limited knowledge had come from her Uncle Osgood and Aunt Rose—the self-seeking nobility. Had her parents thought that the healers were evil?

The captain suddenly spoke from the doorway, "Lady Alice, the practice of healing is forbidden..."

Healing is forbidden. The words struck Alice's mind like a gong and she turned to the captain with a questioning look. Why, she wished to ask?

"Lord Osgood would not—"

"No," Alice cut him off with an upraised hand; she knew very well what Lord Osgood would say— but would his opinion be right? Digging her fingers into the honey-colored curls at her temples, Alice closed her eyes tightly for a brief moment and then looked up at the seaman with sudden confidence, "You may stay."

He gave her a slight smile and a nod of thanks.

"My lady, your uncle!"

"Captain, this castle is my home; I will choose who is to be sheltered by its walls, and I will answer to Lord Osgood if the matter should be of concern to him."

The captain dipped his head in required submission and was silent as Bess appeared in the doorway beside him with a pot of steaming water,

"All is ready downstairs, my lady," the woman spoke as she moved to set the water near the healer.

"Very good, Bess," Alice turned to face the seaman, who seemed to be in charge, "There is a fire built downstairs and food for you to eat, and cots for you all to sleep in...Brentwood does not boast many spare rooms, so I cannot offer you what Druet has here."

He nodded, "Thank you, my lady; you are kind," turning to his comrades he went on, "Talon, Bracy, take Elaina and Renny down. Blunt. Blunt...you go too."

The man Blunt was watching Druet's pain-racked face and looked as if he himself would burst into tears at any moment. Bracy clapped the man's shoulder and gently pushed him out the door after Talon and Elaina, who had coaxed Anvil to go with them. The seaman looked expectantly to Renny, still standing by the opposite wall, and she returned his gaze with one of determination.

"You go down first, Nathaniel."

"I can wait to eat, Renny; you go."

Renny crossed her arms and shook her head, "You've been carrying Druet for the last four or five hours—you go eat and bring food back for Rodney and Sarah, and then I'll go down to eat."

"But Rodney may need my help."

"He'll need you more after he's mixed the herbs and starts to clean the wounds."

Alice stood by the door and looked from one to the other in tentative silence. Renny remained where she was, unmovable, and finally sank to sit by the wall as if to further prove that she would not be swayed. Nathaniel swept a hand through his light-brown hair, causing drops of rainwater to spatter in all directions.

"I'll go, then," he muttered, "but only because I'm too weary to fight just now."

When the door finally closed on Nathaniel, Lady Alice, and the captain, Renny's eyes immediately swung to the healer leaning over Druet. Quickly reaching into a small pouch at her waist she drew out an even smaller leather packet and rose to her feet to make her way to Rodney's side. Reaching out, Renny gave a firm tap to the healer's arm and then glanced to make sure Druet was still unconscious.

Rodney looked up from his plants and blinked several times, obviously trying to clear his mind of herbal cobwebs, "What is it, my dear girl?"

Renny reached out and placed the little packet in the healer's aged hands. The old man gave her a curious glance and then gave the packet's strings a tug; the small sack opened and the healer poured the contents into one hand. A moment later he gave a slight gasp and Sarah turned to see. Both turned wide eyes to Renny.

Rodney stuttered, "Is...is this...what I think it is?"

Renny nodded.

Sarah stared down at Rodney's hand, "But this can only be found—"

"My dear Renny, this means you are—"

"Yes," Renny held her hand up to stop the flow of words; slowly her head began to shake solemnly, "I wanted you to have it to help Druet, but I waited until now to give it to you because I do not want the others to know. You must promise me that you will not breathe a word of this to anyone."

Sarah nodded her understanding and turned to speak in her husband's ear, "Did you hear her, Rodney?"

He nodded and placed a hand on Renny's shoulder, "Your secret is safe with me."

Chapter 22
* A New Friend *

A lice prepared a trencher of food for Rodney and Sarah while Nathaniel fed Druet's dog and filled a trencher for himself. His eyes frequently shifted to glance at the side door where they had taken Druet.

"You are all very fond of him," Alice noted, hoping to bring conversation to the heavy silence that had fallen over the hall.

Talon and Bracy chose that moment to begin arguing over a chunk of bread that both had reached for.

Nathaniel grinned wryly, "Fond of Druet, but not of each other. Talon! Bracy! Give that to Elaina and each of you choose a different piece for the other."

The two young men scowled and pelted chunks of bread at each other.

Alice hid a smile behind her hand.

Nathaniel turned back to the food and explained, "They're clansmen from opposite ends of the kingdom and are determined to keep up their combative reputations. In fact, they were fighting when they met."

Alice tore two portions of bread and set them on the healer's trencher, "And you are a seaman?"

"Yes," his face lit up and Alice knew that she had discovered his favorite topic, "I've been sailing since my first voyage as a cabin boy at the age of thirteen. Are you fond of the sea?"

Alice dropped her gaze as thunder sounded outside; she hated to spoil his brief moment of joy, but knew that she must be truthful.

"Actually, I hate it. I'm terrified of it," she looked up to see his confused frown as he glanced at the window, obviously thinking of Brentwood's close proximity to the sea, "My parents disappeared at sea many years ago and I've been afraid of it ever since. For a long while I lived in Quale with my uncle, but then he...I returned to live in my father's castle on the coast eight years ago."

Nathaniel nodded, "I remember hearing something of your parents...I'm sorry."

Lady Alice nodded and wiped at a tear as she lifted the trencher and followed Nathaniel toward the side door. The two quickly made their way up the flight of steps and into the spare room. Rodney was using mortar and pestle to crush and mix herbs while Sarah replaced the damp cloth at Druet's forehead. Renny sat on the floor by the hearth, rocking back and forth while her lips moved soundlessly.

"Renny," Nathaniel called softly and she looked up, "I'll eat up here; you go down now."

Without a word Renny rose and, with a backward glance at the healer and his wife, left the room.

Rodney turned and caught sight of the newcomers.

"Ah, Nathaniel, my boy! I'm nearly ready for you. I'll have you hold him down while I clean the wound and administer the potion."

The seaman nodded silently and Alice saw his fingers fidget around the edges of his trencher; his strained expression was evidence that he did not look forward to witnessing his friend's pain. Moving to set the healer's food on a small table, Alice quietly asked,

"So, you have two clansmen, a healer and his wife, a blacksmith, and a seaman in your band; who are the others?"

Nathaniel set his trencher by Rodney's, "Blunt is a traveling bard who lost his lute in our recent encounter with the carnatur plants."

Alice's eyes widened and she glanced at Druet, "The carnaturs? And he survived?"

Nathaniel nodded and went on, "Elaina is a simple lass from Ranulf's region, and Renny is a huntress from we-don't-know-where."

Alice nodded as she absorbed the information.

Rodney motioned for Nathaniel to join him at the bedside. The seaman took a deep breath as he crossed the room. Alice left quietly, closing the door behind her. When she reached the bottom of the stairs and stepped into the great hall, the room's occupants froze at the sound of a terrible wail from the sickroom.

Anvil bawled and raced up the steps to scratch at the door and Bracy ran to bring him back down.

Elaina's hands covered her mouth and Renny turned quickly from where she stood at the south window. Blunt crossed his long arms on the table and dropped his head to rest on them, while Talon watched from beside him with a dazed look on his face.

Tears sprang to Alice's eyes as she listened to Druet's roars of pain and watched the effects that his distress had on his followers. She thought of the healer and silently prayed that she had done right in letting him stay to practice his forbidden profession.

Crossing to the central table, Alice sat down across from Talon and bowed her head; *Oh God, I pray that You will bring healing to Druet. Comfort his friends as they watch him suffer. And God, please heal my own heart and help me to accept the great loss of my past and move on in faith to what You hold for my future.*

The next morning Lady Alice lifted her head from where it still lay on the table. Across from where she sat, Rodney smiled at her over his spoon of broth.

"Good morning to you, my dear girl! Rise with the sun and greet the new day over a bowl of this fine substance laid before us!"

Alice blinked and stretched the kinks from her sore muscles, "How is Druet?"

The old man slurped another spoonful and smacked his lips together in satisfaction.

Alice frowned. Was he ignoring her?

Sarah leaned over and spoke loudly in her husband's ear, "The lady asked how Druet is faring!"

Rodney's eyes lifted to Alice, "Ah! He is well; quite well. Asleep for now. The wound is clean and soaking in a strong potion to keep infection from returning. He will not lose the limb, praise God!"

Sarah smiled and leaned toward Alice, "He is hard of hearing, my lady. Thank you for your kindness in opening your home to us and offering a place to sleep and food to eat."

"You're welcome," Alice nodded as a servant placed a bowl of steaming broth before her.

Nathaniel approached the table and sat next to Rodney; motioning toward the hall's large hearth he asked, "Why do you have a tapestry depicting a battle at sea if you…"

Alice held a hand up, "My lord uncle favors the piece; I couldn't take it down without him ordering it back onto the wall."

Nathaniel nodded in silence and cast another glance toward the hearth.

Everyone spent the rest of the day in quiet activity. Alice searched through piles of stored items and found an old lute, which she presented to Blunt in replacement of the one broken. The minstrel thanked her profusely and vowed to write a sonnet in praise of her kindness to their simple band.

Late in the afternoon, Druet opened his eyes and blinked at the ceiling several times before noticing the young man in the chair by the bed.

"Nathaniel," he winced, "how long did I sleep?"

"Not long enough."

"Where are we?"

"Castle Brentwood; southern Osgood. We're on the coast, remember?"

Druet brought his left arm to gingerly feel his right shoulder, "Perfect. We can sail west to Hugh's region and search the Dragon Coast. How long before the band is ready to start?"

"Ho there, mate! Where do you think you're off to in such a hurry? Your arm was nearly torn from your shoulder, Druet. How do you expect it to heal if you don't give yourself a chance to rest? You'll need that limb, you know."

Druet pushed his head back into the pillow that cradled his neck, "I'll manage well enough. I want to go."

Nathaniel grinned and leaned back in his chair, "You give it half a chance and that arm of yours will start to hurt again; then you'll be grateful for a chance to rest."

"I feel fine."

"Do you now? Fine enough to battle a healthy dragon or two?"

"Perhaps."

"You're as stubborn as Renny."

Druet scowled and drummed his fingers impatiently on the bedspread. Scrambling for something to distract his thoughts from restlessness, he asked, "What have you been doing all day?"

"I climbed to the tower's height and sat precariously in an embrasure to watch the sea for two hours."

"Is that all?"

"I ate the noon meal with the others and listened to Blunt's new song about the 'kindness of the lovely Lady Alice' before I came up here to watch over you."

"Who is Lady Alice?"

"The proprietor of Brentwood and Lord Osgood's niece—though nothing like her villainous uncle. She has provided generously for our band's comfort and even gave Blunt the lute that he's been playing with abandon all day."

There was an awkward pause as Druet studied his friend from the corner of his eye.

"And when he played this new song did the lady blush as red as you are now?"

"Druet...!"

Nathaniel lurched forward in his chair and then realized that he would do more harm than good if he tackled his invalid antagonist. Druet gave a hearty laugh just as the door opened and Rodney stepped into the room, followed by an impatient Anvil and a young woman who Druet knew could only be the subject of Blunt's new song. Nathaniel rose as they entered and Druet nodded his head in a respectful gesture. Anvil raced to the bedside and panted his pleasure at seeing Druet awake.

"You're looking better with every passing moment," Rodney came forward to peer at the blacksmith, "It must have been the... And laughter is such good medicine, as the scriptures say. I highly recommend it!"

Casting a sidelong glance at Nathaniel, Druet grinned, "Thank you, Rodney, for using your talents to care for my wounds."

"Think nothing of it! But here is the Lady Alice to see if you have need of anything, and then you must get more sleep."

Druet shifted to look at Alice, "Thank you for your kind hospitality, my lady. I'm in need of nothing at present."

She smiled and nodded, "Rodney told me that your tunic was badly torn by the carnatur. I've placed a new one there on the table for you."

"Thank you."

She nodded and left the room.

Druet yawned, suddenly overcome by the weariness brought on by his healing wounds. Rodney motioned for Anvil to lie down and then shuffled to sit in the chair vacated by the seaman.

"Nathaniel, you may join the others now and I will take a turn with Druet."

Nathaniel quietly muttered his thanks and headed for the door. Druet grinned when the seaman glanced back with a discomfited glare that clearly stated he had not forgotten Druet's teasing of moments before. A short laugh rose in the blacksmith's chest as the door shut on his friend's distress and he could once more sink into the comforting abyss of sleep.

The following morning Blunt begged Rodney to allow him a brief conversation with Druet. Before long the lanky minstrel had been installed in the bedside chair. He waited while Rodney helped the blacksmith to a sitting position and then watched the healer shuffle from the room.

"Druet," Blunt sat at the edge of his seat, "I must thank you for your heroic service to me in rescuing my life from the very jaws of death by vegetation."

Druet smiled at the man's sincerity and lowered his head, "It was nothing, Blunt—"

"Nothing!? My boy, I surely would have been killed! You might have been killed! Nevertheless, you threw yourself before a terrible demise to save the insignificant life of a poor minstrel. You—the hope of Arcrea!"

Druet studied Blunt's face. Tears had pooled in the bard's eyes and his features were drawn in a look of wonder mixed with complete gratitude.

"I don't know that I agree with this talk of 'the hope of Arcrea'; but I am humbled by your thanks, Blunt."

The minstrel gave a small smile as he observed Druet's humble expression.

"I will always remember your kindness to me, Druet; though I may never write a sonnet to tell the tale, for words could not be found that would express my deep gratitude…and I doubt that I would be able to sing such a song without my tears bringing an early termination to its singing."

Druet laughed and held out his hand, "You're a good man, Blunt."

The minstrel took the offered hand and shook it firmly as he stood to leave, "Thank you, Druet. It is an honor to be allowed to follow you on your quest. You are a remarkable man."

Chapter 23
* Dangerous Warning *

A week passed and Rodney pronounced Druet able to travel. Many of Brentwood's inhabitants wondered at the speed of the blacksmith's recovery, but Rodney's only answer to their inquiries was a knowing smile accompanied by a curious wag of his gray head and a muttered comment about "God's goodness".

It was the night before their planned departure.

The small band had insisted that Druet would spend the final night at Brentwood in his comfortable spare room instead of joining them on the great hall cots as he wished. Soon all had retired to get a full night's sleep in preparation for their continuing journey.

In the middle of the night Druet opened his eyes and stared into the darkness.

Something was wrong.

The chair by his bed had been void of a caretaker for several days now, and so it didn't alarm Druet to see it empty now. Anvil had left his place by the hearth but even this was no matter for concern as the dog had taken to the habit of wandering from place to place at night.

Druet frowned warily.

A strange presence had filled the room.

A salty breeze blew across Druet's face and he realized that the window was open. From his motionless position he could just make out that the wooden shutters had been unlatched and swung inward.

Someone was in the room.

With his heart beating at a rapid pace, Druet turned his head and looked to where his sword rested against the wall within reach.

Suddenly, a swift movement caught the young man's eye and he quickly rolled over and lunged for his sword. Just as swiftly, the intruder knocked the sword out of reach and moved into position over Druet, using a knee to shove the blacksmith to his stomach and twisting the young man's right arm over his back. Druet bellowed into his pillow when he felt a muscle tear in the nearly mended shoulder.

"Silence."

The order was hissed into his ear—definitely a man's voice. Druet tried to look around at the stranger but froze when he felt a dagger at his back.

"You must leave this place at once, before your entire band but one are killed at the hands of the seven lords."

"Who are you?"

"I said silence," the dagger was pressed closer, "The lords of Arcrea have heard of your recent injury and will use your disadvantage to their service; they are on their way now from Quale to kill you and to arrest the Lady Alice for sheltering you and the healer."

"How did they...?" Druet grunted fiercely when his arm was pulled tighter.

"It does not matter! Do you understand? You must leave immediately or suffer the consequences. The matter is out of my hands now. Only remember that you have been warned."

Druet felt his arm suddenly released and the dagger was lifted away; breathing heavily, he quickly rolled over to face the window.

The stranger had already vanished.

Chapter 24
* Escape From Brentwood *

Strapping his sword in place only a moment after his frightful encounter, Druet descended the stairway and strode into the great hall with a firm tread. He rubbed his right shoulder with a grimace as his mind scrambled to collect each unanswered question that presented itself.

Who was the stranger who had managed to gain entrance to his room? How had the man become aware of the lords' plans to kill him, and how had news of his recent injury reached all seven of the lords so quickly? Were the seven lords really on their way to Brentwood now? Or was it a trick to draw him out of the castle and into...what?

Using a flint Druet quickly lit a torch and pulled it from its wall sconce. Anvil emerged from the shadows and wagged his tail in pleasure. Druet gave the dog a rough pat on the head.

"God, give me wisdom."

Moving swiftly to the group of cots where his followers slept, Druet gave Nathaniel's shoulder a shove and then moved on to wake Talon.

"Druet?"

"Nathaniel, we have to work quickly—Talon, wake up!—I've just received word that the seven lords are on their way to Brentwood."

Talon sat up, his eyes suddenly alert. Druet continued as he moved to rouse Blunt.

"It seems they know of my injury and plan to use our disadvantage for their own good. Our entire band is in danger of being put to death."

Druet suddenly froze when the stranger's words returned to register in his memory. The man had warned him to leave Brentwood "before your entire band but one are killed".

Why all but one?

Nathaniel and Talon were now helping to wake the others. Druet turned to the other section of cots and saw that Renny was already awake and listening to all that was being said. She studied Druet's expression.

"Who told you this?"

Druet helped Sarah to her feet and answered, "I don't know who it was."

Renny's eyes darted to the door that led up to the spare room, "Then how do you know you can trust them?"

"I don't. But the choice is to either leave now or tomorrow morning. We might as well put a safer distance between our party and theirs."

Bracy's voice suddenly cut off further conversation as he swung his arms wildly and sat up, "Who...? What...? Talon! What's this about? I'll

teach you to wake me in the dead of night, you...
Why is everyone awake?"

"We're leaving Brentwood."

"Now?"

"Immediately and as silently as possible," Druet
cast a glance across the hall to where several servants
had been sleeping along the walls; Bracy's shout had
roused them.

"We're in danger. I'll explain further later, but
now we must prepare to leave and warn Lady Alice—
she's in danger as well."

A loud whisper suddenly sounded from across the
hall and Druet turned to see old Bess coming toward
them, "You there! What are you at in the middle of
the night? Would you rouse the whole castle? The
lady Alice woke with a fright with all your shouting."

Talon finished looking over his swords and
sheathed them with a fluid motion, "It was Bracy's
fault."

"My fault!? I was frightened out of a deep sleep to
see your ugly face staring at me! That's enough to
move any man to defence."

The castle servants began to edge closer in
curiosity. Druet glanced in their direction and then
spoke in a low tone to Bess, telling her briefly of his
plans to leave and adding that he had information for
Lady Alice that must be given immediately. Bess
nodded and scurried away to fetch the young woman.

By the time Lady Alice appeared in the great hall
several moments later, Druet's entire band was awake
and ready to depart. Old Bess bustled alongside her
mistress, muttering nervously as she tended the last
few buttons on the sleeve of the lady's green dress.

Alice studied the faces that surrounded Druet and then looked up at the blacksmith himself.

"What is it? Is there some trouble?"

Druet nodded and quietly told Alice of the stranger's warning. The young woman's eyes widened and she frowned when he mentioned her own impending arrest.

"My lord uncle wouldn't dare…" she gave a stricken look and pressed her fingers to her forehead, "Yes he would. Bess, bring my cloak."

The woman's eyes widened, "My lady, what…?"

"Bring my cloak, Bess; and send the servants out," Alice turned back to Druet, "Will you take me in your company?"

Druet nodded slowly, wondering if the lady was aware of the journey's hardships. Blunt brought these thoughts forward.

"The road is hard, my lady, and will not be a friend to us. Henceforth we are fugitives in our own homeland."

Alice managed a slight smile, "Thank you, Blunt; I understand it will not be easy for me, but by God's grace I believe I will manage."

Elaina yawned, "Do we have to leave tonight?"

"Yes. We have to find a way to get out without the entire district of Brentwood knowing which way we've gone; it may prove helpful to have news of our location kept quiet for a time."

Druet pressed his shoulder with a restraining hand when his torn muscle flamed with new pain. Beside him, Nathaniel observed the signs of discomfort.

"I thought it was nearly healed."

Druet turned and lowered his voice, "Let's just say my visitor was not the gentlest of creatures."

"Did he harm you?"

"Just a torn muscle. I'll have Rodney feel it when we have time for that."

Alice approached adjusting her cloak over her shoulders, "Druet, there is a stairway that leads down to the coast behind the castle. From there we can make our way to the village half-a-mile to the east and then either cross to Geoffrey's region or sail west again to reach Hugh's."

Alice blinked in surprise at her own words. Had she just suggested that they sail on a ship? At sea? With her a member of their party and terrified of the vast waters? Alice fingered the edge of her cloak and drew a deep breath. She would have to trust that God was answering her prayer by beginning to heal her heart of its past pain.

The ten travelers were ready to leave. Alice sent Bess to her room so that the woman might honestly say to any inquiries that she had not seen where Lady Alice and Druet's band had gone. The lady of the castle then led the way to the stairway that led to the spare room. Halfway up the stairs a stone door blended with the wall around it, hidden from casual observance.

Just as the door was pushed open a shout came from the base of the stairs.

"Halt!"

Everyone turned to see the captain of the garrison accompanied by six soldiers.

Lady Alice stepped forward, "It's alright, Captain."

"My lady, you must return to your room."

Alice frowned at the strange order, "Captain, I will do as I please. Leave us now."

Alíce

Nicole Sager

"No Lady Alice," the soldier climbed the first few steps, "I cannot. I know that you are attempting to flee Brentwood and I will not allow you to do so."

"Captain!" Alice's voice held a hint of her anger.

Druet motioned for Blunt and Rodney to start down the hidden stairway with the women. The minstrel took one of the group's torches and led Sarah and Elaina away while Rodney followed behind them. Renny stubbornly remained where she was and fingered her bowstring.

"You are all commanded to remain at Brentwood until Lord Osgood gives permission otherwise."

Druet glanced at Nathaniel. At least now they knew for certain that the seven lords were aware of their stay at Brentwood and were, no doubt, truly heading their way.

Alice descended several steps to meet the captain with a fierce glare, "Captain, Brentwood is my home—it belongs to me. My uncle has no right to say when I may or may not leave its walls."

"Lord Osgood gave strict orders, my lady, that you were never to leave the area of Brentwood without his knowledge or permission."

Alice stared at him, stunned; her eyes narrowed, "When did he give such an order?"

The captain's face was harder than stone, "Eight years ago."

Alice felt her jaw tighten, "He had no right to do so. I am free to leave my castle and its grounds whenever I wish. My lord uncle will not control me as he did my poor father. I will not succumb to his ways of deception and wickedness!"

"How dare you speak such treasonous words against a seat of Arcrea?"

The captain lifted his hand swiftly and would have delivered a harsh slap to the young woman's face, but Nathaniel intervened and suddenly hurled himself at the soldier. The two immediately engaged in hand-to-hand combat and chaos erupted in the narrow stairway as the six other soldiers rushed forward with their swords drawn. Alice retreated and slipped through the door to the hidden stairway when Druet shouted for her to go on ahead. The blacksmith raced down to cover Nathaniel while Anvil followed to protect his master. Talon and Bracy moved to the other side of the stairs and fought the soldiers who met them there.

The work of Renny's bow, Anvil's teeth, Nathaniel's fists, and the four swords of the others brought the fight to a quick close. Two soldiers lay motionless on the stairs; the captain limped disabled from the stairway with an arrow to his leg while the others ushered him out, favoring their own wounds.

Druet quickly turned to survey his own band as they raced for the hidden stairwell. Renny was fine. Talon had a dark bruise and a welt on his cheekbone, and Bracy was complaining about another large hole in his tunic. Nathaniel's left sleeve was ripped from just below the shoulder to the elbow and stained a deep red.

Druet pushed the door shut when everyone was safely inside the narrow passage and the group quickly turned to start down the stairs toward the coast. Druet moved to Nathaniel's side and examined the seaman's arm.

"Was it a dagger?"

Nathaniel nodded, his mouth set in a grim line.

"Rodney will have something—a salve—for you to cover it with."

Another nod and Nathaniel muttered, "The impudent beast. He accuses a lady above his station of treason and then attempts to act against the very laws of chivalry himself! It's beyond reason, mate."

"It's the way of the Arcrean nobility, Nathaniel; and the captain is in the service of an Arcrean nobleman. The laws of Chivalry will mean nothing so long as there is no one in power to uphold and defend them."

∞)(∞

At the base of the cliff on which Brentwood was built, Lady Alice pulled her cloak tighter around her shoulders and winced when the water crashed against the rocks further below. The waves looked dangerous in the moonlight and she was grateful for the wide path that wound among the rocks, making it easier to travel the coast above the waterline.

Alice turned to observe the others, waiting for their comrades at the base of the concealed stone stairway. Alice's blue eyes locked on Elaina and she studied her closely for a long moment. She had tried to befriend the dark-haired girl from Ranulf during the group's stay at Brentwood, but Elaina had always found something else she'd rather do; Alice had come to feel that Elaina was avoiding her. Even the fierce Renny had been easier to talk to than Elaina was.

Finally, Blunt called over the noise of the waves that the others were coming down the steps and Alice went to join in hearing their report. She grimaced at the sight of Talon's swollen face and Nathaniel's bloody arm and gracefully spoke her immense gratitude over the latter's quick defense against the captain's imminent blow.

When her grateful words continued with no end in sight, a bright flush washed over Nathaniel's face and threatened to burn the very tips of his shaggy brown hair. Druet grinned at Talon and Bracy, standing to his right, and then interjected his own voice when Alice came to a pause.

"I think we should move on quickly...before Nathaniel's glowing countenance provides a beacon for our enemies to follow."

Chapter 25
* A Spy *

The small village of Licklee was quickly reached by following the rough coastal path. From a cliff over Licklee, Druet was able to make out the glowing torches of an entourage swiftly moving toward the castle Brentwood.

"A detachment of knights," he spoke to Nathaniel, "And they're on horseback."

"If we take the road from Licklee it won't be long before they catch up to us; but if we find a vessel to carry us to a farther point we may buy time before they discover our whereabouts again."

"We may not be able to keep that a secret," Druet turned to face his closest friend; the seaman's unshaven face reminded Druet that his own appearance must be just as unkempt and ragged.

"Its true the people of Arcrea spread word wherever you go, but…"

"Its not that," Druet started back down the path towards Licklee's small quay, "Nathaniel, the man who brought the warning tonight told me that all my band but one would be killed if caught by the lords of Arcrea."

Nathaniel's brow furrowed, "You think there's a spy among us?"

"It's the only way I can think to explain his words; though I hate to think such a thing about any member of our party."

Nathaniel was silent a moment, his gaze sweeping over the group of travelers on the docks below.

Druet was doing the same, "It can't be Lady Alice; she's just joined us, and news of Rodney's profession was passed to the nobility weeks ago. Rodney wouldn't have reported himself and neither would Sarah."

"Talon and Bracy are far too set against the seven lords to be acting in their service," Nathaniel added, "Unless, of course, it's been a charade."

The two exchanged a look of amusement.

"Not likely."

"Blunt, God bless him, wouldn't have the heart to speak a word against our band."

"True," Nathaniel turned with a serious look on his face, "I hope you know by now that I would never dream of betraying you."

Druet clapped the seaman on the shoulder and nodded, "You have no need to fear on that point. You're the closest I've ever had to a brother, and I thank God for your friendship."

Nathaniel looked instantly relieved, but then his face took on a frown.

"That leaves Renny and Elaina."

"Renny's never trusted Elaina."

"The others have never trusted Renny."

"I trust her."

"So you think its Elaina?"

Druet ran a hand through his hair, "I don't know. No one seems to be a likely choice."

"Not from our point of view. If there is a spy you can be sure they won't act like one to your face."

Druet smiled at the thought.

Nathaniel glanced down at the group, "You know, mate, if I were to judge by the actions of our group I'd say that appearances are against Renny. We know nothing about her; she remains aloof from everybody but you; and there's something about her that suggests she's here for a purpose."

Druet took a rickety set of stairs that led from the path to the docks, and then turned to face Nathaniel, "I trust Renny."

A faint smile of amusement crossed the seaman's face, "So you said; but why?"

Druet turned and spotted a small vessel with several men scampering around its anchoring point.

"Maybe there isn't a spy among us…maybe there's someone following us."

Nathaniel rolled his lips together and nodded in silence. Druet observed him for a moment and then sighed in frustration.

"I don't know what to think anymore, Nathaniel. The entire kingdom is watching my back for one purpose or another—they either want to cover me or kill me. Even some of the peasants along the way have all but spit in my face to show their opinion of me; and now I hear that one of my friends and companions may be just the opposite! Its more of a burden than my mortal shoulders can carry just now, so I'll trust God to carry it for me and pray that He'll keep my eyes open to danger."

Nathaniel's face twisted into a grin. He never ceased to be amazed by Druet's trusting outlook on life and total dependence on God. The blacksmith's words often encouraged Nathaniel to a higher standard of simple faith.

"Then let's go, mate; we've got seven lords breathing down our necks in hot pursuit, and I'm ready to be out at sea again."

"Good. There's a small vessel there that may serve our purpose well."

Chapter 26
* Voyage to Hugh *

The Licklee vessel was hired and Druet's band was soon aboard and ready to depart for the eastern coast of Lord Hugh's region. Rodney took a strangely sweet smelling salve from his pouch and rubbed it over the band's recent wounds, including Druet's torn shoulder.

Nathaniel was in his element; ignoring the awful slash on his arm he assisted the ship's crew and traversed the rigging with ease, a broad smile plastered to his face as the craft kept its coarse along the southern boarder of Osgood.

Druet watched his seaman friend with a knowing smile, pleased that Nathaniel was able to satisfy, even a little, the longing for the sea that was so ingrained into his being that it was clearly first nature to him.

Shifting his gaze, Druet observed the rest of the group. Several were looking a little green and others were sitting silently, hoping they weren't spotted by someone on the cliffs and praying that their seasick neighbor would make it to the vessel's railing in time should the need arise.

Lady Alice sat huddled against a large wooden crate. Her wide-eyed gaze remained fastened on a random point across the deck as she gripped her knees to her chest in child-like fashion. She started when a hand came to rest on her shoulder and she turned to see Renny's violet eyes observing her with a sort of compassion that seemed unnatural coming from the wild young beauty.

"You're thinking of your parents."

It was more a statement than a question but Alice nodded anyway.

"When word came of their disappearance at sea I swore to myself that I would never take passage on a ship. I've always been held captive by the fear that what happened to them would happen to me."

"It sounds to me as if your fear has done to you what the sea did to your parents."

Alice gave Renny a questioning look.

"This fear has kept you hidden away—you've disappeared from the public's eye and denied yourself the pleasures that God has to offer you. Its true the sea is dangerous; but so are mountains and deep chasms, tangled forests, ignispats, carnaturs, catawylds and dragons; even people are dangerous," Renny's voice became quiet, "perhaps they're the most dangerous of all."

The violet eyes held a strange look as they pierced Alice's gaze, "You must face the knowledge of these things with God's assurance that He will be with you and trust that He will show you the good that does surround you."

Alice was stunned.

Renny stood and shifted her weight to brace herself against the vessel's natural tossing. She held her hand out and Alice gripped it firmly.

"Come."

Without a second thought Alice allowed herself to be pulled to her feet. She sidestepped when the deck seemed to fall out from under her, and then readjusted her weight as Renny had done. The young huntress turned and led the noblewoman to the railing. Alice pulled back when a spray of saltwater suddenly rose over the side of the vessel, but Renny continued to pull at her hand until Alice stood beside her at the rail.

Alice's fingers clutched the railing until she thought her nails would leave marks in the smooth wood. Her heart was pounding so strongly that the sound of it in her ears nearly overpowered the noise of the waves. The terrifying waters were closer now than she had ever allowed them to come. Another spray of saltwater rose and Alice braced herself as it washed over her and covered her face in a fine wet film.

Oh God, I trust You to watch over me and I pray that You would help me to follow after You in simple faith.

Alice felt a sweet peace wash over her with even more saturation than the wave before it. Her fears were suddenly swept away with the passing coast and Alice opened her eyes to face the tossing expanse of the Arcrean Sea with new courage.

A strange happiness rose from somewhere deep within her and Alice suddenly laughed outright as tears began to mix with the saltwater that covered her face.

Renny watched the other woman and then turned to glance at Druet, who stood watching from across the main deck. The two exchanged a smile and Druet nodded before Renny felt herself enveloped in Alice's embrace.

"Thank you, Renny, for your kindly spoken words. I will always think of you as my dearest friend and sister in Christ," she gave a knowing smile, "even if you insist on being so distant from the rest of us."

Renny smiled slightly in return, "You are kind, my lady."

"Please," the woman's curls quivered as she shook her head, "call me Alice."

The ship sailed west to the coast of Hugh and deposited its passengers on the docks of a city that was almost as destitute as Morgway. The very buildings looked about ready to collapse into the middle of the street, which was hardly more than a rutted path through the city's core.

The familiar sound of hammer on iron pricked at Druet's ear and he turned to see a blacksmith bent over his work at the anvil.

"Good day to you, sir," Druet stepped in the smith's direction, "Would you tell me—what city is this?"

The blacksmith dragged his weary eyes from the work before him and studied Druet's face.

"It's little more than the grave's edge, boy, and should have been named such. This be the city of Campbell. And who might you be?"

Druet stretched out his hand, "I'm Druet of Oak's Branch in Frederick's region."

Blunt

Nicole Sager

Several passersby stopped and turned when they heard the name, studying the group with open curiosity. The blacksmith ignored Druet's offered hand and lifted his head warily.

"The blacksmith turned adventurer? The man out to gain Arcrea's crown?" he turned to his forge and thrust the cooled iron into the flame, "You'd best take yourself from Campbell as quickly as you came if you'd know what's best for you."

Druet's brow lifted slightly in surprise. The smith turned a cold look over his shoulder and glared.

"You may hear your praises sung to high heaven elsewhere in this miserable kingdom, but not in Campbell, you'll find."

A woman who had stopped began to jeer and Druet was silent as he shifted to listen.

"We've enough trouble here, what wif the lords squeezin' ever' last penny from our pockets and the clans comin' down fro' the mountains to loot us blind. We don' need a cocky young for'ner risin' up an' turnin' the nobles again' us any more'n they are!"

"Druet is far from a cocky young foreigner, my dear woman," Blunt stepped forward with an indignant huff, "Why he is a—"

"Save your song for another crowd, minstrel," the blacksmith started his hammer's rhythmic pounding, "We don't want to hear it!"

"Why, sir—"

"Blunt," Druet held his arm out and stopped the bard's advance, "It's alright."

The crowd of curious citizens had grown and the people began to scoff at the young man before them.

Druet quietly thanked the smith for his time and resumed his walk up the street.

Nathaniel watched his friend's calm response to the building chaos and shook his head at the jeering crowd. He glanced at Renny, walking to his left, and sighed.

"Little do they know; they are mocking the man who will one day be their king, and yet he will never hold this day's actions against them."

Renny glanced ahead to where Druet walked with his head bowed slightly as he watched the road in front of him. She shifted her gaze back to Nathaniel.

"Do you really believe that he will be king?"

"With all of my heart. I see proof of it daily. He has grown throughout this journey and is fast becoming the man who Ulric prophesied would reign on the first throne of Arcrea."

Renny's eyes squinted the slightest bit as if something had pained her, and in that brief moment Nathaniel gathered a clue to what that something was.

Suddenly, a tomato flew through the air and landed at Druet's steadily moving feet. Several heads of lettuce followed and soon the street was filled with flying produce, thrown with as much vengeance as the angrily shouted words that fell on Druet's ear. Druet's band retained the steady pace set by their leader until they had finally left the city of Campbell behind and were on the road heading northwest to an impressive mountain range and, beyond that, Dragon Coast.

Chapter 27
* Hidden Troubles *

Disgraceful! Simply disgraceful! For the people of my native region to treat him thus is a scar on my name!" Blunt fell back against a stump and placed a hand to his head in woeful demonstration.

"It was to be expected, Blunt. Not everyone is going to look on our quest with pleasure."

They were camped for the night in the mountains of Hugh, two days after the events at Campbell, and Nathaniel had lost count of how many times he had been through this conversation with Blunt.

"Nonetheless, I had always thought of my people as open-minded. Never again will I be so mistaken! Never again!"

"Play us a song, Blunt!" Nathaniel called from across the campfire. Talon and Bracy both cast beseeching looks at him, hoping against hope that the request would be denied; but Blunt's face lit up and he situated the lute that Alice had given him and soon lost himself in an original tune.

Druet and Renny appeared at the edge of the clearing, returning from their hunting rotation with a large deer. Druet began to prepare portions of the animal for the spit.

"You've found a friend in Alice, I see."

Renny shrugged, "She is kind."

Druet glanced up to study her face, "But you aren't going to let yourself get too attached."

She shook her head and a thatch of black hair fell over her eye; pushing it out of her face, she bent with her dagger to help with the deer.

"So, Renny, have we come any closer to your home in our travels, or are we just moving farther from it?"

She cast him a sidelong glance, "Nice try, Druet."

"What does your mother think about your being gone so far for so long?"

Renny was silent, turning away from him. Druet bent his head to see her face, a thought suddenly striking him with its shock of possibility.

"Your mother does know...doesn't she?"

Renny's head lifted sharply and she stared at him for a moment. Her wide eyes and slightly furrowed brow gave him the impression that she didn't truly know the answer to his question.

"Renny?"

"My...my father knows."

He returned her pensive gaze with one of surprise until she looked away. Druet's eyes moved to glance at the rest of the group and then he returned his focus to the deer.

Lowering his voice, he asked, "Renny, how could your mother not know?"

"Druet, please; its no concern of yours."

"I want to know."

"Well, you're not going to know!"

Druet glared at her out of the corner of his eye, "You know, I still don't understand you, Renny."

"Good."

"But why?"

"You mean, why don't you understand me?"

"No! Why is that a good thing? The rest of the group are becoming good friends—even Talon and Bracy can stand being within a mile of each other now—but you refuse to let anyone even call you friend."

"I never said that," Renny snapped, "In case you haven't already noticed; I'm not exactly the friendly type."

"I don't believe a word of that," she frowned and Druet grinned, "After all that talk about how much you love your father, and your kindness to Alice on the ship, and all your help throughout our journey...now you want to tell me you aren't 'the friendly type'?"

Renny jerked a hunk of meat from the deer's carcass and took it to Talon for the spit. When she returned, she attempted to change the subject.

"Where do you plan to search next for the heart?"

Druet couldn't keep the grin from his face, "You really are helpless as far as friends go," she scowled darkly and he continued, "because Nathaniel, Alice, Rodney, Sarah, Blunt, Elaina, and I all consider ourselves to be your friends regardless of whether or not you'll have us. We're still working on Talon and Bracy, but I think they'll come around. Anvil's pretty fond of you, too."

Druet rose with more meat and made his way over to the fire. Renny stared briefly at the carcass before her and then turned to watch him go; her gaze then shifted and she realized Nathaniel was watching her. Renny quickly turned back to her work as a tear dripped from her eye and fell to cut a silent path through the grime on her hand.

The rest of the group laughed at something Rodney had said, but the joyful sound only served to twist Renny's heart into further turmoil. Her mind was like a web that insisted on collecting jumbled thoughts and swirling them in a confused mass.

Renny sucked in a deep breath as she sliced at the meat with a bit more force than was necessary.

Druet's words about her mother had pricked her pride; after all, it hadn't been her choice to leave home without any goodbyes. It was true she had wanted to come after Druet's band, but she hadn't realized that she would be leaving in secret. And now that she was here, she was finding it difficult to leave.

She glanced over her shoulder to see Druet returning to help. When he knelt down across from her, Renny muttered without looking up.

"I wish you'd leave me alone."

His head came up in surprise, but nothing further was said. A shrill cry suddenly rent the air and fifty or sixty whooping clansmen leapt into the clearing with swords and clubs drawn. Druet jumped up and reached for his sword, but it was too late. Something struck him from behind and he felt himself falling forward. Reaching up to clutch his throbbing head,

Druet tried to force himself back onto his feet. From all around him came Anvil's barks, cries of pain and fear, and then Renny screamed for help. Someone was shouting in a foreign language.

The world seemed to be spinning at an incredible speed...and then everything went black.

Chapter 28
* More Problems *

When Druet opened his eyes, Rodney was leaning over him with a foul-smelling bottle in his hand.

"Ha ha! It worked!"

Druet's head cleared of the bottle's nasty scent and he sat bolt upright.

"What happened? Where is everyone?"

Rodney shook his head and stood to his feet, "All here...except one."

Druet's gaze darted across the clearing, searching the ranks for the loss of a face. Nathaniel was on his feet and rubbing his head, but the other men were still on the ground. Sarah and Alice were helping Rodney to bring the men back to consciousness. Elaina was sitting with her back to a tree, apparently still in shock. Lying in front of her was a length of rope; Druet quickly gathered that the women had been tied to the tree.

But one was missing.

Druet went to pick up a fallen bow and quiver.

"Renny...where's Renny? Who attacked us?"

Blunt was now standing. He turned toward Druet with a pained expression.

"The clan of Dragon Coast; it must have been. There is only one clan in my native region and I've heard that they are a terrible people—I'm shocked that they allowed us to live! They speak in a tongue unknown to civilized society and carry out rituals of an inhuman nature."

Druet froze, "What kind of rituals?"

Blunt's gaze circled the group and he seemed to realize for the first time that one of them was missing. His eyes widened in horror and he let out a groan.

"They've taken Renny? Oh, my friends, she is in grave danger!"

Druet winced when something tightened around his temples; he hadn't taken notice of the fact that Rodney had been wrapping a strip of cloth around his bruised head. When the cloth was tied, Druet stepped away and looked from one face to the other.

"Which way did they go? Did anyone see? Elaina?"

Elaina swallowed and lifted her arm to point further west, "It was terrible, Druet! Awful," tears streamed down her face, "I could hear Renny screaming all the way up the mountain!"

"Druet."

Nathaniel's somber tone pulled Druet's attention around. On the ground before the seaman lay a heavily breathing form.

Anvil.

Druet felt his heart lurch at yet another painful discovery. He knelt beside Nathaniel and ran his hand over the dog's side.

"He's alive," Nathaniel offered, "A club hit him; I saw it before they hit me."

Druet turned to look west, up the mountain. Somewhere beyond the peak, Renny was in need of their help. Here, his band was in sore shape and his dog was in need of Rodney's assistance. And then there was the heart—when would he search for that?

Druet clenched his jaw and closed his eyes.

God, give me wisdom.

The young blacksmith stood and turned to face his waiting companions.

"Nathaniel, Bracy, and Talon…are any of you able to go on just now?" When the three nodded in firm decision he went on, "We will leave immediately, then. Blunt, Rodney; if you can, return with the women to the base of the mountain and lodge in the village there. Take Anvil with you. We'll return soon."

Elaina leaned forward, "Where are you going?"

"To get Renny," Druet nodded for the three chosen men to follow him up the mountain, "Pray for us."

∞⊙∞

Lord Frederick's cold gaze swept over the peaceful landscape of Osgood, oblivious to the natural beauty before him as his mind writhed in anger.

The young blacksmith had, once again, escaped from his grasp.

Frederick pounded his fist on the embrasure of Brentwood's tower and cursed under his breath. His informant had reported that young Druet was injured—wounded by a deadly carnatur's bite. How could it be that he had healed in the short time it had taken the lords to make the journey from Quale? The seven noblemen had still been lodged at Osgood's castle, and had brought only a selected company of knights to ensure all possible speed for the ride south. And still, this elusive peasant had vanished—injury and all—before their hasty arrival several nights before!

Frederick's gaze swiveled to the village of Licklee, half-a-mile to the east. The villagers swore they knew nothing of Druet's departure from Brentwood. They *had* admitted that a small vessel had departed in the dead of night, earlier than expected, but they knew nothing of its intended destination or whether it had taken passengers.

It had.

Frederick was sure of this.

There was no other way his prey might have disappeared so swiftly from the district. And his men had searched the district thoroughly. With Osgood's permission, the knights of Frederick had pillaged the area surrounding Brentwood and planted a stark fear in the hearts of the citizens. If any local peasant had known of Druet's whereabouts they would have surely confessed the fact by that night's end.

A servant appeared at the top of the stairs and announced Lord Osgood's desire to speak with Lord Frederick.

The summoned lord rolled his eyes. If Osgood would give half-a-thought to consideration, he may find that he had enough strength to lift his generous paunch up the stairs to meet Frederick where he was instead of calling his guest to answer his petty whim.

Lord Frederick found his host seated before the large hearth in the great hall, a young servant handing him a goblet of wine, which Osgood had been sure to include in his load from Quale. The five other lords had returned to their homes to wait until their service was truly needed.

"Nasty business this is, Frederick, nasty. If it weren't for the rebellion on the part of my Alice I would advise that we drop this blacksmith and let him founder to a halt on his own."

Frederick's eyes narrowed as Osgood swallowed a gulp of wine.

"You swore your allegiance to our cause, Osgood. Falling back on your word now would prove very unpleasant for you, I am certain."

"Ha! You mean you'd *make* certain! I am not blind to your true colors, Frederick—all bronzed and polished in a façade of honor. I warn you, sir, do not threaten me under my own roof else your own words speak against you."

Osgood drained his cup and shouted for a servant to refill it. Frederick raised his eyebrows in unaffected poise and motioned for a goblet to be brought for his own enjoyment.

"I am rather upset by this sudden outburst on Alice's part," Osgood redirected his focus to matters at hand, "I don't know why she would prove to be so headstrong all of a sudden. I've kept her here for eight years without any problems!"

Frederick scoffed as he took a seat opposite to Osgood, "You couldn't keep a feather in your hat let alone manage another human's life!"

"How dare you, sir? I manage the lives of my entire region!"

Frederick muttered into his goblet, "Better than your brother would have, I wonder?"

"What's that?"

"What will you do with Alice when you've found her?"

An absent chuckle escaped Osgood as he stared into his cup, "I'll take her back to Quale with me, I dare say. I'll have Rose keep a careful watch over her until I've found a wealthy house to marry her off to— make new connections, you know," Osgood noted Frederick's unimpressed glare, "Or perhaps I'll put her to work for me; teach her to never speak against me or run off with a ragged bunch of commoners."

Frederick grunted and drained his own goblet just as a panting servant approached with a worn scrap of parchment.

"What's this?" Osgood leaned forward in his chair.

"A message just come for Lord Frederick, sir."

Frederick stood and shoved his empty goblet at the servant as he snatched the message. The servant scurried away as the powerful lord unfolded the parchment and read the short piece of news. A slow smile of dark pleasure spread across his face.

"What is it, Frederick? What news?" Too lazy to stand, Osgood impatiently tapped at the arm of his chair with a fat finger.

The captain of Brentwood's garrison, still healing from his recent wounds, approached with a quick salute.

"My lord Osgood, news has just arrived from the village Licklee that the vessel which departed suddenly some days ago has now returned from the west."

Osgood now stood to his feet, "Now Frederick; now we'll have some news!"

Frederick lifted his eyes to observe the other men; holding up the parchment in his right hand, he clutched the pommel of Druet's sword with his left.

"No need to question the vessel's crew, Osgood; I know where Druet has gone."

Chapter 29
* Dragon Coast *

The smell of death clung to the environment like a fixed element of the atmosphere. With every breath, Renny's stomach churned and threatened to heave its contents into the dirt at her feet. Her eyes had been covered with a dirty rag and her hands were tied together in front of her; a massive fist gripped her right arm and guided her through the forest-shrouded mountains of Hugh. They had been walking for two days.

At first, Renny had offered stout resistance and shouted at her captors in hopes that Druet would be able to follow the sound of her screams and come to her assistance; but when night had fallen, Renny had come to realize that Druet's small force was helpless against a company of sixty—she would be better off trying to escape on her own.

So she had tried...and failed.

The clan's leader had then blindfolded her and ordered his largest follower, Grikk, to take charge of her. From what she had seen of him as the rag was being placed over her eyes, Renny had figured Grikk was at least six-and-a-half feet tall and nearly as wide.

Renny knew they were nearing the clan's village when the pungent stench began to intensify. Finally, the gall rose in her throat and the unaffected Grikk paused to let her heave. The respite was brief to say the least. After the space of two breaths Renny felt a tug on the rope at her wrists and she was forced to fall back into the pattern of Grikk's long strides.

Some time later, the sounds of a lively village were heard ahead. Renny tilted her head to listen as each sound began to articulate from the others and she soon felt herself surrounded by an oppressive crowd. Hands came at her from all directions, feeling her hair, clothes, face, and hands; her blindfold became loose and the rag slipped from her face. Renny squinted when the harsh sunlight met her eyes.

Someone shouted in obvious surprise as he pointed at her face and leaned within an inch of her nose. Renny scowled at the stranger and lunged at him, barely missing his own nose with her teeth. A gasp of shock rose from the crowd and someone slapped her from behind. A woman grabbed Renny's face with both hands and leaned in close as the man had done before. Her weathered face wrinkled with wonder as she stared into Renny's angry face and then she turned and passed the captive's face into another pair of hands. With sudden realization, Renny knew they were shocked by the color of her eyes. Everywhere, the members of her captors' clan shoved each other for a chance to get closer, a chance to look into her face and chatter in their strange language.

Finally, Renny could stand it no longer; twisting and turning her head away from anyone who came near, she let out a scream that pierced the clan into a shocked silence.

Renny turned a fierce gaze from one face to another; her voice was raw with indignation, "My father will hear what has happened to me and he will send an army to find me!"

Their faces showed amusement and surprise at her outburst. They could no more understand her than she could them. Renny breathed heavily, praying that her own words would prove to be true. After all, her father had no way of finding out what had happened to her; Druet didn't know where she had come from. But Rodney and Sarah did...

The clan's chief stepped forward, draped in odd-colored robes and decorated with strange designs painted on his skin. A small man, half the chief's height, stepped up beside him and spoke in the familiar Arcrean language.

"Our honored chief says to welcome you to Dragon Coast. What is your name?"

"Renny."

The little man looked up to the chief. The stony-faced man looked down his nose at her and then spoke to his interpreter, who in turn spoke to Renny.

"Our honored chief says that you, Renny, will at last bring our people peace. Our scouts have long searched for the one who would satisfy the sun that it might never dip below the horizon again, for then comes night and the attacks of the dragons. When you have pleased the sun, we will never know night again."

Renny's mouth dropped open, "That's ridiculous! The sun is not a god that hears you, and neither is the moon! There is only one true God—the Creator of all things—and He alone can give you protection from the dragons."

A murmur spread through the crowd as Renny's words were translated. Grikk, still holding the length of rope, stood behind Renny with his usual appearance of indifference.

The chief held his hands up for silence. He continued to stare at Renny as he spoke through the interpreter.

"Our honored chief says that you have spoken blasphemy, but you are still the acceptable one. You will be honored at the banquet tonight and then you will rest for tomorrow when you will satisfy the..."

"Stop saying that!" Renny felt a pit of uneasiness growing in her stomach, "I don't understand what you're talking about."

"AH!" the interpreter's face lit up as if he was about to tell her something pleasant, "Tomorrow we will have a great ceremony, and you will be sacrificed!"

The little man interpreted his own words for the crowd and they began to cheer and dance.

Renny's face had gone pale and she stared at the chaos before her. She leaned over when her stomach heaved again and this time she sank to the ground when she had finished. After two days of tense travel and uncertainty, she had no strength to fight. She would be unsuccessful, anyway. Druet's courageous band would not be able to stand against this crowd, even should they find her in time—that is if they were looking; and her father would have no way of knowing until it was too late.

"God," she moaned into the dirt, "These people have been blinded by foolishness; they do not know You. Save me, please, from their hands."

Towering over her, Grikk listened in unaffected silence to her groaning petitions. The little interpreter approached, prattling some instruction or other to the silent giant. In response, Grikk leaned down and pulled Renny to her feet with little effort. The young woman felt a tug at the rope as he started forward, leading her further into the mountainside village; above the noise of the crowd, the interpreter shouted something about a hut and sleep.

Within minutes, Renny's hands were freed from the binding rope and she was shoved into a one-roomed windowless hut. She fell to her hands and knees as the door was slammed closed behind her and a bar fell into place outside, locking her in.

The sudden quiet was welcoming, but Renny's heart took no comfort in it. Crawling to the far wall, she sat with her back against its uneven face and pulled her knees in close. Lowering her forehead to her knees, Renny allowed one sob to escape her chest.

"Please, God, please," she murmured the only words that would surface through her numb thoughts.

Please, God.

Forced to attend the banquet held in her honor, Renny sat in silence and scowled through the entire evening until she was finally taken back to her hut to sleep.

Alone in the dark, the girl's thoughts drifted to her home and family. Would she ever see them again? Her father—the man she held dearest to her heart; her mother—the loving woman who had raised a spirited daughter with more gentleness and patience than anyone had thought possible; and her brother. Kellen.

Renny paced the oppressive hut in agitation. Thinking of Kellen always made her fidget. She knew her attitude towards him was far from just, but her wounded heart always found reason to condemn him.

Kellen was now fifteen; five years younger than Renny, and heir to her father's honored position in Arcrea.

Renny blinked back tears when she thought of those five years before he had been born. She had been her father's pride and joy, his prize companion through every venture possible; he had even begun to teach her the bow in those years. But the birth of a son had changed her father's focus. Renny had had to share his attention and time. Kellen had shared her lessons with the bow and taken her place at her father's side.

Renny gave a loud huff of frustration over her own pettiness. Kellen had had no choice. It had been expected of him—a boy in line to take his father's seat. And every child had to share their parents' attention with other children in the family—it was never a "firstborn takes all" condition.

A shadow filled the cracks in the hut's door and Renny knew her groans had attracted attention from outside. Moving to the threshold, she pounded her fists on the rough wooden door and shouted,

"Go away, Grikk! I'm just feeling sorry for myself. Can't a person breathe without every person within a mile's distance coming to see what its about?"

A soft grunt was her only answer. Renny had begun to wonder if the giant spoke at all...even when he *could* understand what was being said to him.

The young prisoner returned to her pacing, her thoughts too stormy to let her sleep.

What was wrong with her? Did she think that her father had stopped loving her just because another child had been born into their family? Renny shook her head; she knew that was a ridiculous thought. Her father had continued to show his love for her in every way possible throughout the years; he had simply needed to share his time in order to show the same devotion to his son as well.

The fault had been with her. Renny saw it clearly now. She had allowed her heart to cultivate the seeds of bitterness and jealousy until they had grown into weeds more vicious than the carnaturs.

Renny bowed her head as tears began to flood her vision, "God, forgive this sin that I have performed toward my brother. He has been so good to me."

Renny sank to sit against the wall, leaning her head back. How she longed to see her family again and to beg Kellen's forgiveness for her anger toward him. Her violet gaze shifted to study the door, guarded by Grikk. There seemed to be little hope of ever seeing anything beyond this hut but death itself.

&)C&

Druet crawled on his belly to the edge of the clearing. Talon and Bracy crawled at his left, while Nathaniel advanced by his right. The putrid air forced them to pause on occasion to breathe in the cleaner scent of the earth beneath them. For three days they had followed the vague trail left by Renny's captors, ever west toward the Dragon Coast. Now a vast encampment appeared on the mountainside before them, swarming with a population of vicious clansmen and their families.

Nathaniel tilted his head to look out over the trees on the lower slope. Beyond them lay the western sea, lined for many miles by cliffs that soared nine hundred feet or more above the tossing waves. It was in the walls of these cliffs that hundreds of dragons made their homes in caves and burrows. At night they could be heard screeching as they flew over the countryside in search of food. The people of Hugh's region kept the dragons from terrorizing their homes by lighting bonfires that were stoked all through the night. Fire seemed to be the only source that could keep the beasts away.

Talon's bright green eyes darted over the Dragon Coast village and then shifted to exchange a glance with Bracy. The two grinned in spite of themselves, each knowing the other's thoughts without speaking a word; here, at last, was the type of battle they were accustomed to: clan against clan…though their present clan was a rather undersized one.

An hour passed and the group had still seen no sign of Renny. The clansmen had begun forming a large pile of sticks and brush around a wooden stake at the camp's center. Everyone was scurrying in excitement, dressed in what looked to be their finest robes and covered with signs painted on their skin. Druet thought of Blunt's words regarding the clan's inhumane rituals and silently prayed for Renny's safety.

The sun had not yet risen over the highest peaks of the Hugh Mountains, and so the village was still bathed in shadows. When a thin line of sunlight finally framed the western edge of the village, the scene before Druet and his friends changed to one of frightening bedlam. Amid chilling cries and foreign chants, the people of Dragon Coast made their way to a small hut at the camp's perimeter. Standing at the door was a man of enormous stature; as the wild crowd approached he entered the hut, quickly reappearing with Renny close behind him. The young woman's wrists were bound by a rope that the giant was pulling in the direction of the wooden stake and its surrounding pile of kindling.

The crazed mob grew louder as they neared the center of their village. Renny's eyes were wide and she began to pull against the rope, shouting for the "big oaf" to let her go.

"Are these mad creatures really Arcrean?" Bracy asked in a hushed voice, though the crowd's chants were loud enough to shield their voices from detection.

"How have they been allowed to grow so wicked?"

Druet didn't answer. His eyes were trained on the scene before him, quickly revealing itself to be a ritualistic sacrifice. His mind screamed at him to give the signal to charge into the scene, come what may, in an attempt to rescue their friend from disaster; but something deeper held him back—like a restraining hand on his shoulder, something kept him in place.

Wait.

The word stuck in his mind like a barb—impossible and yet unmistakable.

"Druet…?" Talon's voice held concern as they watched Renny being tied to the stake. Torchbearers danced wildly around the brush pile.

Wait.

"Wait, Talon," Druet held his hand up.

Nathaniel eyed his friend closely; noting the struggle Druet was experiencing and marveling once again at the blacksmith's ability to remain calm under pressure—after all, they were about to risk their lives in battle against an entire clan.

Clan members dropped to their knees and lifted their hands to the sky, singing noisily to the tune that a group of musicians were playing. The giant guard finished tying Renny to the stake and paused to look down at her for a long moment before turning to move away from the site of sacrifice.

An angry-looking man, probably the clan's chief, stepped forward and raised his hands over his head, bringing the music and chanting to an abrupt halt. Without the deafening screams of the mob, the four young men could now hear Renny's angry shouts directed at her captors.

Bracy grunted, "Well, she hasn't lost her tongue, that's for sure."

Suddenly, the air was rent by a fierce shriek that sent chills up Druet's spine. All eyes lifted in shocked silence to search the sky, and then the entire clan quickly turned to chaos as everyone ran for shelter from the imminent danger. Their sacrifice momentarily forgotten, the clan seemed eager to vanish from sight.

Druet jumped to his feet and his three companions did the same. Simultaneously, three beasts of incredible size rose above the treetops on leathery wings, hovering with angry glares over the far side of the village.

Dragons!

Chapter 30
* Of Dragons & Deliverance *

The screaming villagers collided with one another in their attempts to gain cover. Frantic cries of "Drago! Drago!" filled the air as the hovering beasts observed the chaos with glassy eyes. The dragons' long necks arched like striking ignispats and their thick tails swayed like snakes as their leathery wings waved noiselessly to keep them floating in midair.

Without warning, the smallest of the three beasts dipped its head and dove toward the camp. It sailed just above the huts, devastating homes in it powerful wake and coming to land on a pile of boulders at the vast clearing's edge. Turning to survey its work of terror, it shrieked and stretched its neck in apparent pleasure.

Druet drew his sword and immediately heard the ring echoed as his followers did the same. The four stood for the space of a heartbeat, preparing for the duty that laid before them—a duty which none had predicted when setting out on a seemingly simple quest through Arcrea.

The two larger dragons started their plummet to earth with unnerving screams.

"God help us," Nathaniel shook his head.

Druet led the band from the cover of the trees and they quickly made their way into the village. Clansmen cast them confused looks as they moved against the flow of frightened people, but no one attempted to stop the four strangers on their mad dash toward obvious death.

The two large dragons pulled up before hitting the ground and seemed to float just above the packed earth as they flew through the village with their massive claws stretched out before them, heading straight for Druet's band. At the last minute, Druet shouted "Drop!" and the four young men quickly hugged the earth. The beasts swept by, mere inches above them and let out cries of disappointment when their claws remained void of prey.

Druet was on his feet an instant after the danger had passed, and sprinting toward the stake where Renny was tied. The young woman was franticly trying to pull the ropes away, but unsuccessfully.

"Hold on, Renny!"

Renny looked up in shock when she heard her name.

"Druet—behind you!"

Without looking, Druet threw himself down a second time and instinctively rolled to one side. The smaller dragon flew by in a flash of scales and leathery wings, clawing at the dirt where Druet had just been.

Druet jumped up just as the thwarted dragon flapped his wings in quick strokes and brought himself to the ground some yards away. The furious monster turned and stretched his neck toward Druet with a hiss.

Nathaniel appeared beside him, "The boys have the other two distracted, but not for long."

Druet nodded. At any other time he would have thought it comical that Talon and Bracy had just been referred to as "the boys", like a pair of children; but at the moment it mattered little.

The blacksmith swung his sword when the dragon's face lunged closer and the beast quickly drew back.

"We'll have the upper hand once I get Renny's bow to her."

"Done," Nathaniel nodded and sprinted toward the dragon with sword ready.

Druet ran in the opposite direction, towards Renny, when the dragon turned to strike out at Nathaniel. The top of the brush pile was quickly reached and Druet cut the ropes free. Tearing the bow and quiver from his own shoulder, he shoved the articles at Renny and then, grabbing her arm, helped her from the pile and to the ground.

"Hit the dragons, not the people; and try to stay out of their sights!" Druet shouted over his shoulder as he raced to Nathaniel's assistance.

Renny drew an arrow from her quiver and shouted back, "I know what to hit and what not to hit, Druet!" A rush of energy flooded her being as the realization of freedom dawned on her and she clutched her familiar bow.

She muttered a swift prayer of thanks to God for her miraculous rescue as she set the arrow to the bowstring and eyed the smaller dragon. Ducking beneath a cart by the side of a hut, Renny positioned herself to aim. Nathaniel was at the beast's back while Druet was trying to distract it at the front. Tilting her head, Renny eyed the shot and yelled as loudly as she could,

"Druet! *DUCK!*"

Druet's head whipped around and he ducked just as the arrow zipped across the space and lodged in the dragon's torso. The dragon shrieked and began to thrash at the sudden impact. Nathaniel jumped clear of the tail and then thrust his sword into the monster's side. Another arrow struck the beast's heart and it fell with a jarring crash.

"*LOOK OUT!*"

Talon's bellow came just in time. Nathaniel and Druet dove for the sheltered doorway of a nearby hut just as the two large dragons flew to a landing beside their fallen companion. With furious hissing and thrashing, the two twisted and turned in the narrow village street, crumbling the walls of many homes with the strength of their sweeping necks and tails.

Renny's cart was suddenly struck and tossed like a child's plaything across the road. The impact knocked Renny from her feet and she fell backwards, spilling arrows from her quiver. The largest dragon peered down at her and flicked its forked tongue as it reared back to strike at its prey. Her shelter gone, Renny scrambled to her feet and grabbed one of the dropped arrows to fit on her string; but before she was ready, the dragon dropped to its front legs and lunged forward with open jaws.

Renny took a step back and tripped. Anticipating the dragon's bite, she quickly covered her face with her arm and cringed. But nothing happened. A strange noise caused her to look up and Renny's eyes widened in shock. Grikk had appeared and stopped the dragon's mouth with a massive club!

The giant suddenly let go of his end of the club and retrieved a long spear from where he had dropped it at his feet. The dragon spit the chunk of wood in disgust and shrieked at the man who had interrupted his kill.

Renny crouched to retrieve a handful of arrows, keeping a constant eye on the dragon. Druet and Bracy were cautiously approaching the monster from behind.

The dragon swiveled its neck back and forth, trying to confuse Grikk as he blocked each advance with the shaft of his spear. Renny aimed and missed two shots as the animal easily dodged the small group's efforts.

Druet cast a glance toward the other dragon and then shouted at Renny, "Talon and Nathaniel need an arrow!"

Renny nodded and ran in that direction.

Talon's swords were a blur of skilled expertise as he kept the dragon at bay while also distracting it from Nathaniel's advance to one side. As Renny approached, the beast suddenly turned and lurched in her direction, knocking Nathaniel over and pinning the seaman beneath its tail. Talon leapt forward and swung one sword in an overhead arch, catching the side of the dragon's face.

"RENNY," Talon shouted, "Have an arrow ready!"

Breathing heavily, Renny reached back to her quiver and felt with alarm that she had only one arrow left! She couldn't afford to miss again.

The dragon hissed at Talon and with a swift motion knocked the blonde clansman to the ground. Talon quickly crossed his arms over his chest as the beast brought one foreleg to pin his shoulder to the dirt.

"Get ready, Renny!"

Renny's heart raced thunderously as she fit the arrow to the string. Her hands began to shake and she remembered that she hadn't eaten anything since the morning before. A sleepless night had rendered her exhausted until the arrival of her friends had renewed her hope. Now it was all catching up to her in a moment when she couldn't afford the luxury of relaxation.

"God, help me," she murmured and bent her head to eye the shot, "I'm ready, Talon!"

The dragon lifted its second foreleg to strike its captive, alleviating its weight the slightest bit from Talon. In that instant, Talon delivered a forceful kick to the dragon's belly and the creature pulled back in surprise.

"NOW!" Talon sat up, uncrossing his swords across the dragon's scaly torso. Simultaneously, Renny let her arrow fly and it struck true in the vicious dragon.

When the beast lay prostrate, Renny and Talon ran to help a breathless Nathaniel from under its tree-trunk-sized tail. The three turned toward the other skirmish just as Druet's sword found its target; the final dragon fell to the earth with a shriek and then lay still.

For a moment no one spoke. The six warriors looked over their fallen enemies and then turned to glance at one another. Druet turned toward Grikk and nodded breathlessly.

"Thank you."

The giant man gave a single nod, seeming to perceive what the young foreigner was saying to him. Druet marveled at the man's impressive height—a head taller than himself—and wondered if this Grikk might be the tallest man in Arcrea.

Druet's attention shifted when he realized the people of Dragon Coast were beginning to emerge from hiding. Their stunned gazes drifted from the five strangers to the fallen dragons. Renny appeared at Druet's elbow.

"They believe the sun requires a sacrifice that, when given acceptably, will result in the end of dark nights and dragon attacks."

Druet lifted an eyebrow incredulously and a spark of anger flashed in his eyes, "That's ridiculous!"

"That's what I said," Renny's eyes swept across the front ranks of the clansmen, "The attack today in broad daylight will confuse their ideas by proving that the dragons do not regard night and day as boundaries."

"Who is that little man coming toward us?"

"The interpreter. He is the only clansman permitted to learn the Arcrean tongue."

The little man approached cautiously and bowed low before Druet. The clan's chief was behind him.

"Our honored chief asks, are you warriors of the sun, good sirs?"

"Absolutely not," Druet's voice was charged with a sense of unarguable authority, "The sun is not a god, nor does it deserve service from any man; but rather it serves the one true God Who created all things. It is in His name—in the name of the Lord Jesus Christ—that we have fought against evil this day. He is our Strength and our Shield!"

Bracy shifted uncomfortably from one foot to another.

The interpreter was silent, struck speechless until the chief reached out and slapped the back of his head. The little man started and quickly interpreted Druet's words. The chief stiffened as he listened and stared at Druet in amazement.

Before the chief could say a word, Druet snapped his sword into its sheath and stepped forward.

"By my God's strength, I will not permit you to sacrifice my friend," he motioned toward Renny, "but if you desire peace and safety, I will tell you of the sacrifice made by Jesus Christ, for the deliverance of all men."

The interpreter seemed to quake as he turned to stutter Druet's words to his chief. The taller man listened with a frown and then spoke a harsh command.

"Our honored chief says that you will not speak these words here."

Druet's steady gaze made the man lower his eyes.

"Then my friends and I will leave."

Druet motioned for his comrades to follow him out of the village. The four young men created a ring around Renny and started off.

Seeing his intended sacrifice slipping away, the angered chief shouted at his clan to stop the small group; but the people, still stunned by the scene they had just witnessed, watched in marveling silence as the five strangers began their journey back up the mountain.

Druet didn't look back until he heard the interpreter coming closer and shouting.

"Please, sir; wait!"

The group turned to see Grikk some yards behind them and the interpreter following at a brisk pace. The little man pointed at Grikk and spoke to Druet in a condemning manner.

"Grikk believes that his orders to guard the acceptable sacrifice must force him to follow you. Our honored chief says that you must tell Grikk that he is to remain here."

Druet stepped toward the interpreter and towered over the little man.

"Does Grikk want to stay in this place?"

The interpreter opened his mouth to speak and then dropped his gaze, unable to utter the words he knew were false. Druet glanced at the silent giant several paces away and then spoke to the small man.

"You tell your 'honored chief' that I wouldn't order a rat to stay in this place if it didn't want to, let alone a grown man created in the image of God."

The interpreter looked up with fearful eyes and then quickly scurried away without another word. Druet turned to continue up the rough path, motioning with his head for Grikk to join them. The giant waited for them to advance several paces and then began to follow at a distance.

"Why do you think he wants to follow us?"

"Do you think he'll try to take Renny back?"

Druet glanced back at Grikk and shook his head, "I don't think so. I think perhaps he's drawn to the presence of God in our group."

"Speak for yourself," Bracy spoke defensively as he examined a tear in the sleeve of his ever-suffering tunic.

"I do," Druet grinned at the ruffled clansman.

Renny cleared her throat and glanced around the ring of protectors, "Thank you for coming for me."

Talon grunted, "We thought about letting them run off with you, but in the end decided it just wouldn't be civil."

"Or chivalrous," Bracy added.

Renny cocked an eyebrow.

"I never thought of you as chivalrous, Bracy; but for your assistance in my rescue, I'll allow the description to apply…until further notice."

They traveled for some time through the forested hills before stopping to let Renny sleep. It was while the four young men sat around the small cook fire waiting for a rabbit to roast that Grikk approached and knelt beside Druet.

Druet held out his hand and it disappeared in the other man's massive grasp.

"I'm glad you joined us," the blacksmith smiled.

Grikk tilted his head to one side and then spoke haltingly, "Ques-tion."

Druet's brow rose in surprise, "You speak Arcrean?"

Grikk squinted as he tried to grasp each word.

"Words."

Druet nodded his comprehension and spoke slowly, "You know a little of the language."

Grikk's voice was as big as his powerful physique; sounding deep as the Arcrean Sea, but made husky from little use. He repeated his first statement.

"Ques-tion."

"You have a question."

Nathaniel, Talon, and Bracy were now leaning forward, listening curiously.

Grikk studied Druet for a long moment until the younger man felt that his soul had been searched. When the giant finally spoke again it was with an expression of hopeful yearning.

"Jesus…?"

Druet shifted to face the clansman, "You want to know more about Jesus?"

Grikk grasped enough of Druet's words to give an answering nod. Bracy and Nathaniel exchanged glances. Talon's gaze remained riveted on the two in conversation; a powerful giant of a man brought to his knees by the desire to know Druet's God.

Druet's words came slowly, with several pauses to ensure his audience understood.

"Jesus Christ is the perfect Son of God, Who came to earth as a man to die on a cross as the spotless sacrifice of atonement for the sins of the world. Three days later He rose from the dead and is now at the right hand of God in Heaven. He delights in redeeming the souls of men who will admit their sinful status before Him and believe that His work on the cross was indeed done for them."

"That's all there is to it?" Talon voiced his surprise.

Druet smiled, "That's all, Talon; but it's nothing trivial; accepting Christ is a life-changing decision— one that will alter the way you think and live; all to the glory of God."

Bracy suddenly shoved to his feet and walked away. For a moment the only sound to be heard was the crackling flames of the cook fire. The rabbit was left forgotten on the spit. Nathaniel glanced from one face to another, afraid to breathe and thereby shatter the moment.

Grikk slowly rose to his feet and stood towering over the campsite. His face retained its usual collected look, except for the small smile and look of pleasure that pulled at the corners of his eyes and mouth.

He nodded at Druet, "I...believe...Jesus."

Druet stood and looked up into the giant's face with a smile, "I'm very happy for you, Grikk."

Nathaniel finally exhaled and blinked to clear his suddenly blurry vision. Turning, he found Talon leaning forward with his face buried in his hands. A tear found its way through Talon's fingers and dripped like a sparkling diamond into the grass at his feet. Nathaniel gripped his friend's shoulder and wiped his own eyes, conscious that another soul had come to Christ for redemption.

A moment later, Talon rose to receive Druet's firm embrace. The blacksmith's smile was radiant with inexpressible joy.

"Now, whether I find the heart of Arcrea or return home empty-handed, I can say with conviction that my journey was not in vain."

Chapter 31
* Painful Parting *

Grikk continued his earlier assigned duty with obvious sincerity and commitment; wherever Renny went, the giant followed a short distance behind. The young woman assured him that he was not bound to this responsibility now that she was free from the Dragon Coast clan, but Grikk continued to guard his young charge with immovable steadfastness. Despite the giant's brutish appearance, it was quite obvious that Grikk had the gentlest heart of gold. Renny finally shrugged and let him have his way.

After traveling east for nearly three days, the troupe was reunited with those who had stayed behind in the small village where Druet had sent them. The blacksmith was relieved and grateful when he heard Anvil's bark, and the dog came running to greet them.

The eleven travelers rejoiced at being reunited, and welcomed Grikk into their company. When the tale of Dragon Coast had been shared, and Blunt had exclaimed his anticipation of a sonnet in memory of the story, the group stood in a ring as they had done several times before, and Nathaniel led them in a prayer of thanksgiving to God for His blessings and protection.

The following day, they continued on their journey north through Hugh, once more turning their attention to the search for Arcrea's mysterious heart.

On asking Alice and Grikk their opinion of a heart, Alice replied that it was "something too easily taken for granted"; Grikk, once he'd been made to understand the question, placed his hand over his own heart and simply said, "Close". Their thoughts were recorded with the others' on the reverse side of the map.

Two days after leaving the village, Druet stopped the band for a night's rest in a grove of trees some miles southwest of the large city of Kally. It was late in the afternoon, but the sun would not set for several more hours.

Druet was gathering wood for a cook fire when he glanced up to see Renny standing several yards away with a blank expression on her face. Druet grinned when he spotted Grikk standing not far off.

"Renny? Would you—"

"You told me once that I should tell you if I planned to wander away from the group so that you wouldn't worry."

Druet looked up with a knowing smile, "No need to worry now; Grikk won't let you out of his sight. Where do you—"

"I'm leaving."

Druet's smile disappeared, "You're what?"

"I'm leaving. I need to go home," Renny shifted from one foot to the other, seeming uncomfortable with having to tell someone her plans.

Druet blinked and stuttered for words.

"But, uh... Now?" she nodded, "This is...rather sudden."

"My father is sure to hear of my nearly being sacrificed and will want to see with his own eyes that I'm safe. I should have left sooner—I had planned to actually—but I...I couldn't."

Renny turned to glance at the others nearby, laughing at Blunt's silly songs and Nathaniel's good-natured teasing. Talon and Bracy would soon return with meat for the evening meal and everyone would enjoy a time of rest before an early start the next day. Knowing that she wouldn't be there to take part in any of it, Renny blinked hard to keep tears from coming.

Druet ran his free hand through his hair and several strands stood on end. The look on his face showed that he was trying to reason with what he had just heard.

"Will you come back after you've seen your father?"

She shook her head no.

"I see. Renny, you're a part of our group now...we wouldn't feel right without you."

Renny pressed her fingers to her forehead and then dropped them to her sides again.

"Druet, what you hoped for has actually happened," she sighed in frustration at her own admission, "I've grown attached to the people in your group—some more than others..."

"Then—"

"...But that's not what I came for!" she took a step forward and lowered her voice to a hoarse whisper, "I had a purpose and I fulfilled it; so now I must go."

Renny crossed her arms and muttered something about staying too long, but Druet didn't hear. Her words had reminded him of his conversation with Nathaniel about the possibility of a spy in their midst. He couldn't believe that it may have been Renny; nevertheless, his brow furrowed slightly and he tilted his head to ask,

"What purpose were you here for?"

There was a long pause.

"Renny?"

She wouldn't look at him. She stared at the grass and her jaw worked back and forth until she finally decided on what she could tell him.

"To seek out your intent."

Druet lifted one eyebrow in further confusion, but Renny shook her head.

"That's all I can say."

"Then you were sent by someone else...your father?"

She ignored his question, "You are far different from what I had prepared myself for, Druet. All my life I learned to fear the man who would be Arcrea's first king; but now I see that I had no reason to. You will be a remarkable king. Thank you for letting me join your quest for a time; I've learned much and I'm grateful to you."

She turned to go, but Druet stopped her.

"Renny, wait! Where can we find you? When the quest is over—whether the heart is discovered or not—the others will want to see you again. I'd like to see you again. There's a question…Renny, I'd like to ask you…"

Renny's head had begun to move from side to side, and her face had taken on a nervous expression. She had guessed what he was about to say.

"No, Druet. You can't… It will be better if you don't know where I am."

Renny's voice was firm and her words sounded final. Druet closed his mouth with a resigned sigh. Renny couldn't bear to see his hurt expression and was grateful that she had decided not to say goodbye to the others.

She glanced at her giant shadow and tried to sound lighthearted, "I'm sorry to take Grikk from you, but he wouldn't stay if I chained him to a tree."

Druet forced a smile, "He'd take the tree and find you. I'm glad he'll be with you. Renny, you need more arrows."

"I plan to purchase some in Kally tonight and start for…" she broke off when her destination nearly slipped her tongue, "…I'll start for home tomorrow morning."

Druet was silent.

Renny took a deep breath, "Goodbye, Druet. Tell the others I said goodbye…" she grinned, "…especially Talon and Bracy," he nodded, "Find the heart and serve our kingdom well; I'll look forward to hearing news of your quest."

She turned to go but paused to look back with a suddenly wary expression, "And Druet…"

"Yes?"

"I still don't trust Elaina."

Druet tried to reply, but could only manage a single nod. He watched as Renny and Grikk made their way across the meadow to the northeast. Nathaniel approached to help with the kindling, but stopped when he saw the two disappear in the distance.

"Where are they going, mate? Druet…?"

"Home."

The young blacksmith bent to gather more wood. Nathaniel's face looked as shocked as Druet had been moments before.

"Home? Renny's home? She's leaving and not coming back?"

Druet nodded.

The seaman stared at his friend for an everlasting moment.

"Well…she's always been stubborn—I guess there was no stopping her once she'd set her mind to go. Ever since the incident at Dragon Coast she seemed to have something on her mind—maybe she has something that needs to be settled at home."

"She told me she was here to learn my intent. She had planned to leave sooner…"

"Was she the spy?" Nathaniel paused and then grinned, "I think she came to enjoy our unlikely group of wanderers. And I saw enough to know that you had both begun to hope for the same thing;" Druet turned with a questioning glance and Nathaniel gave him a pitying smile, "Marriage."

Druet made a face at Nathaniel's direct and indelicate way of putting things.

"She gave up on the idea, though, when it became clear that you're to be king—a peasant learns not to hope for more than their station in life will allow."

Druet surprised his friend when he dropped his armload of kindling, suddenly reaching the limit of his composure.

"Why has everyone come to the conclusion that I'm the man to find the heart and become Arcrea's first king? It was never written that, when asked about the matter, Ulric the Ancient thought of Druet the blacksmith and prophesied accordingly! I don't want the crown! I only wanted to learn what this heart is and aid in its discovery so that I might have a way of freeing my father from Lord Frederick's chains. Maybe it would be better for me to return to Oak's Branch and let the hopeful mob get over their disappointment now!"

For a moment Nathaniel stared at Druet, his brow wrinkled with disbelief. Taking a step back, he spread his arms wide.

"Druet, the only way to know what the heart is, is to find it yourself or wait for another man to do so and then tell the rest of us!" His voice became low, "But that isn't going to happen," the seaman stepped closer and pierced his friend with a confident gaze, "It's true that you've inspired many men to search for the heart, but no other man has the innocent *passion* for the mission that you do. No other man has the honest strength and ability—the desire or willingness—to lead a band of people who hate—*can't stand* each other, and work to keep peace among them. You know that I've believed all along that you will be king. In our small group, you have already shown you are capable of joining the hands of the seven regions…"

Stunned into silence, Druet leaned his back against a tree and stared at Nathaniel's earnest face.

"Don't you see, mate? You've already begun to fulfill Ulric's prophecy. If you give up now, all of Arcrea would, as you say, be disappointed; but they would also lose hope. If the one man who has ever earned their support in this quest crumbles beneath the pressure, how can they expect that another man will ever be able to surpass his efforts?"

Druet lowered his head, humbled by the seaman's words and ashamed by his own hasty complaints. Nathaniel bent to gather the load of kindling. When he stood up, he studied Druet with a gleam of respect.

"I will always believe that you are the man who Ulric wished to crown one hundred thirty years ago, and that God has called you to make this journey. I look with anticipation to a future day when I may serve you as my king."

Nathaniel turned and made his way to the spot designated for the cook fire. Druet watched him go and then closed his eyes.

"God, I believe that You sent me to search for the heart—I've lost focus of that mission. Give me the strength to go on and the wisdom to know where I should go. Renew my purpose and joy."

A commotion in their small camp signaled that Talon and Bracy had returned from hunting. Druet felt a smile stretch his face when he heard their usual bantering—Talon's teasing, lately of a good-natured quality, and Bracy's irritation over his failed attempts to rile the other clansman.

Druet's eyes lifted to the point where Renny and Grikk had disappeared. Two people who he'd come to associate with his quest: suddenly gone. He shifted to observe the eight companions who remained and in their faces saw the thousands of Arcreans who were praying, as he had done, for a king who would rule in honor and justice.

His purpose was still alive.

Taking a deep breath, the blacksmith leaned away from the tree and moved toward the fire. A sense of new energy surged through his being and he smiled with anticipation over the morrow's journey.

Somewhere, Arcrea's heart was waiting to be discovered; and he was a man ready to find it.

Chapter 32
* Falconer *

Falconer moved with a purposeful stride through the crowded streets of Kally, an impressive city located in northeastern Hugh. His eyes scanned the oblivious mob with alert focus. Word was quickly spreading that Druet was in the area.

A child darted across Falconer's path, nearly toppling them both to the cobbled street. With a scowl, Falconer turned to watch the child race away with a shout to his young friends. As his eyes shifted forward again, the informant collided with yet another person.

Pulling back in irritation, Falconer muttered under his breath and looked up to see that the man he had run into was nothing less than a giant. The enormous Arcrean stared down at him with an unaffected expression. He was bald, and his massive arms were decorated with painted signs that were beginning to fade from a lack of being refreshed.

"Excuse me, sir," Falconer sidestepped the mountainous man. The giant didn't reply; he didn't seem to understand what had been said and his eyes studied the crowd with a sense of confusion. Falconer suddenly remembered rumors he had heard of a clan in Hugh who spoke a language strange to traditional Arcreans. Perhaps this man was a member of the detached clan.

"Grikk! Over here!"

A young woman's voice suddenly cut into Falconer's reverie and he saw the giant turn to answer her call. Instinctively stretching his neck, Falconer was only able to catch a glimpse of the dark-haired girl as she turned toward the city's eastern gate. A full quiver was strapped to her back, and a bow slung over her shoulder. The crowd quickly made a path for the giant as he moved to follow her.

Falconer turned to resume his walk, turning once to glance in the direction of the gate. From behind, the young woman had nearly resembled...

Falconer grit his teeth and ducked through the door of the Catawyld's Den. The impressive creature painted on the sign over the inn's door was one of mystery and legend; not many Acreans had ever come into contact with one of the angry beasts, and those who claimed they had were usually doubted. Except for Druet. Everyone had heard of the blacksmith's band battling a pack of catawylds, and the majority of listeners believed every word of it.

Falconer climbed the stairs and moved along the corridor to his small room at the back of the inn. Closing the door, he leaned against the wall and stared out through the window at the constant flow of people.

Falconer

Nicole Sager

Arcreans.

Commoners waiting to hear the next piece of news concerning the blacksmith from Frederick's region.

Falconer wondered if Druet knew how his quest had consumed the thoughts of Arcrea. His own thoughts included. Everywhere he turned, Falconer was met by his need to make a choice—Frederick or Druet? Nobleman or peasant?

Falconer moved to a small table by the wall and removed his sword belt; the strap needed to be rethreaded through one of the buckles. As his fingers began to work, his mind retraced the past few weeks.

He had thought that he had decided in favor of Druet's cause. He had ridden to Brentwood and warned Druet of the lords' advance on his position. In secret, it was true; but he had warned him nonetheless. It had pleased him to learn that his warning had been heeded, and Druet had escaped the imminent danger.

Falconer had left Brentwood before Lord Frederick's arrival, determined to separate himself from the vicious ruler. But Falconer knew that his absence would be nothing new to Frederick—he was often gone for weeks on one assignment or another, and the northern lord would suppose that this time was no different.

Falconer jerked the strap into place and replaced the belt around his waist. Removing his dagger, he turned it to the light to inspect the blade.

He knew that he would have to decide once and for all whose cause he sided with.

Frederick's or Druet's?

Nobleman or peasant?

Injustice or honor?

Pride or humility?

The characteristics of the two men in question flooded Falconer's mind and he was once more grounded in his decision. He longed to be joined to Druet's mission.

But he was afraid of what this decision might cost him.

Replacing the dagger, Falconer moved to draw his sword for inspection. As his arm crossed his torso, he remembered the torn message that he had long been carrying in his doublet. Removing the pieces, Falconer stared at the parchment and felt anger rise like gall in his chest when he glanced at Lord Frederick's seal on one half of the page.

What kind of man—ruler—allowed his daughter to venture into danger as Frederick had done?

Falconer thought of the night in Coswell when she had delivered Frederick's order, this message, stating that she was to join Druet's band as the key informant for matter's concerning the blacksmith's location and status.

Falconer stared at the parchment and nearly tore it into even smaller pieces.

Did Frederick have no dignity? Could he not govern his own family with care? Falconer knew the nobleman's daughter to be a stubborn young woman, eager to have her share in the work against threats to Frederick's seat as lord; but shouldn't her safety be of more importance than her involvement?

Falconer eyed the message with disgust and thought of the young woman's order to burn it.

No.

Falconer folded the pieces and returned them to his doublet. He would keep it as he had the past few months. It would serve as a reminder of his decision; and this time he would not falter. He would openly join himself to Druet's cause.

The spy stepped to the window and searched the busy streets again. A cloaked figure caught his eye and habitually he moved to one side of the pane, watching from a point where he would not be seen. The familiar figure ducked into an alleyway across the street and exchanged a few words with someone already in place there. Falconer frowned as the first figure left the alley and the man's face at last came into view.

Things would be happening sooner than he'd anticipated.

Chapter 33
* Druet's Sword *

I wish I knew where to find Renny."

Alice readjusted the strap of Sarah's bag on her shoulder; she was walking beside the older woman and had offered to carry the bag. At her other side, Nathaniel lifted his head to survey the group ahead.

"So do I. As ready as Druet seemed to be starting out this morning, everyone else seems to be amiss now; Grikk and Renny's leaving has created a void in our way of thinking."

"Talon and Bracy have been quiet ever since Druet told us last night that they'd gone."

Nathaniel glanced at the two moody clansmen and nodded, "Something is definitely wrong."

"Did she ever give anyone a clue to where she lives?"

The seaman shook his head and a thatch of brown hair in his eye reminded him that he needed to have it trimmed short the way he liked it.

Alice saw Sarah fidget with her shawl and she noted the way the elderly woman's lips rolled together in agitation.

"Are you alright, Sarah?"

She nodded, "Just thinking about Renny, dear child."

Alice nodded and looked up as the city of Kally came into view. The city was the grandest in Hugh and housed the regional lord's castle of residence. Alice wondered if Lord Hugh was aware of Druet's presence in the area; and, more importantly, if he cared. Were the seven lords still at Brentwood? Or had they scattered when they discovered that Druet had already left?

They entered Kally quietly, trying not to attract too much attention. The city was holding a sort of festival for the local farmers and herdsmen to try and earn a few coins for their summer of hard work. An auction was taking place in the city square that could be heard from outside the gates.

The band separated, planning to meet in a side street off of the square in one hour's time. Blunt walked off to sing for pennies while Nathaniel, Talon, and Bracy took Alice to see the festival's sights. Rodney stated the need to buy a few more clay jars, and a moment later Sarah and Elaina accompanied him down the street.

Druet made his way to the appointed side street with Anvil, and leaned against the outer wall of a shop to wait, listening to the cries of the auctioneer in the square and enjoying a moment of ease. His thoughts turned to the air of misery that hung over his group today and he prayed that God would give them grace to accept that two of their friends would no longer travel with them.

"Two and a piece!"

The auction kept up a lively rhythm. The auctioneer's shouts were so loud Druet thought they might be heard in Oak's Branch. He smiled when he thought of his father bidding on a cow from Frederick's tower; and Gregory would do it too.

"Who will give me two and a half?"

"Druet!"

"Two and a half! Where is three?"

"Druet!"

"Who will give me three?"

"Druet!"

Anvil barked.

Druet's eyes shot open when a voice, nearly drowned out by the auctioneer, continued to call his name in the square. Moving to the end of the side street, Druet searched the masses and saw Elaina trying to make her way through the crushing mob in his direction. The young woman's face was a picture of fright and Druet saw tears trying to spill from her eyes.

"Druet!"

He left the street and moved into the square to meet her halfway. Anvil followed at his heels.

"Elaina, what's wrong? Where's—"

"Rodney!" Elaina grasped a handful of his sleeve and pulled him in the direction she had just come.

"What happened to Rodney?"

"There was an accident!"

Elaina's tears started to fall now and her words became sobs; Druet continued to wade through the crowd, trying to catch everything she said.

"The jars...street...large cart...driver yelling!"

Druet's heart was racing as he grasped at her words, "Elaina, what about the cart?"

"It's overturned in the road and Rodney is..."

"Will someone give me five and a piece?"

Druet winced when the auctioneer's bellow landed like a clap of thunder on his ear.

"Rodney is WHAT?"

"STUCK!"

Druet's face went pale, "Under the cart?"

Elaina had already turned toward their destination. Elbowing their way across the square, the two followed a northbound street for thirty paces and then Elaina led him through another side street.

"It's the next street over," her voice sounded as tense as Druet's heart felt. Would they make it on time? Rodney was an old man—not strong enough to...

"Ahgh!"

Druet gave a cry of shock when something collided with his abdomen with the force of a galloping horse. He gasped for breath and reached for the wall to keep himself from falling over. The powerful force shocking his body was suddenly removed and Druet realized it had been cold steel. Wrapping an arm over his stomach, he leaned into the wall and panted for each breath.

Anvil was barking ferociously; Druet had never heard him become so vicious.

A coarse laugh suddenly brought Druet's head up. It was the laugh he had heard so often in his dreams—the laugh that set his nerves on edge.

"So, we finally meet again, boy!"

"Frederick," Druet's mouth could barely form the word; his stomach felt like a pit of angry fire. He felt a sense of overwhelming betrayal and defeat when he realized the weapon in Frederick's hand was the one fashioned by Druet. Druet had been pierced by his own sword!

Lord Frederick looked down at Druet with haughty disdain, "Had I known it would be so easy to corner you, I would have done so months ago."

"You couldn't have done it when Renny was around, Father; she would have spoiled everything."

Willing his eyes to focus, Druet saw Elaina standing in the shadows beyond Frederick. She stood watching with her arms folded in indifference.

I don't trust Elaina. Renny's words collided with his memory and he grit his teeth.

Anvil's barking heightened to a feverish pitch.

"God, help me," Druet could barely mutter the words.

Looking down, he saw that a bright stain was quickly covering the front of his tunic. Legs shaking, he tried to lower himself to the ground easily, but only half succeeded; collapsing the rest of the way, he lay in the grimy alleyway and listened to Lord Frederick's taunts.

"You should have stayed in Oak's Branch and minded your own business, blacksmith. Look at what your quest for glory has brought you. You have failed!"

Druet thought of Grikk and Talon and shook his head, "No...Frederick," he gasped for breath, "I have...not failed."

Frederick's face became red with rage and he towered over Druet in fury, "You discovered the heart?" He turned to Elaina with a questioning glare and she shook her head in confusion; turning back to Druet, he shouted, "Where is it?"

Druet shook his head, unable to explain further.

In a blind rage, Frederick lifted his sword—the one stolen in Gregory's shop so long ago—and prepared to finish the helpless young man. In a flash, Anvil leapt forward and claimed Frederick's arm with his teeth. Elaina shrieked in alarm and Frederick roared in pain. In another instant Anvil was shoved aside with a yelp, and Druet saw Frederick turn on the animal.

"No!"

Druet's roar fell on deaf ears. The young man squeezed his eyes shut to block out the sight that he knew would meet his eyes. His shout had drained him of any strength and sent his wounded stomach to new levels of pain. Tears of agony and grief fell freely from his face.

The alley was blanketed in silence. The auctioneer's booming voice still shouted the latest bid, and Druet knew that no one would hear if he yelled for help. His friends would wait for him in the alley until it was too late to search the vast city for which way he had gone.

"And now, Druet," Frederick turned back around, "I'll settle your score; but first," he leaned down and drew his old sword from Druet's sheath, "I believe this belongs to me."

"As this belongs to him."

Druet's eyes had slid shut, but they flew open again when he heard another voice above him—it was the voice that had warned him to flee Brentwood!

A dark-clad man had come up behind Lord Frederick and now had his hand around the pommel of Druet's sword, still held in Frederick's grasp.

"Falconer…?" Lord Frederick eyed the newcomer with uncertainty.

"My lord, if you desire the return of your sword, I think it only right that the favor is returned. *It will make a fair exchange.*"

The words jarred Druet's memory and he saw once again the sultry day in Oak's Branch, when Lord Frederick had stolen his sword, arrested his father, and threatened Druet's freedom; and this man—this stranger—had stood in the door of the smith and watched!

"Falconer! Do you dare to oppose me in this matter?"

"I oppose you in all matters, and I will not stand idly by and let you kill an innocent man as carelessly as you did his dog!"

Druet groaned inwardly when his fears concerning Anvil were confirmed.

Falconer jerked the pommel of Druet's sword from Frederick's grasp before the stunned lord had time to react. The spy then moved to stand before Druet, silently confirming his declaration to protect the helpless man.

Lord Frederick was seething, "You realize this is treason?"

Falconer narrowed his gaze, "Treason to whom? A man who unjustly uses his power in Arcrea or the man who will be her first king?"

Frederick's face was crimson, and his voice came as a hiss, "This…peasant has infected your mind as he has done to all other Arcrean commoners. Like dumb sheep you all follow any man who carries your shepherd's staff."

Falconer quirked an amused eyebrow, "My lord, dumb though they may be, I believe sheep recognize the shepherd, not the staff."

Frederick turned on his heel and stalked several paces away. With two swords in Falconer's possession and only one in his own, he knew it would be foolishness should he challenge the better swordsman to a duel at this time.

Never mind. He had accomplished his goal.

"Take him, then," the ruler turned to Falconer and pointed at Druet with a condemning air, "Lift your future king up out of his own blood and see if he lives to fulfill your expectations!"

The foreboding words echoed across the narrow alley as Lord Frederick sheathed his sword and quickly disappeared from sight, followed by Elaina.

Keeping a wary eye out, Falconer turned to kneel beside Druet. Tearing a wide strip from his cloak, he wadded it into a ball and pressed the piece against Druet's stomach.

"Forgive me for not reaching you sooner; I lost track of them in the crowds."

"Thank you," Druet panted the words and then grimaced in pain, "My dog?"

"Dead."

Druet winced as he sucked in a sharp breath, "You...sure?"

Falconer nodded absently as he examined Druet's wound, "I saw him struck. I'm sure."

Something of a sob escaped Druet and Falconer quickly spoke, "It is not safe for us to remain here; I'll take you to the inn where I am staying and then have someone locate your friends," a thought struck him and for a moment he hoped, "Is the healer still traveling with you?"

Rodney! The cart!

Druet's eyes shifted wildly and he tried to sit up, "Rodney...stuck under...a cart!"

Falconer eased him back again, "Druet!" the blacksmith paused and Falconer gave him a pitying gaze, "There was no cart."

Druet closed his eyes and exhaled, "Thank God."

Falconer studied the younger man in amazement. There he lay in his own blood in a strange alleyway, and yet he still had the wherewithal to thank God for his friend's safety and ask after his dog's condition!

Falconer was beginning to wonder how he would get Druet back to the Catawyld's Den, when a voice suddenly sounded from the other end of the alley.

"Hello, sir! Do you need help?"

The spy turned and immediately recognized Druet's seaman friend...Nathaniel! Beyond him, two more of Druet's companions stood peering in his direction.

Druet recognized the voice.

"Nathaniel!"

Nathaniel's face went pale and he rushed forward, his face twisting with grief when saw his friend's condition.

"Druet, what happened?" He dropped to his knees.

"Frederick."

Talon and Bracy came running, slowly coming to a halt behind Nathaniel.

Bracy studied Falconer warily, "Who are you?"

"Bracy…" Druet grimaced, "he's alright."

Falconer tore another strip off his cloak and exchanged it for the one already soiled.

"I have a room at the Catawyld's Den inn. If we find a cot, we can carry him there. Is the healer with you?"

Nathaniel nodded, never taking his eyes from Druet's face, "Bracy, search out a cot. Talon, go back to the street off of the square and tell the others what's happened. Meet us at the inn."

The two clansmen darted off immediately.

Falconer carefully removed Druet's sword belt; wiping the blacksmith's sword clean, he slid it into the sheath.

"I'm glad to see this back in his possession at last; though I thought it would been under circumstances far different."

Nathaniel eyed the weapon as tears filled his eyes, "You were always mentioning that blade, mate."

Druet gripped his friend's hand firmly, "Never…thought it would…be the one to…finish me."

Nathaniel's head shook in determination, "You're not finished, mate; you hear me? Your quest is far from complete."

Druet closed his eyes to wait.

Bracy soon returned with a cot. Placing their injured leader carefully on it, they lifted him and started off for the Catawyld's Den.

Chapter 34
* Ulric's Rose *

Nathaniel gripped the windowsill and stared with unseeing eyes at the street below. The events of the day had come about so suddenly. The small group had learned further details from the man Falconer, and had been shocked to hear of Elaina's involvement. Nathaniel thought back to the attack of the clan in Stephen that had brought her to their group, and wondered if it had been planned.

Falconer had offered to purchase a meal at the inn for Druet's band, and so most of the group was downstairs now. Behind Nathaniel, Rodney muttered over his herbs, trying to talk himself into one being more effective than another, while Sarah waited patiently beside him. Druet lay unconscious and deathly pale on the bed.

"Hazel Nut...infection...Yarrow...or the Vervain. Perhaps the Nettle... Nathaniel, I'll be ready to clean the wound in a moment; I'll need you to hold him steady."

Nathaniel's grip tightened; the task before him would be unpleasant, but it was absolutely necessary. Druet's wound looked awful. Rodney's murmurs continued.

"Arnica or Butterbur...no better than the Common Comfrey! Sarah what I wouldn't give to get more of Ulric's Rose before its too late..."

"Rodney!" Sarah glanced at Nathaniel and motioned for her husband to be quiet.

Nathaniel continued to stare through the windowpane, trying to prepare himself for cleaning the place where the sword had been thrust through Druet's abdomen. As a seaman, Nathaniel had seen many wounds in his time, but it was different with Druet. Druet was the little brother he had never had. Seeing his brother in pain hurt Nathaniel almost as much as Frederick's sword would.

Ulric's Rose.

Rodney's comment drifted belated through Nathaniel's mind. He knew of the small yellow flower; it grew only in the Heartland. It was said that the rose had incredible healing abilities. When administered correctly, it could heal the sick or wounded faster than one would think possible.

Like Druet had healed from the carnatur's bite...

Nathaniel blinked.

Rodney wanted more of the roses.

More.

Nathaniel turned from the window with a shove and met Sarah's startled gaze.

"Where did he get it before?"

Sarah glanced at Rodney, sifting deep within his bag; she shook her head, refusing to speak.

"He used it on Druet after the carnartur, didn't he?"

Her wide-eyed stare was all the answer he needed. Nathaniel stepped closer, "Sarah, the flower only grows in the Heartland. Where did he get it for Druet?"

"I can't say...I promised."

Rodney suddenly let out a cry of delight. Pulling his hand from the bag, he held up a small yellow flower and smiled first at Sarah and then Nathaniel.

"My dear, I still have one left! If we hurry, this may be enough to keep the infection away until we can get more of the roses!"

Nathaniel glanced at Sarah. The woman followed Rodney to the small table and quickly set out mortar and pestle. She spoke to Nathaniel as she began to crush the flower into powder.

"We'll give it two hours to set into the wound and then we must go to the Heartland for more. We'll need a means of conveyance;" she looked up with concern, "Druet will have to come with us."

"In his condition?"

Sarah nodded, pressing her lips tightly together.

"Shouldn't we send someone—myself even—for the rose and bring it back? The trip may kill him before the infection does!"

"It will be a risk; but at this distance the roses wouldn't be back here before the effects of this one wear off. Besides, Lord Frederick knows where he is here, and would be supported by Lord Hugh's army."

She was right.

"I'll send one of the boys to ask after the use of a cart and horses, and then return to help with Druet," Nathaniel turned toward the door, but suddenly stopped and looked back, "It was Renny, wasn't it? Renny had Ulric's Rose and gave it to you that night at Brentwood."

Sarah hesitated only a moment. Finally, she gave a small nod and quickly returned her gaze to her work.

Nathaniel made his way downstairs to tell the others of the planned journey. In spite of the day's anxiety, he felt the smallest bit of pleasure at having discovered one long-kept mystery.

Renny was a native Arcrean.

She lived in the Heartland.

∞∞

Several days after leaving the city of Kally, Renny and Grikk reached the border of the Heartland. They traveled through forests, highlands, and fields, rather than taking the indirect roads, and reached the western meadowlands of Arcrea's ancient encampment.

They were met by a border guard who quickly sent them ahead, and then signaled across the meadow with news of their arrival. Within hours, word had traveled to Olden Weld to her father, Leland, and he came to meet her. Dismounting, the natives' chief ran to embrace his daughter.

"Aurenia, my rose, I should have sent for you sooner."

Renny shook her head, "I should have returned before on my own."

273

"Word only just reached us of the events at Dragon Coast—were you the young woman they spoke of?" she nodded and he cupped her face in his hands, "I shouldn't have let you go; I don't know what I was thinking! Perhaps I'm crazy, as the other elders suggest."

Renny laughed, "You know I wanted to go, and at the time there would have been no keeping me here. I'm sorry for my stubbornness and pride that have made me so disagreeable. I believe God used this journey, though, to work in my heart. I needed to go."

Leland studied the girl's face until Renny lowered her gaze. The chief's eyes then shifted to the giant several yards away. Renny introduced the two men and then the three turned toward the horses brought by Leland and his guard for the ride home.

As they mounted and turned the horses around, Leland eyed Renny, "The way is clear, then?"

Renny nodded solemnly, "Very clear," she glanced away and started to rub her horse's neck, "We have nothing to worry about where Druet is concerned."

A sudden suspicion caused Leland to wonder if Renny was mistaken—perhaps this Druet had given him reason for more careful attention. He said nothing, but instead pressed his heels to his horse's flanks and urged the group eastward. The elders had gathered for a council meeting the day before, and now that Renny had returned, she would be able to share with them the details of Druet's cause. Why would a blacksmith take to the road so suddenly in search of an ancient legend? Leland's brow furrowed in concentration. He trusted his Renny; he would just have to take her word for it. Trust that the way was indeed clear.

೫〇೧

Renny sat perched in a tree that stretched over the roof of her family's cottage in the village Olden Weld. The home was built at the head of the main street, a well-worn route that passed between the rows of natives' dwellings.

Renny's fingers moved with experience to finish the last arrow for her quiver. Those purchased in Kally had served her well on the trip home, but she preferred to make her own. A gentle breeze passed through the village and picked leaves from the trees. One leaf fastened itself in Renny's hair and she absently removed it with a sweep of her hand.

On the limb above her, a boy with sandy-colored hair tried to coax a squirrel into his hands. Renny shook her head with a smile.

"Kellen, it's a squirrel—a flighty creature that doesn't want you to tame it."

"I had him last week, Ren; you should have seen me!" Kellen laid flat on the branch and peered down at her with a mischievous grin, "Besides, just because it's a flighty creature doesn't mean it can't be tamed. Take you for instance!"

"Ha!" Renny kept her eyes on the arrow, "Who says that I've been tamed?"

The squirrel moved away and Kellen swung down to straddle the branch in front of her.

"I knew from the moment you returned two days ago that there was something different about you," Kellen's mouth twisted into his signature grin—

Renny had never seen another face that could copy it, "And after our conversation that night, I knew for sure."

Renny gave a satisfied nod and slid the arrow into her quiver, hanging on a branch to her right. Leaning back against the tree's trunk she studied her brother. As a direct descendant of Ulric the Ancient, Kellen would one day take Leland's place as the Heartland's chief elder. The honored position would be a trying load for his shoulders to bear, but she knew he would carry the responsibility with admirable patience. Their father had trained him well. Already, he was a young man of Godly honor and humility, who respected his elders and fellow-natives, yet he still managed to expend an amazing amount of boyish behavior. When Renny had condemned him for this about a year before, Kellen had simply stated that he "may be in line for greatness, but that was no reason to rob him of his childhood".

Kellen returned Renny's stare for a long moment and then made a face at her, only confirming her train of thought. She laughed and Kellen gave a look of feigned shock.

"My dear sister," he placed a hand over his heart and leaned back dramatically, holding onto the limb with his legs, "Did I just hear a laugh escape your lips? What unearthly surprise will you next bestow upon such mortals as I? Why, your face is enlightened when you smile; one might even say that you're pretty today!"

Renny playfully swung after him as he scrambled back to the upper tree limb. Gathering her quiver, she swung it onto her shoulder just as Grikk called from his seat at the base of the tree. Renny had taught him more of the Arcrean tongue on their recent journey, and Grikk was at last able to communicate with a little more ease.

"Renny!" the giant was on his feet and pointing down the road, "Horse is coming."

Renny felt Kellen return to the lower limb and both looked in the specified direction to see two riders approaching with urgent speed.

Kellen pointed, "The man on the left is a western border guard."

Renny nodded as they watched the horses draw closer. Suddenly, her violet eyes widened and her face paled; she recognized the second rider.

"Nathaniel!"

Chapter 35
* The Crisis *

L ady Alice had purchased horses and a cart for the band's journey to the Heartland. Blunt and Alice had driven the cart, with Rodney and Sarah tending to Druet in the back. Nathaniel, Falconer, Talon, and Bracy had ridden mounts of their own, the "boys" taking turns riding out from the group in search of food.

When they had crossed the western border of the Heartland, they had been stopped and questioned by a lookout. When he heard that the strangers were none other than Druet's band, the lookout had solemnly declared "The way is clear" and offered to ride east with Nathaniel to inform the elders of Druet's arrival and ensure that a clean place was prepared where his wound could be treated. The two had ridden off and the others had continued at a slower but steady pace, taking time enough to collect Ulric's Rose where it still grew in thick clusters along the way.

Renny was shocked to tears at the sudden change in her friend. Just a short time ago, she had seen Druet in perfect health, battling dragons and standing firm against a dangerous clan of hundreds. Now he lay weaker than a newborn in the back of the cart. Frustration welled inside of her as Renny reprimanded herself for not investigating Elaina further.

The Arcrean natives emerged from their homes and neighboring fields to watch the strange procession with open curiosity. Heads shook with sorrow when they heard that this was the promising young man the elders had hoped would be "Ulric's king".

The cart finally stopped and Falconer and Nathaniel carefully moved Druet inside a small hut. The old woman who lived there had offered to stay with a willing neighbor during the length of Druet's stay.

Talon and Bracy helped Rodney and Sarah from the cart, and the healer quickly used his walking stick to propel himself through the hut's door. Sarah followed and immediately began to set things in order for her husband.

Great beads of sweat covered Druet's forehead, dripping through his hair to soak his collar and pillow. His chest rose and fell quickly as he all but gasped for each breath. Occasionally, his arms moved to clutch his stomach before a grimace, accompanied by a sharp gasp, warped his features in pain.

Rodney's aged hands selected several roses as he glanced at the invalid, "The potion applied in Kally has been used up—his body is quickly losing its defenses and infection has begun to set in."

Falconer and Nathaniel exchanged glances, neither wanting to remind the other that stomach wounds usually proved fatal. Druet's followers each clung to the hope that Rodney's God-given knowledge of medicine would defy common opinion, and that God Himself would touch their young leader with His healing hand.

When Rodney had applied the first batch of rose tonic, Talon turned and offered his right fist to Nathaniel; the seaman clutched Talon's wrist with his left hand and offered his own right wrist to Bracy. The familiar pattern was followed until the group stood in a ring to pray for Druet. Renny and Grikk appeared in the doorway and quietly joined the circle. When the prayer ended Alice turned to embrace her friend with a happy cry.

Renny returned Alice's greeting and then glanced around the ring of familiar faces; Nathaniel offered her a small smile that teased.

"Found you."

Falconer recognized Grikk and then Renny—the young woman in Kally who had been accompanied by the giant. When he learned of Renny's background, he was reminded of Elaina and again wondered how a father could send his young daughter on so dangerous a mission; and yet Renny's involvement with Druet's mission didn't seem to bother him as Elaina's had. Perhaps, he thought, it was their purposes or lifestyles that made the difference in his thinking.

The days gradually lengthened into weeks, passing in a slow procession of sameness and little variation. The village was strangely quiet, as if the natives feared any loud noise would send the blacksmith to his grave. Blunt strummed his lute in a hushed and absent manner; his sad songs carried an air of melancholy through the streets.

Rodney's potions kept Druet alive, but a fever still burned within him. Occasionally, he would thrash about, muttering incoherently. The old healer would place a hand to Druet's forehead, hot to the touch, and then glance at Sarah with a sad shake of his head.

"Only God can save him now, my dear."

Sarah nodded and reached to change the quickly-drying compress with tears in her eyes and a pleading prayer on her lips. This young man, whose life hung precariously in the balance, had truly become the hope of Arcrea; if he should die, Sarah firmly believed that the heart, wherever it may be, would die with him.

Sarah's eyes shifted to watch Rodney's hands; Arcrea's lords had forbidden their gentle work of healing, and now it seemed the kingdom's future rested in those weathered fingers. The elderly woman let out an overwhelmed sigh and changed the compress again.

Only God could help Rodney now.

Only God could save Druet.

Only God could save Arcrea.

Late that night, the crisis came. Druet's hoarse breathing filled the small hut and grated on every ear present. They listened as his moans told his pain and his delirious words called for help; twice he begged for his father's deliverance.

Suddenly, the young blacksmith exhaled deeply and he was still. The silence in the room was suffocating as everyone stared, unable to move…unwilling to accept that he was gone. Tears spilled from every eye in silent grief. Finally, Rodney approached the cot and felt for Druet's pulse; at the same time, Druet's chest rose and fell in a deep breath that sounded peaceful, and Rodney sank to his knees in relief.

"Thank God," he wept, "Thank God! The fever has broken!"

Chapter 36
* The Heart of Arcrea *

Druet opened his eyes and stared at the unfamiliar ceiling. The strange room was bathed in the deep yellow glow of late afternoon. Closing his eyes again, he breathed in the warm scent of baking bread, and felt the crisp autumn air surround him with cheerful welcome. Somewhere in the distance a blacksmith's hammer rang a familiar tune on hot iron.

A stiff presence at his stomach brought Druet's hand down to investigate the bandage wrapped around his middle.

He'd been wounded!

Druet's brow furrowed and he rubbed his forehead in confusion until his memory returned with a jolt.

Frederick! The evil lord had used Druet's own sword against first him, and then Anvil! Druet groaned and laid his arms over his face, telling himself that he should have been more careful that day.

A soft noise told Druet that his groan had roused someone in the chair by his cot. Shifting his head, he peered through his crossed arms at a grinning Nathaniel.

"Afternoon, mate! Guess I fell asleep," the seaman paused, seeming to search for words, "It's good to see you awake, Druet. We thought you'd left us for Glory."

"A preferable arrangement, you must admit."

Nathaniel's smile broadened at Druet's comical tone. The blacksmith rubbed his hands over his face and murmured, "Where are we?"

"Just down the road from Renny's home."

Druet lifted his head in surprise and then dropped it back to the lumpy pillow when the sudden motion strained his stomach. His eyes searched Nathaniel's face.

"Where?"

The seaman leaned his elbows onto his knees, "Olden Weld. The Heartland."

Registration slowly dawned on Druet's face and he shifted to study the ceiling again, "How did we not figure that out before?"

Thoughts scrambled through his mind as Druet remembered his conversation with Renny. She had been sent to seek out his intent. The natives of the Heartland had great reason to fear the reign of Arcrea's first king—the man who, rumor said, would be given possession of their homeland. It was only natural that they would want to know a determined heart-seeker's purpose and character.

"I don't understand how we didn't see through Elaina's plot," Nathaniel spoke quietly, "I wish I had been there for you, mate."

"I know you would have been, Nathaniel. Thank you. Your loyalty means a lot to me."

Nathaniel nodded as tears clouded his eyes. He silently praised the Lord again for Druet's recovery as the young blacksmith slipped once more into a deep sleep.

The next few days were joyful ones as news spread through the Heartland and beyond of Druet's recovery. Druet's smile spread the widest when his entire band of followers, including Renny and Grikk, crowded into the hut to see him. He was pleased to officially meet Falconer and thank the man for coming to his rescue in Kally.

Renny's father, Leland, came to visit Druet, and the two talked at length about Druet's purpose for finding the heart. The native chief was impressed with the young blacksmith, and prayed that God would see fit to bless his quest with success.

As usual, Druet soon became anxious to continue his journey for the heart, but Rodney refused to let him budge from the small cot. Druet scowled at the healer and ranted and raved at his friends, but they only laughed at his ill humor and opened the hut's door and one shuttered window. That was the closest to "outside" that he would be getting for a while.

Finally, Druet yielded to their wise counsel and contented himself with sitting up in the cot and laying the worn map over his lap to study it and plan where he would search next.

"Please, God, let it be soon," he whispered a prayer as his eyes scanned the regions yet to be traveled, "You know what is best...I trust You. You spared me from death; though Heaven, in Your presence, is a place far better than Arcrea, I feel that You have left me here to fulfill a purpose. Lead me to it, God; I'll follow."

One afternoon, Renny and Kellen brought Druet's midday meal and stayed to talk while he ate. Druet liked Renny's brother; relaxed manners and a singular grin made Kellen an enjoyable friend who was easy to exchange smiles with.

When Druet had finished eating, Renny took the platter and Kellen handed him the requested map of Arcrea.

Renny watched him unfold it, "Where will you search next?"

Druet looked up, "I haven't decided yet. I haven't searched the regions of Ranulf, Quinton, or Geoffrey."

Kellen leaned against the doorframe, "Do you think Frederick will come after you again when he learns that you survived his last attack?"

Druet's eyes swiveled to observe the boy, "No doubt; only next time I don't think he'll be alone."

Renny shifted her hold on the platter, and Kellen studied the far wall, his expression veiled in thought. Finally, the yellow-haired boy straightened with a sigh,

"We'd better let you rest now. Come along, Ren."

Kellen reached to take the platter from Renny and then disappeared through the door. Renny started to follow, but turned on the threshold.

"Nathaniel said that he'll be in to check on you in a while."

Druet shook his head, "He's more anxious than a mother hen in the rain."

Renny laughed at the idea and then the two fell silent for a moment.

Druet picked at the edge of the map, "Are you glad to be home?"

She nodded, "There were some things that I needed to make right...with Kellen and my father."

Druet grinned, "I like them both."

"And they like you. Mother is pleased that Kellen looks up to you; she says you are a good influence on him."

Druet shook his head; "Your mother has a lot of faith in me."

"She is a good judge of character," Renny turned to go, but once again stopped, "The Heartland is taken with you. Everyone believes that you are Ulric's king."

"Ulric's king?"

"The man who Ulric himself would have chosen to be the first king...had you been alive one hundred thirty years ago."

Druet's eyes danced with mischief and he shrugged, "I guess I missed it. Then again, if I'd been there then, I wouldn't be here now."

Renny cocked an eyebrow and shook her head, "Should you become king, I will pity your future councilmen; how ever will you find a group of men willing to endure your endless humor?"

Druet feigned an expression of perplexity and rubbed his chin, "I'll have to convince Nathaniel to stay..."

"Hmm," she turned once more, "I have to go; I promised Bracy I'd find him a new tunic."

"Ha! Make it something colorful!"

"I'll do my best," she laughed.

Druet watched as Renny disappeared from the doorway and then his gaze shifted to the map in his lap. He had accidentally placed it map-side down and now his eyes scanned the written list on the back:

What is a heart?
~The very depth of a man.

~His inner self—that which is hidden from the world's view, yet expressed in his desires and actions.

~The core or reason behind a matter.

~A delicate, yet powerful member of the body, without which one cannot survive.

~The organ which pumps life through a body.

~That which carries the weight of one's emotions; whether hatred or love, triumph or defeat.

~Essential.

~A thing too easily broken and then never restored to its former state of perfection.

~It needs the blood as much as the blood needs the heart. They give each other purpose and keep each other active.

~Something too easily taken for granted.

~Close (always near).

Druet's eyes studied the words, remembering each person who had spoken them, and the circumstances that had brought them to cross his path—the quest that had produced these friendships as well as these thoughts.

His eyes scanned the list again. He was the only one who had never answered the question.

What is a heart?

Closing his eyes, Druet thought hard, trying to produce an answer that would satisfy his longing to know. He could state that a heart was something that God deeply cared for...and He did. Or he could say that a heart was an unknown mystery...which it was.

Druet ran both hands through his dark hair.

What had Ulric wanted the seven explorers to find? Was it a place? A person? A particular thing? Was it something entirely different from every one of these?

Druet's mind returned to Oak's Branch and the life he had led there with his parents. Had he come any closer to finding the heart than he had been the day he started out on this quest? There was no way of knowing.

He who discovers the heart of Arcrea...

Druet reviewed the words in his mind.

Discover. Discovering something meant that it had not been known before, and it would not be known until the day of discovery. What was something in Arcrea that Ulric would have been aware of, and that the ancient explorers had failed to see?

Druet's gaze focused again on the list of observations. What was the heart of a kingdom? What was the very depth of Arcrea? The reason behind it? The member which pumped life through it? What carried the weight of Arcrea's emotions? What was essential in Arcrea, yet too easily broken or taken for granted?

Taken for granted.

Leaning his head on the wall at the head of the cot, Druet closed his eyes and saw again the mother in Morgway with her starving child, the crowd of children begging for a single coin, the husband who had given up hope of an income, Rodney's near arrest in Quale, and his own father in prison.

Suddenly, Druet's eyes shot open and he stared, unseeing, at the space before him. Beginning to tremble, he looked down and read over the list yet again. Coming to Nathaniel's comment about the heart needing the blood, Druet paused.

The blood.

Blood circulated through the body, needing to reach every member, every limb, with an uninterrupted flow if it would maintain life.

Druet's breathing became heavy.

Money—economy circulated through a kingdom, needing to reach every member with an uninterrupted flow if it would maintain life—survival.

Druet's heart was pounding in his ears.

What was it, then, that acted as a heart and pumped the blood—the economy—through Arcrea?

The people.

The thought was so small Druet nearly missed it. The young blacksmith leaned against the wall, nearly gasping for air. His hands were shaking so hard, it was impossible to hold the map steady; laying it to rest in his lap, he read through the list a final time, inserting his thoughts into each comment. Everything fit. It was clear.

The people—commoners, peasants—were Arcrea's heart! They were everything his companions had observed and more.

Druet thought back to the ancient day of prophecy. The seven explorers had, themselves, been the heart until they had placed themselves in authority over their fellow man. The people *needed* a leader, Druet knew; God had established an order of authority for men to follow. What the seven explorers had failed to see was that the lowly peasant was just as essential as a king—the common masses would populate the land and create economy, giving the ruler a reason to occupy his position in the first place. If a ruler took his people for granted, cutting off the blood's circulation, the heart—and, consequently, the entire body—would die.

Druet thought of the ancient explorers. If any one of them had simply realized the need for humility—the importance of building up a kingdom from the lowest levels—and resigned his claim to the throne, he would have reaped the opposite and been crowned king.

Druet exhaled deeply. Satisfied. Hardly believing that his quest was complete. His thoughts drifted to his father in Frederick's tower; he thought it ironic that a member of the heart itself had been his motivation to start out on this journey to discover it.

His father was of the heart.

His mother was of the heart.

His companions were of the heart.

He was of the heart...

Druet's smile faded when he realized that he was no longer the man he had been ten minutes ago. He had discovered the heart of Arcrea and even begun, as Nathaniel had said, to join the hands of the seven regions; this could only mean one thing...

Nathaniel stepped through the doorway into the hut, whistling "Clouds o'er an Arcrean Sea" in a lively manner; he looked up to greet his friend and suddenly froze.

"Druet...? What is it, mate? Are you in pain?"

Druet stared back in stunned silence. Everything—his way of life, his friendships, and even his kingdom—would forever be altered by the discovery hidden for the moment in his thoughts. Once spoken, the words could never be taken back. The discovery had been made and his destiny had been sealed. He—Druet the blacksmith of Oak's Branch in Frederick's—was the first king of Arcrea.

"Druet...?" Nathaniel's voice was filled with apprehension as he came to lean over the cot, "Should I send for Rodney?"

Druet shook his head numbly, "No...Nathaniel, no; I...I know."

The words hadn't come out like he'd expected. Then again, what had he expected? He hadn't made plans for the discovery...God, in His power and wisdom, had taken care of that.

Nathaniel placed the back of his hand on Druet's forehead, "You know? What do you know? Druet, mate, you have to make some sense or I'm running for Rodney."

Druet took a deep breath; the moment of truth had come. He looked up and stared at Nathaniel, but no words of explanation would come.

None were needed.

Nathaniel searched Druet's gaze for understanding and his face suddenly paled with it. Pulling away from the cot, the seaman took several steps back, breathing heavily.

"You...you...you..."

"I know."

"You know."

Druet nodded.

"You really know."

"I really know."

Nathaniel took a deep breath and ran his hands through his hair, slowly turning in a circle in the middle of the hut. Facing the cot again, a smile of wonder split his face.

"Say it—let me hear the words!"

Druet smiled and shook his head at his friend's request, but obliged anyway.

"I've discovered the heart of Arcrea, Nathaniel."

The seaman laughed outright and jumped into the air with a whoop. Pulling the chair closer, he sat beside the cot.

"You did it! You really did it," his voice could barely contain his excitement, "Well, tell me—what is it?"

Druet laughed, "It's the people."

"The people?"

"Yes; the commoners," Druet picked up the map and showed Nathaniel the list, explaining his thoughts and reasoning. Nathaniel's smile broadened and, when Druet had finished, he stood and paced the hut with excitement.

"We'll have to get word out."

"Nathaniel, I haven't joined the hands of the—"

Nathaniel waved Druet's comment aside, "In order to join the people together, they have to know first that there's a reason to join together! You're that reason!"

The two stared at each other in silent disbelief for a moment, and then Nathaniel stepped to the cot and slowly knelt on one knee beside it. His face shone with brotherly pride and his voice shook with emotion.

"I have served as your friend to this day, and will strive to continue as such in the future; but allow me to be the first to offer you my humble submission as your subject...my king."

Druet placed a firm hand on Nathaniel's shoulder, "You have been far more than a friend; you have been, and will always remain, my brother."

A twinkle appeared in Nathaniel's eye and he grinned, "You honor me, Sire."

Druet leaned back and shook his head; Nathaniel was growing accustomed to this change far too quickly.

Chapter 37
* Realization & Rage *

"Y ou found it?"

"Here in the Heartland?"

"What is it?"

"Where is it?"

"You mean to say it was randomly hidden in the old woman's hut?"

Druet shook his head, "No, Bracy, it wasn't hidden here…well, in a way it was—but not the way you're thinking."

Bracy squinted one eye in confusion, "What!?"

"The woman herself is a part of the heart. The heart of Arcrea is the people like you and me; the commoners—a delicate but powerful source so easily taken for granted, but without which Arcrea cannot survive. The people create economy in the land like the heart pumps blood and life through the body."

Druet's ten companions, Leland, and Kellen stared back in mute surprise—except for Nathaniel, who stood grinning from ear to ear. Druet found himself wondering how they had all managed to fit inside the little hut, when Bracy found his voice.

"That's it?"

Druet gave a firm nod, "That's it."

The dark-haired clansman looked down, "We found the heart of Arcrea and all I got was this stupid tunic."

"We?" Talon turned to eye Bracy, "*We* didn't find the heart, Druet did!"

"He knows what I meant, Talon!"

Renny crossed her arms defensively, "I searched high and low for that tunic; don't give me grief about it now!"

"It's green!" Bracy all but wailed, "I'd much rather wear something brown or black—dark! Now every time I look at myself, I'll be reminded of Talon's eyes!"

The blonde clansman delivered a stiff shove to Bracy's shoulder, "Leave me out of this!"

Druet cleared his throat loudly and the three warring parties turned to look at him.

"Well...the discovery of the heart changes almost everything else, but apparently it hasn't done a thing to change the three of you."

Renny, Talon, and Bracy glanced at one another guiltily, and then Blunt broke the moment of silence by rushing forward to congratulate their leader.

"Bless you, Druet, bless you! I knew from the first day I met you that you would be the man to rescue Arcrea from the chains of injustice and cruelty."

Druet smiled and dipped his head at the praise, "It is God who will rescue Arcrea, Blunt. If I can be used as a tool in His hand to accomplish this, then I would be greatly honored."

Slowly, the realization of Druet's discovery impacted the group in its fullest sense and everyone followed Blunt's example in excited conversation and congratulations.

Standing at the door of the congested hut, Falconer habitually appraised the young blacksmith as he had done months before in the smith at Oak's Branch. Any other man of Falconer's acquaintance would have been filled with pride over such a life-changing discovery; Druet's obvious humility contrasted this mental picture so starkly it was hard for the former spy to wrap his mind around the truth. This simple peasant from an obscure village had solved a mystery one-hundred-thirty-years old and would soon claim the throne of a kingdom yet to be ruled by one man; yet he would willingly have passed the honor to another, asking only for his father's release from prison in return.

Falconer saw, as Druet had, that humility was the final element to discovering the heart—if a man held his head aloft in pride, refusing to lower his gaze to the common masses, then he would also fail to observe the truth that was hidden there.

Falconer made his way across the room to the cot where Druet sat with his back propped against the wall at its head. Removing a second belt from its place of safekeeping at his waist, the spy knelt on one knee by the bed and held the belt in outstretched hands to Druet. The group behind him became quiet. Druet's eyes swept over the object held before him and he smiled as Falconer spoke.

"I have kept this sword for you since the events at Kally and have long awaited the day when I might return it to your possession."

Druet took the belt and slowly drew his sword, made to match his confident grasp so long ago. The blade had been cleaned and polished to perfection, speckling the walls of the hut with reflections of sunlight as he turned the pommel in his hand.

Leland observed the weapon and spoke with a sense of wonder, "Fashioned by the hand of our future king, who could foresee that it's first mission would be to assassinate the same man? Formed in innocence and simplicity, it was destined to become the sword of Arcrea."

Tears formed in Druet's eyes when the sword produced a flood of memories about his father. Shifting his gaze, he nodded his thanks to Falconer, still kneeling by the cot.

Falconer drew his own sword and laid the fisted pommel over his heart, "My sword and my service I pledge to you this day. May God bless your reign, Sire."

A small smile appeared on Druet's lips as he moved to imitate Falconer's salute.

"For Arcrea."

Falconer's head dipped in the slightest of nods. His mind raced back to the night in Quale when the seven lords had lifted their voices and swords—including Druet's—in this same cry, but with motives far different.

One by one the other men in the hut drew their swords, placing the weapons over their hearts in agreement with Druet's words.

"For Arcrea."

Druet closed his eyes, trying to grasp the life of responsibility that stretched before him. The knowledge that God alone could help him to reshape an entire kingdom produced an adjustment to his cry of commitment;

"May my life, as my sword, be wielded for God; and may God be the Help of Arcrea. For God and for Arcrea!"

෫෬

Elaina slipped through the door into the great hall and stood in the shadows, listening as Lord Frederick's new chief informant was ushered into her father's presence near the large hearth. Gavin, the man who had replaced Falconer was a short, squatty man with shifty eyes. His manner and appearance weren't nearly as striking as Falconer's, and his persona gave little hope that his skills would manage to surpass his predecessor's great abilities either.

It had been one month since Druet's certain death in Kally, and yet Gavin hadn't produced any definite proof of the blacksmith's demise.

Lord Frederick was losing patience.

Elaina heard her father question Gavin with a short clipped tone, and then Gavin answered in a voice that always reminded Elaina of the slimy sea grasses near Brentwood.

"My lord, I have at last discovered proof that Druet the blacksmith is…"

" 'At last' is correct! I've waited one month to hear a report that Druet is—"

"…alive."

Elaina stiffened as the room became deathly still. Lord Frederick had turned away from Gavin but now whirled to face the stout man with an incredulous glare.

"*What* did you say?" he hissed.

Gavin seemed unaffected by Frederick's rage, "He is alive, my lord; taken by his followers to the Heartland, he is there regaining strength."

Elaina's eyes widened and her clenched jaw began to tremble with anger; all the work and effort she had put into placing Druet in harm's way in Kally…and he had lived through the ordeal!

"You are sure of this?" Frederick took a step toward Gavin.

"I have no reason to doubt them, my lord; if he were dead, then his followers would not easily get away with spreading word of anything different."

"His followers are spreading word of these happenings?" Frederick bellowed and then swore as he turned away.

"Yes, my lord…which brings me to another piece of news," for the first time, Gavin seemed nervous about what he had to say.

Frederick looked over his shoulder and narrowed his gaze on the suddenly quiet informant, "What is it? Spit it out, man!"

"The blacksmith's followers are riding throughout all of Arcrea with word that…the…that he—"

"WHAT IS IT?!" Frederick raged as he towered over Gavin.

The informant cowered slightly and then answered as Frederick's demand echoed across the

Elaína

Nicole Sager

heights of the hall, "The blacksmith has discovered the heart."

A moment of stunned silence followed as the news settled in the minds of those present.

Suddenly, the air was rent by a shriek of wrath, and the two men turned to see Elaina coming toward them.

"Send for the other lords," she pinned her father with an angry glare; her voice shaking as uncontrollably as her small frame, "Call for an assembly and gather the armies—bring them all home from the border wars if you must—I don't care! Just corner Druet once and for all and kill him! And this time make *sure* he's dead!"

Chapter 38
* The Goat *

Druet stepped out of the hut and stood for a moment to bask in the warm rays of the sun. It had been weeks since he had last stood on his own two feet outside the confines of the small home. His eyes studied the neat, if primitive, street of the native village, and his hand moved to rest with satisfaction on the hilt of his sword.

Shifting to glance down the road, Druet wondered when his companions would return from their mission. After hearing of the heart's discovery, Nathaniel, Blunt, Talon, Bracy, Grikk, Falconer, Kellen, and a number of native Heartlanders had ridden out in pairs to spread word of Druet's news throughout the kingdom. As a precaution, it had been decided that no one would reveal the heart's identity, only say that it had been discovered.

Leland had wisely nodded and pointed out, "If the people wish to know, they will come; then you will have the advantage of revealing the truth before hundreds—even thousands of witnesses. If the truth is revealed prematurely, there is the risk of many people attempting to join the hands of the seven regions and laying claim to the throne on the grounds of your knowledge."

Druet's mind was jarred into focus when a goat sprinted by and disappeared around the corner of the hut. A moment later the old woman who owned the hut appeared out of breath, hobbling in the same direction as the goat.

"Ornery critter," she murmured as she paused before the door to glance at Druet, "Feeling better today?"

Druet nodded, "I am, thank you. You were kind to offer your home for my use," he glanced after the goat and grinned, "Would you like some help?"

Her glance flickered momentarily to his stomach, which, it was known, was still wrapped in a bandage.

"I feel fine," Druet assured her.

The woman nodded, her breathing still a bit heavy, "Well…if you're sure it won't do more harm to those wounds of yours, it would be of great assistance to me if you managed to catch the animal."

Druet dipped his head and stepped from the doorway to follow the runaway; the elderly woman promised to catch up as soon as she caught her breath.

Behind the hut was a small clearing where the woman had planted a small garden. At the far edge of the yard was a line of brush at the base of tree-spotted embankment that climbed to form the edge of a broad meadow.

Druet immediately spotted the goat, gnawing on a bush that grew beside the open gate of its pen. The blacksmith crept closer, hoping to shove the goat into the pen and close the gate before the creature knew what was happening.

The goat had other ideas.

When Druet had moved close enough to lunge for the animal, it suddenly turned and bolted for the brush line. Druet gave chase, calling to the goat in the most coaxing tone he could conjure. "Ornery" weaved in and out of the bushes, pausing to munch on the foliage only when Druet tripped and landed on his knees. From this vantage point, Druet studied Ornery with a rueful glare; the goat returned his look with one of total indifference and continued to inhale the stringy branch in its rotating jaw.

Retreating on his knees behind the cover of the brush, Druet crept along the row of shrubbery until he came to be opposite Ornery's position. In a flash, his arm shot out and his fingers closed around the unsuspecting goat's leg. Ornery dropped the branch and bawled pitifully, bucking and rearing against Druet's hold. The blacksmith clutched the animal and tried to move into a position to grab it around its middle. Suddenly, Ornery twisted away and forced Druet to loosen his grip. The goat gave a bleet of victory and dashed up the embankment toward the meadow; Druet gave a huff of irritation and jumped up to follow.

In spite of the stubborn creature's triumph, a grin crept onto Druet's face as he scrambled up the bank after the goat. He hadn't had this much fun since he'd helped the Osgood farmer catch his cows!

Ornery was frolicking triumphantly along the edge of the meadow. With a cry of "Charge!" Druet darted after the creature, dodging this way and that when the goat veered away from his path of pursuit at sharp angles. Druet felt himself chuckle as he gained ground and the animal cast a look of distress over its shoulder.

"Ha! Too close for comfort, Ornery? Come here, you ridiculous animal!"

Druet dove for the goat and missed by a few inches. Jumping up, he moved to cut off the goat's path of retreat. Suddenly, the two froze simultaneously and stared at each other. Druet inched forward a step.

"Mutton is beginning to sound like a wonderful choice for supper, Ornery."

The goat took a step back, still staring warily at Druet.

Finally, Druet made a successful dive and pinned Ornery to the ground. The goat thrashed for a moment, but gradually became calm as Druet brushed his large hand over its back.

"Now…how do I get you back to your pen?" Druet new that lifting the heavy goat in his arms would send Rodney into a state of panic; he was nearly healed, it was true, but still wrapped in linen around the middle.

Hearing a noise coming from the tree-lined embankment, Druet turned, expecting to see the old woman. Instead, he found Renny with her arms crossed, leaning against an oak's trunk and trying with all her might to keep a laugh from surfacing.

Druet rolled his eyes, barely able to suppress a laugh himself, "I know; it looked ridiculous. Go ahead and have your laugh before you burst."

Renny immediately burst into a fit of mirth. Ornery twitched nervously at the sound of another human. Druet shook his head and tried to frown at the goat.

"You're a lot of trouble, you know."

Renny approached and Druet saw she was holding a length of rope, "Marie said you might need this."

"Perfect. Tie it around his neck, will you?"

Renny crouched by Ornery's head and knotted a loop around his neck, "I've never laughed so hard in my life."

Druet stood up, pulling Ornery to his feet, "Well, I'm glad to offer you a bit of amusement. How are you managing without Grikk following five paces behind you?"

Renny grinned, "He has been very good to me, but I'm glad he was able to ride as a messenger. I wanted to go too, but Father explained it would be best for me to stay here."

"I'm glad you did."

"So am I...now," she glanced at Ornery, "I might have missed your goat-chase."

"Very funny."

The motley three started back toward the village, Druet all but dragging the goat behind him when the creature sat down and refused to budge.

Renny laughed again, "I wonder what your subjects would say if they could see their king warring helplessly against a goat."

Druet yanked on the rope and flashed a rueful grin, "I'm not king yet."

"But you will be."

"I haven't joined the seven regions' hands."

"But you will."

Druet paused to stare down at Renny, "I'm not even sure how to begin such a task. The seven regions of Arcrea are so diverse, it will be a miracle when they unite together beneath the banner of one cause."

Renny studied him for a moment, "You don't realize, do you, how deeply the people of Arcrea are craving a just cause that is worth uniting for? Its true they are diverse, but they are still one people. Its true that there are seven regions, but they are one kingdom."

Druet took a deep breath, "You're right. I'll just have to keep trusting that God knows what He's doing."

Renny nodded and glanced at the goat, munching obliviously on the branch of a low shrub. She started when Druet suddenly took her hand.

"Renny, I—"

The old woman's voice cut him off, "Druet, are you alright up there?"

The goat stood stock-still, fully aware that it was his owner calling.

"Yes, ma'am!"

"Did you manage to catch Humphrey?"

Druet shifted an incredulous glance between Renny and the goat—Humphrey?

"Yes, ma'am!" He called, "I'll bring him down in a moment," turning back to Renny he quickly tried to begin again, "Renny, I wanted to—Ouch!"

Renny's hand flew to her mouth when Humphrey the goat suddenly bolted down the incline toward old Marie's voice, dragging a surprised Druet behind him. The blacksmith clutched his end of the rope and barely managed to keep his footing as he trailed the goat down the bank, through the bushes, across the yard, and into the pen. Marie quickly closed the gate behind him and Druet leaned against a post to catch his breath.

Marie clasped her wrinkled hands together and smiled, "Druet, you're a miracle worker!"

Druet gave a slight smile in response as he hurdled the gate, unwilling to open it and so offer Humphrey another chance for escape. Marie moved to toss an armful of dried grass into the manger.

Renny appeared at the base of the incline and crossed the yard to meet Druet, this time doing nothing to suppress her laugh. Druet shook his head and grinned as they started toward the front of the hut. When they rounded the corner, they found Leland in the doorway.

"Ah, there you are," he cast a glance between the two and then studied Druet a bit closer, "Are you well, Druet? You're looking flushed."

"I'm fine, thank you, sir—just working up an appetite for mutton."

Leland looked confused, but quickly went on, "We have received word that our messengers are nearing the Heartland's border. God willing, they will have spread word of your discovery and the Arcrean people will follow them."

Druet nodded and Leland continued in a somber tone, "There is other news. It has been discovered that Frederick sent word to the other lords only days ago, and they are now preparing their armies for battle."

Renny's jaw dropped, "They would bring their armies to war against one man?"

"It would seem so, Aurenia."

"But they surround the Heartland; they'll trap him here."

Leland shifted his gaze to Druet, "If you wish to flee, I will assign a guard…"

Druet shook his head, "Thank you, but I wish to remain here. I escaped Frederick once, and now he is gathering an even greater force; if I escaped again, he would be sure to follow me until the day of my death. I have to face them, Leland—particularly Frederick—or I will never be rid of them."

Leland nodded in agreement and observed Druet with a look of respect, "The men of the Heartland are at your service, Druet. We will defend you to the death."

಄಄

The pairs of messengers began to arrive back in Olden Weld the next morning, and the following evening all were accounted for when Talon and Bracy rode into the village. A council was held and reports given to the elders and Druet's band of followers.

The word had been spread throughout the Arcrean masses: The people were now aware of Druet's discovery.

಄಄

A week passed and a distinct rumble could be heard in the vast meadows of the western Heartland. Like the noise of distant thunder, the sound steadily grew in strength.

Druet stood in old Marie's doorway and listened.

Nathaniel reined his horse to stop before the hut and dismounted with a grin.

"Is it true, Nathaniel?"

The seaman nodded, "As true as true can be, mate."

Druet drew a deep breath and exhaled slowly.

"How many?"

Nathaniel shook his head and his smile broadened, "Thousands—too many to count. Like a living sea! Druet, the people of Arcrea's seven regions are gathering to hear of your discovery."

"What can be done to shield them from the armies of the nobility?"

"Druet, the people outnumber all seven armies combined! You have built a reputation of honor, justice, humility, and honesty; and the people have sworn, even before hearing of the heart's identity, that they will stand together for your cause and defend you."

Druet stared, overwhelmed, at his friend, "They are here to help me?"

"You discovered them, Druet; and now the heart of Arcrea beats for you."

Druet shook his head, "May they serve God before me; and may I serve them in His name to the best of my abilities."

"Druet, do you understand what this means?" Nathaniel grasped Druet's shoulders with firm hands, "You've joined the hands of the seven regions, mate. You are king."

Chapter 39
* A King *

Blunt stood with the rest of Druet's band as the young leader—the novice king—stepped forward to address the gathered throng. The minstrel's poetic senses were alive as his gaze roamed the length and width of the meadow; the people—the heart—truly looked like a model of that wondrous organ as they shifted for a better view of Druet. Blunt was sure he would never be able to find words adequate enough to write a sonnet describing the sights, the sounds, and the emotions that surged through his own being let alone Druet's.

Nathaniel stood to one side, his heart swelling with brotherly pride. They were at the eastern head of the meadow on a large rock formation, from which Druet's voice would have a chance of reaching even half of the people by echoing across the hills.

A moment later, as Druet began to speak to the hushed crowd, Nathaniel's mind retraced the steps of Druet's quest, and of his own journey north from

313

Dormay before that. He thought of Druet's arrival in Roughton, when Nathaniel had rushed to his aid against Frederick's men, and he smiled; Druet had seemed so lost that day—without any purpose or direction beyond a desire to bring justice to Arcrea.

Nathaniel thought of the ignispats and catawylds, the carnaturs and dragons, the storms and disappointments that had met them at every turn; and yet, here they were at the end of their quest. Successful.

Glancing to his right, Nathaniel saw Alice and Renny standing together, each with her arm around the other's waist and tears in her eyes; Nathaniel knew that one woman cried out of happiness, the other—acceptance. The two had become close friends during the weeks spent in the Heartland. The thought made Nathaniel wonder for the first time what would happen to the group after Druet was officially crowned as king. They would most certainly have to go their separate ways.

The crowd listened with rapt attention as Druet revealed the heart's identity…them. They gazed with silent amazement as he told them of his reasoning behind the matter and finally explained that his quest had been successful only by God's hand, and that God was willing to guide the life of each man, woman, and child present.

Silence hung like a thick veil over the meadow as Druet bowed his head and took a step back. Leland stepped up to stand by Druet and lifted his voice in authority.

"You have heard the testimony of Druet of Oak's Branch this day; is there any who would deny his words?"

Silence.

"Then let it be known, people of Arcrea, that I Leland, direct descendant of Ulric the ancient and chief elder of the Heartland, approve of this man, Druet, as Arcrea's first king," drawing his sword, Leland thrust it into the air and shouted, "Long live King Druet!"

The crowd roared with approval and echoed Leland's cry again and again. Druet's gaze scanned the innumerable faces and then he turned to his companions of the past months. Holding his right fist out to Bracy, he waited as the clansman took it in his left grasp and in turn offered his own right fist to Talon. When the ring was complete, they waited for Druet to begin the prayer. When the blacksmith-king remained silent, the group looked up to see his features twisted and his jaw clenched with emotion. He nodded, signaling that he was ready to pray, and they bowed their heads again; this time Druet's voice was lifted, only to break with his first words.

"Thank You, God!"

Chapter 40
* Rescued *

The people of Arcrea remained in the Heartland for three days, waiting for some sign of the seven noblemen's armies, but Frederick's desire for battle was never satisfied. On the third day, scouts discovered the seven lords' camp where they were bickering over various strategies—they hadn't expected the entire kingdom to uproot and relocate, blocking their paths to the Heartland.

Lords Frederick, Geoffrey, Hugh, Osgood, Ranulf, Stephen, and Quinton were bound and brought to Olden Weld; charged with attempts to assassinate the king.

When they arrived at the meetinghouse where Druet and his band were gathered in discussion, the young king looked up and scanned the group until his gaze collided with Frederick's.

Stepping away from the room's long table, Druet marched toward the northern lord and quickly drew his sword. Several gasps were heard across the room at this uncharacteristic behavior, but Druet continued at a steady pace until he stood several paces away from Frederick. With a quick movement, Druet thrust the blade; the evil lord winced, waiting for death, but when it didn't come he opened his eyes to see that Druet had stayed the weapon just short of his heart. Frederick lifted his eyes to meet Druet's—filled with authority, they were yet void of malice.

"Why do you not kill me?"

Druet held the sword steady, "Frederick, as loathsome and deserving of death as you are, I am aware that you have a wife and daughter who still need you. Also, as none of you will retain your positions as noblemen in Arcrea, you are all now members of Arcrea's heart...and I am a defender of the heart. Your families will need you even more now, as you all learn to live lives of simplicity."

Frederick grimaced.

Druet turned the man around and cut the ropes binding his wrists, "Frederick, with this sword you tried to take my life, and with it I now grant you yours," his eyes scanned the seven prisoners, "Only do not allow yourselves to gain a false sense of security in your new lives; you will be watched very closely."

Druet turned to go, but paused to address the scouts' leader, "Where are their swords?"

The man motioned to one his scouts; "We retrieved them as soon as we had captured them."

Druet eyed the armful of swords and, finally selecting one, turned back to Frederick.

"This was yours," it was a statement, but Frederick answered with a nod anyway, "I'm of a mind to keep it in memory of my quest—it being the one I used. I'll pay you for it."

Frederick studied Druet in astonishment, trying to find fault with the young man, but failing miserably; even in his newfound position of royalty Druet showed no signs of pride or malice. Even now his expression was one of humble question.

"Would you mind?" Druet waited until Frederick shook his head, "Thank you," he stepped forward and purposefully placed a coin in Frederick's palm; he grinned, "I wouldn't want to take it without asking."

ഇൻൻ

The people of Arcrea returned to their homes with joy and a newfound hope for their future. Druet appointed Leland and the other Heartland elders to be his founding councilmen and to help him set the details of his reign in order. The council quickly began to draw up documents and lists of things to be considered, while Druet rode out from the Heartland on his first mission of justice as Arcrea's king.

ഇൻൻ

Gregory lay on the floor of the tower's cold cell. The one small window let in too little light, and too much chilled air. Months had passed, and the only word that had reached him was that his wife was being held under house arrest. Where was Druet? Had he too refused Frederick's demands for the mending of his force's arms and been thrown in prison? Or, worse, had he been put to death? Was his Ruth coping with the hard blows dealt to their family?

Had Frederick destroyed the clans? Was his brother still alive?

"Take care of them, dear God," his chapped lips formed the prayer as they had every day, "Provide for their needs. Bring justice and peace to Arcrea. I praise you…"

Voices from outside the door interrupted Gregory and he forced himself to a sitting position. Though the months in prison had done nothing to dampen his spirits, they had succeeded in weakening his body. The blacksmith ran a hand over his unshaven face as the bolt on the door gave way to a key. No doubt, he would receive another platter of what the guards insisted was food, and a mug of cloudy water.

The door swung open and Gregory blinked.

It wasn't the guard.

The next instant, Gregory felt Ruth's arms thrown carefully around his neck. He blinked fiercely and tried to get a clearer view of her tear-streaked face.

"Ruth, don't tell me they're throwing you in here too!"

Ruth sobbed and shook her head, unable to speak. Gregory's gaze returned to the door for some sort of explanation and there he saw his son's form filling the open space. The young man was working hard to blink persistent tears from his eyes as well.

"Druet?"

"Father," Druet came forward and joined the family embrace for a moment before pulling away and resting a firm hand on Gregory's shoulder, "Father, I've come to take you home. We must get you back to Oak's Branch; there is work to be done."

Gregory knew Druet must be joking, but his son looked serious.

"Druet, I'm in no condition to man a forge just yet."

"You will be soon. There is a healer downstairs who will tend to your needs…"

Gregory opened his mouth to question, but stopped when Druet continued.

"…and when you are strong again, there is a task that I'd…" Druet paused as tears pooled in his eyes again; a sudden suspicion made Gregory start to tremble, "I'd like for you to…Father—would you honor me by fashioning my crown?"

Gregory's lip trembled and his shoulders shook heavily as a wave of many emotions washed over, around, and through him. His head began to nod and he tried to answer that the honor would be his, but his lips would only form one word as he took Druet's face in his large hands and gazed into his son's eyes.

"Remarkable."

Chapter 41
* A Singular Dilemma *

Druet looked up from signing the last of several documents and met the gazes around the table. The councilmen had done an admirable job of thinking through many details that he himself would have overlooked in his inexperience. Druet passed the document to his left and Nathaniel, acting as his witness, signed below Druet's signature.

"Thank you, sirs," Druet stood, "Is there anything further that you wish to discuss before we finish for the evening?"

Clearing his throat, Leland too rose from his seat, "There are two matters, Sire, that must be addressed soon...if possible."

With a slow grin, Nathaniel propped his arms on the table's surface and rested his chin on his hands. As it had been with him, Druet never ceased to amaze the council with his ability to make a decision and successfully run with it. The seaman always enjoyed the looks of relief and surprise that were directed at Druet when a matter had been settled with impossible speed and effectiveness.

Druet placed his palms on the table and motioned for Leland to continue.

"These matters may seem trivial, Sire, but they must be addressed. First, the elders of the Heartland wish to know your intentions regarding our encampment. All of Arcrea knows that the first king was given the right to claim this land for his own use…"

Leland stopped when Druet lifted a hand for silence.

"Leland that decision was made by seven self-seeking explorers whose motives had just been frustrated by the Heartland's chief. As far as I am concerned, it is of no effect."

The elders looked relieved.

"Thank you, Sire, you are gracious. It was supposed that these would be your thoughts on the matter," Leland studied a parchment spread before him, "However, this brings up another aspect of this issue. Where will you live? The seven regions' boundaries are no longer in place, but it will take some time before the boundaries are erased from the minds of the people, and they will be prone to jealousy in situations such as this."

Druet tapped a finger on the table, "You are suggesting that if I were to return to live in northern Arcrea, the people would still see it as Frederick's region and find fault with my choice of residence."

Another elder stood, "There will be those who wish to find fault with everything you do. Every action on your part will be scrutinized by discontented people who will always be bent on mischief and discord."

Leland nodded in agreement, "The elders have discussed this issue at length and we have decided, after much prayer, that we would like to offer you a plot of land in the western Heartland. You will be free to employ the many craftsmen who have offered their services in building the royal palace—drawing their wages from the overabundant taxes retrieved from the former lords."

Druet's expression showed his surprise, "I don't know what to say…"

A white-haired elder leaned forward with a grin, "Do you accept our gift?"

"Yes!" Druet nodded, "I accept, of course; and thank you!"

Nathaniel leaned back in his chair, glancing from one face to another. For once, it was Druet who had been surprised by the problem's swift resolve. The young king studied the smooth table before him until he seemed to remember something.

Druet shifted his gaze to Leland, "There was another matter?"

"Yes…in a way it is the same issue as the one before—dealing with the jealousy of the people. Only…" Leland glanced at the other elders.

Druet followed his gaze to the other faces, all appearing to be uncertain, "Only what?"

Nathaniel leaned forward curiously as Leland turned back to Druet with a sheepish grin.

"This matter should really be of no concern to anyone but you; however, the elders thought it wise to warn you that if the people are expected to show jealousy over the region of your residence, they are sure to also be discontent with the region of your..."

Leland broke off and rubbed at the back of his neck, trying to hide his discomfort. Druet stared at him for a moment and then glanced around the table in confusion. Nathaniel stood up and did the same.

"What is it, Leland?"

The white-haired elder leaned forward again to complete Leland's sentence, "Your bride."

A moment of silence followed. Nathaniel glanced to his right and saw a bright flush cover Druet's face.

Leland spoke again, "As I said, this matter really should be your concern alone; only now that you are king your choice in marriage will decide Arcrea's first queen. Therefore, you must prepare yourself for the opinions of the people being made known to you. No matter where the woman comes from, the people from the other former regions will be discontent that she was not chosen from theirs."

"Oh, is that all?" Nathaniel dropped back into his chair, unable to wipe the grin from his face. An air of discomfort hung over the room, as each man considered the awkward dilemma.

"Well," Druet brought his palms down on the surface before him and lifted his flushed features to smile at the elders, "Sirs, allow me to relieve your concerns about this matter. The first and similar issue was solved by the decision to build my home in a place wholly unconnected with the seven former regions of Arcrea. This second matter can be solved in exactly the same way," Druet's face was a picture of innocent compliance, "I'll just have to marry a woman from the Heartland."

Nathaniel swallowed a laugh and nearly choked on it in the process. The elders' eyes widened in surprise at Druet's readiness to make such a decision so quickly; Druet's glance shifted to Leland, and he noticed the chief didn't appear quite as shocked as the others.

The young king cleared his throat, "And to further relieve your distress, kind sirs, I feel that I should confess—the woman has already been chosen."

"You did *what!?*" Renny's eyebrows shot upward as she turned a look of shock to Druet in the meetinghouse half-an-hour later.

Druet rubbed his jaw and flashed her a grin, "Volunteered you to be queen."

Renny's face flushed crimson as she crossed her arms and seared him with an annoyed glare, "The stress has done nothing to your sense of humor, has it?"

"Just improved it," Druet's eyes scanned the table of elders, waiting for Renny's decision…the situation couldn't be any more awkward, "I need to marry someone from the Heartland in order to escape the criticism of my subjects."

Renny tilted her head sarcastically, "Oh, now I'm begging for the opportunity."

Druet's face turned serious, "You know I'm teasing."

Renny turned to her father, "If the people are going to be jealous of a queen from another region, they're going to be just as jealous and filled with contempt for a queen from the Heartland; especially if Druet chooses to live here as well!"

"The choice was Druet's, Aurenia."

"It will give the impression that he favors the Heartland over the rest of Arcrea."

The old white-haired elder rose to his feet and eyed Renny closely, "Are you saying that you do not wish to accept Druet's hand in marriage?"

For a moment Renny stood speechless, returning the old man's gaze; and then her eyes shifted to her father and he raised his brows, requesting an answer to the elder's question.

"No," her voice sounded small, "I didn't mean to imply that; but I don't want to be chosen out of obligation."

"You weren't," Druet quickly confirmed, "You know I would have chosen you whether I found the heart or not."

Renny turned to face him with one eyebrow quirked, "Ha! You didn't know where I lived!"

Druet crossed his arms, "I would have found you! Nathaniel figured it out..."

"The only reason he did was out of necessity when you had a sword thrust through your stomach."

Druet grinned and dramatically placed a hand over his heart, "I would have endured such treatment seven times over if only it meant that I would be led to you!"

Renny gave an exasperated huff and turned back to the table. Nathaniel's face was red and her father's amused expression clearly stated his desire to laugh.

"Aurenia, are we to understand that you accept Druet's hand?"

Renny's face flushed again—she'd never been so embarrassed in her life! But she knew that if she chose to answer out of pride now, she would immediately regret her words. Forcing her head to nod up and down, she finally answered, "Yes...I accept."

In the next instant, Druet gave the elders yet another surprise when he swept Renny off of her feet and danced her in wild circles around the room.

Chapter 42
* Parting Words *

The kingdom was in a state of celebration on the day Druet was officially crowned the first king of Arcrea. Leland performed the ceremony before the thousands gathered in the western meadow where Druet had announced his discovery one month before. A simple golden circlet, fashioned with care by Gregory's hands, was placed on the young man's head to the backdrop of great applause. A second crown was brought and Druet gently lowered it to grace the head of his new bride. Taking her hand, Druet then turned with Renny to face the cheering heart of Arcrea as king and queen.

After the ceremony, the gathered masses slowly took their leave and returned to their homes, where festivals were held for another week.

A site was chosen in the western Heartland for the royal palace; plans were drawn up and craftsmen were hired to begin the work. It was expected to take at least a year, and so Druet and Renny found a temporary home in Olden Weld while they waited for the structure to be completed.

Another month passed and life in Arcrea began to settle into its new routine.

Gregory and Ruth returned to Oak's Branch to make preparations for moving south, closer to their son. The king's father had asked to be included among the craftsmen who were building the palace, and his offer had been accepted.

The law against healers was annulled and Rodney began to train others in the forgotten art. The healer and his wife were hired as members of the royal staff.

Blunt the minstrel made his farewells and set out to ply his trade once again. The traveling bard became distinguished among his peers, being known as one of Druet's companions and therefore trusted to tell the truth in his sonnets and songs.

Talon and Bracy, unbeknownst to each other, both expressed a desire to remain in Druet's following. They were assigned positions as couriers and scouts in Falconer's division of informants...as a team.

Grikk had never left off his protection of Renny, and no one was inclined to put a stop to his service now. He readily included Druet's safety in his vigilance and soon became an expected shadow wherever the royal couple went.

It was at the end of the first month of his reign when Druet was faced with the most difficult parting since his quest's completion. Standing alone in the meetinghouse, looking over plans for Morgway's reconstruction, Druet looked up when a form filled the doorway and its shadow stretched across the floor.

"Nathaniel!"

"Sire," the seaman grinned and tipped his head in greeting.

Druet straightened to work the kinks from his back, "How many times do I have to tell you that I want you to continue calling me Druet? My mother and father still use my name, and it shouldn't be any different for my brother."

Nathaniel's smile was forced and his gaze dropped to study the floor between them.

Druet's grin disappeared, "What's wrong?"

Nathaniel took a deep breath and lifted his gaze, apparently deciding to jump into the distasteful topic that was on his mind.

"Its time for me to leave, mate. I've enjoyed my time on land far more than I ever dreamed I could; I was thrilled to be a part of your adventure—I enjoyed meeting new friends, seeing new places; but now the quest is over, my job is done...at least for now, and I'm anxious to be out at sea again."

Druet studied his friend for a moment of strained silence.

"I understand, Nathaniel. You've been of more help to me than you'll ever know and I'll miss you, brother, but I do understand."

Nathaniel nodded and the two gave each other a firm embrace. Druet clapped the seaman on the shoulder.

"Come back to us when you've had enough voyaging...mate."

Nathaniel grinned at the use of his favorite word, "I'll be back. I want to see your palace when it's complete."

Druet nodded, "You'll always have a place here, Nathaniel."

"Thanks, mate," Nathaniel turned toward the door and paused when he reached the threshold, taking a deep breath, "By the way, I took the liberty of sending word to the craftsmen to cover the mortar tonight…its going to rain."

"Nathaniel, what will I do without you?"

The seaman gave a lopsided grin and shrugged, "You'll survive…somehow or other!"

Outside, Nathaniel gathered the reins of his horse and started down the road. Coming to a hut noisy with women's chattering, he shook his head and grinned; he looked forward to seeing his mother and sisters again. Alice stepped outside with a basket under her arm and smiled when she spotted Nathaniel; the smile quickly disappeared when she assessed the situation.

"You are leaving, then?"

He nodded and stroked the horse's muzzle; "I have the sea in my blood, Alice."

She clasped her hands around the basket, "Will you be back?"

Another nod, "I told Druet I'd be back to see his palace. He keeps saying he'll find a place for me if I decide to give up my inborn profession. I'll think about it—pray about it," he smiled, "Only God could make a true land-lover out of me."

Alice nodded and turned away to glance up the road.

Nathaniel watched as old Marie appeared and dragged Humphrey around the corner of her hut; he turned back to Alice.

"Have you decided, yet, what you'll do?"

"I offered to help Renny plan the castle gardens—it isn't exactly a noted skill of hers," she gave a significant grin, "And Renny asked if I would consider staying at the palace as her companion instead of returning to Brentwood."

"You'll be here, then...with them?"

"Yes. I sent to inform Bess of my plans and when the palace is complete she will bring my belongings and come to stay with me."

Nathaniel nodded, running a hand through his finally-trimmed hair and then scratching the back of his neck; he cleared his throat and turned to face Alice again.

"You know, the Arcrean Sea is uncertain—well, of course you're aware of that—uh..." he cleared his throat again, "I can't ask you to promise—"

Nathaniel's words were cut off when Humphrey bolted back across the road, followed by a crowd of five shouting children in pursuit. Alice covered a laugh as she and Nathaniel watched goat and pursuers disappear in a mass of flailing arms, legs, and hooves around the corner of another hut.

After a second of recovery, Nathaniel went on, "Alice, if I return—"

"*When* you return," Alice corrected, and then smiled, "I'll be praying for you, Nathaniel; and I'll be waiting...to show you the plans for Renny's garden."

A smile spread across Nathaniel's face, "I'll look forward to it."

The seaman mounted his waiting horse and bowed to Alice and the other ladies who were gathering in the doorway behind her.

"God be with you, Nathaniel," Alice called and waved as the seaman pressed his heels to the horse's flanks and disappeared from sight.

Epilogue
* The Mizgalian *

Talon and Bracy followed the base of the Brikbone Mountains, along the border of Quinton's region. They were returning from delivering a message to the captain of the Arcrean army stationed there. Riding into a thickly forested area, they stopped to rest for the night in a small clearing.

Suddenly, three men clad in the apparel of foreign soldiers appeared and immediately attacked the weary travelers. Talon's swords quickly felled one man and he turned to set eyes on the third assailant just as Bracy dropped his own opponent. Talon's eyes widened in alarm when he spotted the third man situated beyond the preoccupied Bracy, and with a ready bow in his hands. With a cry of fierce determination, Talon dropped his swords and dove to shove his comrade out of harm's way.

Bracy fell to the dirt and immediately heard the sickening thud of an arrow meeting flesh—Talon's flesh. In an instant Bracy was on his feet, infuriated and ready to meet the archer and finish him off. But the warrior was gone.

Keeping his sword at hand and an eye on the surrounding trees, Bracy turned and dropped on his knees beside Talon. An arrow protruded from the other man's shoulder and he was fast losing blood.

"Talon!" Bracy rolled the wounded man over, relieved to see that the green eyes were open, "Talon, are you alright?"

Talon gave Bracy a sarcastic glance, "Yes, Bracy, I'm dandy as a sunflower on a bright spring morning."

Bracy's eyes darted to the trees and then focused on the arrow, "Mizgalian."

Using his knife, Bracy cut the dart in two and pulled the pieces out of Talon's shoulder. Talon roared in pain. Ripping two strands from the hem of his green tunic, Bracy wadded the pieces and pressed them firmly to both of the wound's openings.

Talon managed a weak grin, "Now you need a new tunic."

Bracy's jaw was clenched tightly as he drew a vial of the Ulric's Rose tonic from his pouch and poured several drops into Talon's mouth and then into his wounds. Talon hissed to keep from bellowing again.

"You could have died, Talon," Bracy's tone sounded strained.

"I know," Talon blinked when sweat dripped into his eyes, "I *could* have; but if I hadn't done anything, then you *would* have."

Bracy paused in the act of replacing the vial, and stared at Talon.

"Bracy," Talon looked his comrade steadily in the eye, "I didn't die for you, but Jesus did."

Bracy seemed frozen. He stared down at Talon for a full minute before a noise from behind pulled him to his feet and whirled him around.

A young man, about eighteen years of age, stood at the edge of the clearing. He was dressed in a simple but clean tunic and pants. Blond hair neatly covered his head and tried to curl around his ears and at the base of his neck. His fingers clutched the pommel of a sword at his waist and his light blue eyes darted from Bracy to Talon and then back to Bracy.

"I thought I heard some trouble over this way. Is everything alright?"

His bass voice was extremely rich for one so young. He spoke with a thick foreign accent that Bracy and Talon recognized all too well, nevertheless he appeared to be fluently familiar with the Arcrean tongue.

Bracy eyed the boy suspiciously, "Who are you? What are you doing on this side of the Brikbones?"

"I am Trenton," the boy's head lifted with a measure of dignity, "and yes, I come from Mizgalia. I am journeying south to find the one called Druet."

Bracy stiffened, "What business do you have with King Druet?"

"Word has reached my people of his Arcrean coronation. I have listened with great interest to tales of his recent quest for your kingdom's heart, and now I wish to meet this remarkable man."

Bracy glanced back at Talon; he needed to get his comrade back to Rodney in case the tonic and his own attempts to staunch the loss of blood failed. If he left this Mizgalian youth here, the boy was sure to eventually find Druet on his own—Bracy might as well take him to the Heartland himself and keep a close watch over him. He motioned with his head for Trenton to come closer.

"We are riding to see King Druet as well. Help me get my friend onto his horse and you're welcome to ride with us."

Trenton nodded gratefully, "My own horse is tied fifty yards or so back. I'll fetch him and return directly to help you."

Bracy nodded and Trenton disappeared into the trees. Helping Talon to a sitting position, Bracy motioned after the boy.

"What do you think of him?"

Talon grimaced over his throbbing shoulder, "We'll just have to make sure he isn't being followed—that we're not being followed because of his presence."

Bracy nodded, "There's something about him…"

"Something familiar," Talon agreed with Bracy's unfinished statement.

"You noticed it too?"

Talon nodded.

"But how could it be possible that we would both recognize him? You and I came from two different ends of Arcrea."

"I don't know how it could be true; but something tells me that meeting Trenton today was not by chance. God has a purpose for every encounter, Bracy, and I feel in my bones that there's something peculiar about Trenton's case."

§) Q

Nicole Sager

ABOUT THE AUTHOR

Nicole Sager is a homeschool graduate and an avid reader. She has lived in both Virginia and Texas with her wonderful parents and five siblings. Besides reading and writing, Nicole also enjoys music, tap-dancing, theatre, and drawing illustrations for her books. *The Heart of Arcrea* is Nicole's first published book.

"In writing each book, I pray that it will bring honor and glory to God, and that He will use it as a tool to bring at least one person to the saving knowledge of Jesus Christ. I pray that my books would be a blessing to readers (individuals & families alike) as they search for wholesome yet exciting reading material for all ages."

~ *N.S.*

LOOK FOR BOOK 2 OF
THE ARCREAN CONQUEST
COMING SOON!

The Fate of Arcrea

Return to the kingdom of Arcrea, where the stage is set for an epic battle between good and evil.

Trenton is a young Mizgalian caught up in the deadly beliefs inspired by a life in his father's garrison. When a simple mission in Arcrea unearths the shocking truth of a mystery two decades in the making, he is left with a choice that may decide the fate of an entire kingdom. Join old friends and new on a journey of discovery, where battling vicious beasts and conquering a coast of dragons will test the mettle of men and set the pace for an adventure like no other.

For more information or updates on upcoming books, contact at
pocoauthor@gmail.com

Made in the USA
San Bernardino, CA
22 August 2014